I0688098

George Meredith

The Tale of Chloe

George Meredith

The Tale of Chloe

ISBN/EAN: 9783744661683

Printed in Europe, USA, Canada, Australia, Japan

Cover: Foto ©Andreas Hilbeck / pixelio.de

More available books at **www.hansebooks.com**

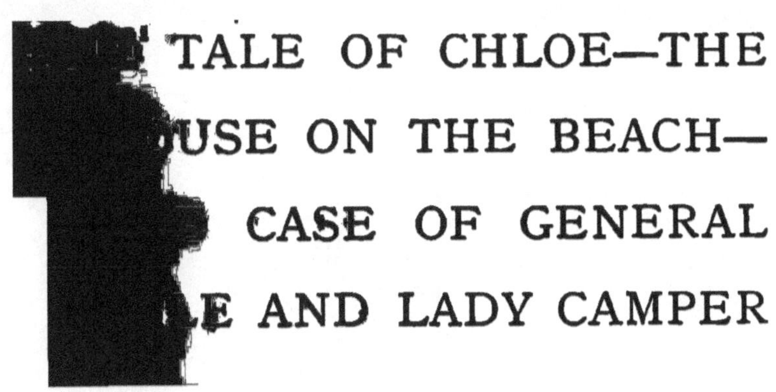

TALE OF CHLOE—THE
USE ON THE BEACH—
CASE OF GENERAL
E AND LADY CAMPER

BY

George Meredith

CONTENTS

B

" Fair Chloe, we toasted of old,
  As the Queen of our festival meeting ;
Now Chloe is lifeless and cold ;
  You must go to the grave for her greeting.

Her beauty and talents were framed
  To enkindle the proudest to win her ;
Then let not the mem'ry be blamed
  Of the purest that e'er was a sinner !"

Captain Chanter's Collection.

THE TALE OF CHLOE

CHAPTER I

A PROPER tenderness for the Peerage will continue to pass current the illustrious gentleman who was inflamed by Cupid's darts to espouse the milkmaid, or dairymaid, under his ballad title of Duke of Dewlap: nor was it the smallest of the services rendered him by Beau Beamish, that he clapped the name upon her rustic Grace, the young duchess, the very first day of her arrival at the Wells. This happy inspiration of a wit never failing at a pinch has rescued one of our princeliest houses from the assaults of the vulgar, who are ever too rejoiced to bespatter and disfigure a brilliant coat-of-arms ; insomuch that the ballad, to which we are indebted for the narrative of the meeting and marriage of the ducal pair, speaks of Dewlap in good faith :

O the ninth *Duke of Dewlap* I am, Susie dear !

without a hint of a domino title. So likewise the pictorial historian is merry over "Dewlap alliances" in his description of the society of that

period.   He has read the ballad, but disregarded
the memoirs of the beau.   Writers of pretension
would seem to have an animus against individuals
of the character of Mr. Beamish.   They will treat
of the habits and manners of highwaymen, and
quote obscure broadsheets and songs of the people
to colour their story, yet decline to bestow more
than a passing remark upon our domestic kings:
because they are not hereditary, we may suppose.

The ballad of " The Duke and the Dairymaid,"
ascribed with questionable authority to the pen of
Mr. Beamish himself in a freak of his gaiety, was
once popular enough to provoke the moralist to
animadversions upon an order of composition that
" tempted every bouncing country lass to sidle an
eye in a blowsy cheek " in expectation of a coronet
for her pains—and a wet ditch as the result !   We
may doubt it to have been such an occasion of mischief.   But that mischief may have been done by it
to a nobility-loving people, even to the love of our
nobility among the people, must be granted ; and
for the particular reason, that the hero of the ballad
behaved so handsomely.   We perceive a susceptibility to adulteration in their worship at the sight
of one of their number, a young maid, suddenly
snatched up to the gaping heights of Luxury and
Fashion through sheer good looks.   Remembering
that they are accustomed to a totally reverse effect
from that possession, it is very perceptible how a
breach in their reverence may come of the change.

Otherwise the ballad is innocent ; certainly it is innocent in design. A fresher national song of a beautiful incident of our country life has never been written. The sentiments are natural, the imagery is apt and redolent of the soil, the music of the verse appeals to the dullest ear. It has no smell of the lamp, nothing foreign and far-fetched about it, but is just what it pretends to be, the carol of the native bird. A sample will show, for the ballad is much too long to be given entire :

> Sweet Susie she tripped on a shiny May morn,
> As blithe as the lark from the green-springing corn,
> When, hard by a stile, 'twas her luck to behold
> A wonderful gentleman covered with gold !
>
> There was gold on his breeches and gold on his coat,
> His shirt-frill was grand as a fifty-pound note ;
> The diamonds glittered all up him so bright,
> She thought him the Milky Way clothing a Sprite !
>
> "Fear not, pretty maiden," he said with a smile ;
> "And, pray, let me help you in crossing the stile."
> She bobbed him a curtsey so lovely and smart,
> It shot like an arrow and fixed in his heart.
>
> As light as a robin she hopped to the stone,
> But fast was her hand in the gentleman's own ;
> And guess how she stared, nor her senses could trust,
> When this creamy gentleman knelt in the dust !

With a rhapsody upon her beauty, he informs her of his rank, for a flourish to the proposal of honourable and immediate marriage. He cannot wait. This is the fatal condition of his love : apparently a characteristic of amorous dukes. We read them in the signs extended to us. The minds of these august and solitary men have not yet been sounded ; they are too distant. Standing upon their lofty pinnacles, they are as legible to the rabble below as a line of cuneiform writing in a page of old copybook roundhand. By their deeds we know them, as heathendom knows of its gods ; and it is repeatedly on record that the moment they have taken fire they must wed, though the lady's finger be circled with nothing closer fitting than a ring of the bedcurtain. Vainly, as becomes a candid country lass, blue-eyed Susan tells him that she is but a poor dairymaid. He has been a student of women at Courts, in which furnace the sex becomes a transparency, so he recounts to her the catalogue of material advantages he has to offer. Finally, after his assurances that she is to be married by the parson, really by the parson, and a real parson—

> Sweet Susie is off for her parents' consent,
> And long must the old folk debate what it meant.
> She left them the eve of that happy May morn,
> To shine like the blossom that hangs from the thorn !

Apart from its historical value, the ballad is an example to poets of our day, who fly to mythological Greece, or a fanciful and morbid mediævalism, or—save the mark !—abstract ideas, for themes of song, of what may be done to make our English life poetically interesting, if they would but pluck the treasures presented them by the wayside ; and Nature being now as then the passport to popularity, they have themselves to thank for their little hold on the heart of the people.   A living native duke is worth fifty Phœbus Apollos to Englishmen, and a buxom young lass of the fields mounting from a pair of pails to the estate of duchess, a more romantic object than troops of your visionary Yseults and Guineveres.

CHAPTER II

A CERTAIN time after the marriage, his Grace
alighted at the Wells, and did himself the
honour to call on Mr. Beamish. Addressing that
gentleman, to whom he was no stranger, he com-
municated the purport of his visit.

"Sir, and my very good friend," he said, " first
let me beg you to abate the severity of your countenance, for if I am here in breach of your prohibi-
tion, I shall presently depart in compliance with it.
I could indeed deplore the loss of the passion for
play of which you effectually cured me. I was then
armed against a crueller, that allows of no interval
for a man to make his vow to recover !"

"The disease which is all crisis, I apprehend,"
Mr. Beamish remarked.

"Which, sir, when it takes hold of dry wood,
burns to the last splinter. It is now "—the duke
fetched a tender groan—" three years ago that I
had a caprice to marry a grandchild !"

"Of Adam's," Mr. Beamish said cheerfully.
"There was no legitimate bar to the union."

"Unhappily none. Yet you are not to suppose
I regret it. A most admirable creature, Mr.

Beamish, a real divinity! And the better known, the more adored. There is the misfortune. At my season of life, when the greater and the minor organs are in a conspiracy to tell me I am mortal, the passion of love must be welcomed as a calamity, though one would not be free of it for the renewal of youth. You are to understand, that with a little awakening taste for dissipation, she is the most innocent of angels. Hitherto we have lived . . . To her it has been a new world. But she is beginning to find it a narrow one. No, no, she is not tired of my society. Very far from that. But in her present station an inclination for such gatherings as you have here, for example, is like a desire to take the air : and the healthy habits of my duchess have not accustomed her to be immured. And in fine, devote ourselves as we will, a term approaches when the enthusiasm for serving as your wife's playfellow all day, running round tables and flying along corridors, before a knotted handkerchief, is mightily relaxed. Yet the dread of a separation from her has kept me at these pastimes for a considerable period beyond my relish of them. Not that I acknowledge fatigue. I have, it seems, a taste for reflection ; I am now much disposed to read and meditate, which cannot be done without repose. I settle myself, and I receive a worsted ball in my face, and I am expected to return it. I comply ; and then you would say a nursery in arms. It would else be the deplorable spectacle of a beautiful young woman yawning."

"Earthquake and saltpetre threaten us less terribly," said Mr. Beamish.

"In fine, she has extracted a promise that this summer she shall visit the Wells for a month, and I fear I cannot break my pledge of my word ; I fear I cannot."

"Very certainly I would not," said Mr. Beamish.

The duke heaved a sigh. "There are reasons, family reasons, why my company and protection must be denied to her here. I have no wish . . . indeed my name, for the present, until such time as she shall have found her feet . . . and there is ever a penalty to pay for that. Ah, Mr. Beamish, pictures are ours, when we have bought them and hung them up ; but who insures us possession of a beautiful work of Nature? I have latterly betaken me to reflect much and seriously. I am tempted to side with the Divines in the sermons I have read ; the flesh is the habitation of a rebellious devil."

"To whom we object in proportion as we ourselves become quit of him," Mr. Beamish acquiesced.

"But this mania of young people for pleasure, eternal pleasure, is one of the wonders. It does not pall on them ; they are insatiate."

"There is the cataract, and there is the cliff. Potentate to potentate, duke—so long as you are on my territory, be it understood. Upon my way to a place of worship once, I passed a Puritan, who was complaining of a butterfly that fluttered prettily abroad in desecration of the Day of Rest. 'Friend,' said I to him, 'conclusively you prove to me that you are not a butterfly.' Surly did no more than favour me with the anathema of his countenance."

"Cousin Beamish, my complaint of these young people is, that they miss their pleasure in pursuing it. I have lectured my duchess——"

"Ha!"

"Foolish, I own," said the duke. "But suppose, now, you had caught your butterfly, and you could neither let it go nor consent to follow its vagaries. That poses you."

"Young people," said Mr. Beamish, "come under my observation in this poor realm of mine—young and old. I find them prodigiously alike in their love of pleasure, differing mainly in their capacity to satisfy it. That is no uncommon observation. The young have an edge which they are desirous of blunting ; the old contrariwise. The cry of the young for pleasure is actually—I have studied their language—a cry for burdens. Curious ! And the old ones cry for having too many on their shoulders : which is *not* astonishing. Between them they make an agreeable concert both to charm the ears and guide the steps of the philosopher, whose wisdom it is to avoid their tracks."

"Good. But I have asked you for practical advice, and you give me an essay."

"For the reason, duke, that you propose a case that suggests hanging. You mention two things impossible to be done. The alternative is, a garter and the bed-post. When we have come upon cross-ways, and we can decide neither to take the right hand nor the left, neither forward nor back, the index of the board which would direct us points to itself, and emphatically says, Gallows."

"Beamish, I am distracted. If I refuse her the visit, I foresee dissensions, tears, games at ball, romps, not one day of rest remaining to me. I could be of a mind with your Puritan, positively. If I allow it, so innocent a creature in the atmosphere of a place like this must suffer some corruption. You should know that the station I took her from was . . . it was modest. She was absolutely a buttercup of the fields. She has had various masters. She dances . . . she dances prettily, I could say bewitchingly. And so she is now for airing her accomplishments : such are women ! "

"Have you heard of Chloe?" said Mr. Beamish. "There you have an example of a young lady uncorrupted by this place—of which I would only remark that it is best unvisited, but better tasted than longed for."

"Chloe? A lady who squandered her fortune to redeem some ill-requiting rascal : I remember to have heard of her. She is here still? And ruined, of course ? "

" In purse."

"That cannot be without the loss of reputation."

"Chloe's champion will grant that she is exposed to the evils of improvidence. The more brightly shine her native purity, her goodness of heart, her trustfulness. She is a lady whose exaltation glows in her abasement."

"She has, I see, preserved her comeliness," observed the duke, with a smile.

"Despite the flying of the roses, which had not her heart's patience. 'Tis now the lily that reigns. So, then, Chloe shall be attached to the duchess during her stay, and unless the devil himself should interfere, I guarantee her Grace against any worse harm than experience; and that," Mr. Beamish added, as the duke raised his arms at the fearful word, "that shall be mild. Play she will; she is sure to play. Put it down at a thousand. We map her out a course of permissible follies, and she plays to lose the thousand by degrees, with as telling an effect upon a connubial conscience as we can produce."

"A thousand," said the duke, "will be cheap indeed. I think now I have had a description of this fair Chloe, and from an enthusiast; a brune? elegantly mannered and of a good landed family; though she has thought proper to conceal her name. And that will be our difficulty, cousin Beamish."

"She was, under my dominion, Miss Martinsward," Mr. Beamish pursued. "She came here very young, and at once her suitors were legion. In the way of women, she chose the worst among them ; and for the fellow Caseldy she sacrificed the fortune she had inherited of a maternal uncle. To release him from prison, she paid all his debts ; a mountain of bills, with the lawyers piled above —Pelion upon Ossa, to quote our poets. In fact, obeying the dictates of a soul steeped in generosity, she committed the indiscretion to strip herself, scandalizing propriety. This was immediately on her coming of age ; and it was the death-blow to her relations with her family. Since then, honoured even by rakes, she has lived impoverished at the Wells. I dubbed her Chloe, and man or woman disrespectful to Chloe packs. From being the victim of her generous disposition, I could not save her ; I can protect her from the shafts of malice."

" She has no passion for play ? " inquired the duke.

" She nourishes a passion for the man for whom she bled, to the exclusion of the other passions. She lives, and I believe I may say that it is the motive of her rising and dressing daily, in expectation of his advent."

" He may be dead."

" The dog is alive. And he has not ceased to be Handsome Caseldy, they say. Between ourselves, duke, there is matter to break her heart. He has been the Count Caseldy of Continental gaming tables, and he is recently Sir Martin Caseldy, settled on the estate she made him free to take up intact on his father's decease."

" Pah ! a villain ! "

" With a blacker brand upon him every morning that he looks forth across his property, and leaves her to languish ! She still—I say it to the redemption of our sex—has offers. Her incomparable attractions of mind and person exercise the natural empire of beauty. But she will none of them. I call her the Fair Suicide. She has died for love ; and she is a ghost, a good ghost, and a pleasing ghost, but an apparition, a taper."

The duke fidgeted, and expressed a hope to hear that she was not of melancholy conversation ; and again, that the subject of her discourse was not confined to love and lovers, happy or unhappy. He wished his duchess, he said, to be entertained upon gayer topics : love being a theme he desired to reserve to himself. " This month ! " he said, prognostically shaking and moaning. " I would this month were over, and that we were well purged of it."

Mr. Beamish reassured him. The wit and sprightliness of Chloe were so famous as to be considered medical, he affirmed ; she was besieged for her company ; she composed and sang impromptu verses, she played harp and harpsichord divinely, and touched the guitar, and danced, danced like the silvery moon on the waters of the mill pool. He concluded by saying that she was both humane and wise, humble-minded and amusing, virtuous yet not a Tartar ; the best of companions for her Grace the young duchess. Moreover, he boldly engaged to carry the duchess through the term of her visit under a name that should be as good as a masquerade for concealing his Grace's, while giving her all the honours due to her rank.

"You strictly interpret my wishes," said the duke; "all honours, the foremost place, and my wrath upon man or woman gainsaying them!"

"Mine! if you please, duke," said Mr. Beamish.

"A thousand pardons! I leave it to you, cousin. I could not be in safer hands. I am heartily bounden to you. Chloe, then. By the way, she has a decent respect for age?"

"She is reverentially inclined."

"Not that. She is, I would ask, no wanton prattler of the charms and advantages of youth?"

"She has a young adorer that I have dubbed Alonzo, whom she scarce notices."

"Nothing could be better. Alonzo : h'm! A faithful swain?"

"Life is his tree, upon which unceasingly he carves his mistress's initials."

"She should not be too cruel. I recollect myself formerly : I was . . . Young men will, when long slighted, transfer their affections, and be warmer to the second flame than to the first. I put you on your guard. He follows her much? These lovers' pantings and puffings in the neighbourhood of the most innocent of women are contagious."

" Her Grace will be running home all the sooner."

" Or off!—may she forgive me! I am like a King John's Jew, forced to lend his treasure without security. What a world is ours! Nothing, Beamish, nothing desirable will you have which is not coveted! Catch a prize, and you will find you are at war with your species. You have to be on the defensive from that moment. There is no such thing as peaceable possession on earth. Let it be a beautiful young woman!—Ah!"

Mr. Beamish replied bracingly, " The champion wrestler challenges all comers while he wears the belt."

The duke dejectedly assented. " True ; or he is challenged, say. Is there any tale we could tell her of this Alonzo? You could deport him for the month, my dear Beamish."

" I commit no injustice unless with sufficient reason. It is an estimable youth, as shown by his devotion to a peerless woman. To endow her with his name and fortune is his only thought."

" I perceive ; an excellent young fellow ! I have an incipient liking for this young Alonzo. You must not permit my duchess to laugh at him. Encourage her rather to advance his suit. The silliness of a young man will be no bad spectacle. Chloe, then. You have set my mind at rest, Beamish, and it is but another obligation added to the heap; so, if I do not speak of payment, the reason is that I know you would not have me bankrupt."

The remainder of the colloquy of the duke and Mr. Beamish referred to the date of her Grace's coming to the Wells, the lodgement she was to receive, and other minor arrangements bearing upon her state and comfort; the duke perpetually observing, "But I leave it all to you, Beamish," when he had laid down precise instructions in these respects, even to the specification of the shopkeepers, the confectioner and the apothecary, who were to balance or cancel one another in the opposite nature of their supplies, and the haberdasher and the jeweller, with whom she was to make her purchases. For the duke had a recollection of giddy shops, and of giddy shopmen too; and it was by serving as one for a day that a certain great nobleman came to victory with a jealously guarded dame beautiful as Venus. "I would have challenged the goddess!" he cried, and subsided from his enthusiasm plaintively, like a weak wind instrument. "So there you see the prudence of a choice of shops. But I leave it to you, Beamish." Similarly the great military commander, having done whatsoever a careful prevision may suggest to insure him victory, casts himself upon Providence, with the hope of propitiating the unanticipated and darkly possible.

CHAPTER III

THE splendid equipage of a coach and six, with footmen in scarlet and green, carried Beau Beamish five miles along the road on a sunny day to meet the young duchess at the boundary of his territory, and conduct her in state to the Wells. Chloe sat beside him, receiving counsel with regard to her prospective duties. He was this day the consummate beau, suave, but monarchical, and his manner of speech partook of his external grandeur. " Spy me the horizon, and apprise me if somewhere you distinguish a chariot," he said, as they drew up on the rise of a hill of long descent, where the dusty roadway sank between its brown hedges, and crawled mounting from dry rush-spotted hollows to corn fields on a companion height directly facing them, at a remove of about three-quarters of a mile. Chloe looked forth, while the beau passingly raised his hat for coolness, and murmured, with a glance down the sultry track : " It sweats the eye to see ! "

Presently Chloe said, " Now a dust blows. Something approaches. Now I discern horses, now a vehicle ; and it is a chariot ! "

Orders were issued to the outriders for horns to be sounded.

Both Chloe and Beau Beamish wrinkled their foreheads at the disorderly notes of triple horns, whose pealing made an acid in the air instead of sweetness.

"You would say, kennel dogs that bay the moon!" said the wincing beau. "Yet, as you know, these fellows have been exercised. I have had them out in a meadow for hours, baked and drenched, to get them rid of their native cacophony. But they love it, as they love bacon and beans. The musical taste of our people is in the stage of the primitive appetite for noise, and for that they are gluttons."

"It will be pleasant to hear in the distance," Chloe replied.

"Ay, the extremer the distance, the pleasanter to hear. Are they advancing?"

"They stop. There is a cavalier at the window. Now he doffs his hat."

"Sweepingly?"

Chloe described a semicircle in the grand manner.

The beau's eyebrows rose. "Powers divine!" he muttered. "She is let loose from hand to hand, and midway comes a cavalier. We did not count on the hawks. So I have to deal with a cavalier! It signifies, my dear Chloe, that I must incontinently affect the passion if I am to be his match : nothing less."

" He has flown," said Chloe.

"Whom she encounters after meeting me, I care not," quothed the beau, snapping a finger. "But there has been an interval for damage with a lady innocent as Eve. Is she advancing ? "

" The chariot is trotting down the hill. He has ridden back. She has no attendant horseman."

· " They were dismissed at my injunction ten miles off: particularly to the benefit of the cavaliering horde, it would appear. In the case of a woman, Chloe, one blink of the eyelids is an omission of watchfulness."

" That is an axiom fit for the harem of the Grand Signior."

"The Grand Signior might give us profitable lessons for dealing with the sex."

" Distrust us, and it is a declaration of war ! "

" Trust you, and the stopper is out of the smelling-bottle."

" Mr. Beamish, we are women, but we have souls."

" The pip in the apple whose ruddy cheek allures little Tommy to rob the orchard is as good a preservative."

" You admit that men are our enemies ? "

" I maintain that they carry the banner of virtue."

" Oh, Mr. Beamish, I shall expire."

" I forbid it in my lifetime, Chloe, for I wish to die believing in one woman."

"No flattery for me at the expense of my sisters!"

"Then fly to a hermitage; for all flattery is at somebody's expense, child. 'Tis an essence—extract of humanity! To live on it, in the fashion of some people, is bad—it is downright cannibal. But we may sprinkle our handkerchiefs with it, and we should, if we would caress our noses with an air. Society, my Chloe, is a recommencement upon an upper level of the savage system; we must have our sacrifices. As, for instance, what say you of myself beside our booted bumpkin squires?"

"Hundreds of them, Mr. Beamish!"

"That is a holocaust of squires reduced to make an incense for me, though you have not performed Druid rites and packed them in gigantic osier ribs. Be philosophical, but accept your personal dues. Grant us ours too. I have a serious intention to preserve this young duchess, and I expect my task to be severe. I carry the banner aforesaid; verily and penitentially I do. It is an error of the vulgar to suppose that all is dragon in the dragon's jaws."

"Men are his fangs and claws."

"Ay, but the passion for his fiery breath is in woman. She will take her leap and have her jump, will and will! And at the point where she will and she won't, the dragon gulps and down she goes! However, the business is to keep our buttercup duchess from that same point. Is she near?"

"I can see her," said Chloe.

Beau Beamish requested a sketch of her, and Chloe began : " She is ravishing."

Upon which he commented, " Every woman is ravishing at forty paces, and still more so in imagination."

" Beautiful auburn hair, and a dazzling red and white complexion, set in a blue coif."

" Her eyes ? "

" Melting blue."

" 'Tis an English witch ! " exclaimed the beau, and he compassionately invoked her absent lord.

Chloe's optics were no longer tasked to discern the fair lady's lineaments, for the chariot windows came flush with those of the beau on the broad plateau of the hill. His coach door was opened. He sat upright, levelling his privileged stare at Duchess Susan until she blushed.

" Ay, madam," quoth he, " I am not the first."

" La, sir ! " said she ; " who are you ? "

The beau deliberately raised his hat and bowed. " He, madam, of whose approach the gentleman who took his leave of you on yonder elevation informed you."

She looked artlessly over her shoulder, and at the beau alighting from his carriage. " A gentleman ? "

" On horseback."

The duchess popped her head through the window on an impulse to measure the distance between the two hills.

" Never ! " she cried.

"Why, madam, did he deliver no message to announce me ? " said the beau, ruffling.

"Goodness gracious ! You must be Mr. Beamish," she replied.

He laid his hat on his bosom, and invited her to quit her carriage for a seat beside him. She stipulated, "If you are really Mr. Beamish?" He frowned, and raised his head to convince her ; but she would not be impressed, and he applied to Chloe to establish his identity. Hearing Chloe's name, the duchess called out, "Oh! there, now, that's enough, for Chloe's my maid here, and I know she's a lady born, and we're going to be friends. Hand me to Chloe. And you are Chloe ? " she said, after a frank stride from step to step of the carriages. " And don't mind being my maid? You do look a nice, kind creature. And I see you're a lady born ; I know in a minute. You're dark, I'm fair ; we shall suit. And tell me —hush !—what dreadful long eyes he has! I shall ask you presently what you think of me. I was never at the Wells before. Dear me ! the coach has turned. How far off shall we hear the bells to say I'm coming? I know I'm to have bells. Mr. Beamish, Mr. Beamish ! I must have a chatter with a woman, and I am in awe of you, sir, that I am, but men and men I see to talk to for a lift of my finger, by the dozen, in my duke's palace —though they're old ones, that's true—but a woman who's a lady, and kind enough to be my maid, I haven't met yet since I had the right to wear a coronet. There, I'll hold Chloe's hand, and that'll do. You would tell me at once, Chloe, if I was not dressed to your taste, now, wouldn't you? As for talkative, that's a sign with me of my liking people. I really don't know what to say to my duke sometimes. I sit and think it so funny to be having a duke instead of a husband. You're off!"

The duchess laughed at Chloe's laughter. Chloe excused herself, but was informed by her mistress that it was what she liked.

"For the first two years," she resumed, "I could hardly speak a syllable. I stammered, I reddened, I longed to be up in my room brushing and curling my hair, and was ready to curtsey to everybody. Now I'm quite at home, for I've plenty of courage —except about death, and I'm worse about death than I was when I was a simple body with a gawk's 'lawks!' in her round eyes and mouth for an egg. I wonder why that is? But isn't death horrible? And skeletons!" The duchess shuddered.

"It depends upon the skeleton," said Beau Beamish, who had joined the conversation. "Yours, madam, I would rather not meet, because she would precipitate me into transports of regret for the loss of the flesh. I have, however, met mine own and had reason for satisfaction with the interview."

"Your own skeleton, sir!" said the duchess wonderingly and appalled.

"Unmistakably mine. I will call you to witness by an account of him."

Duchess Susan gaped, and, "Oh, don't!" she cried out; but added, "It's broad day, and I've got some one to sleep anigh me after dark;" with which she smiled on Chloe, who promised her there was no matter for alarm.

"I encountered my gentleman as I was proceeding to my room at night," said the beau, "along a narrow corridor, where it was imperative that one of us should yield the *pas*; and, I must confess it, we are all so amazingly alike in our bones, that I stood prepared to demand place of him. For indubitably the fellow was an obstruction, and at the first glance repulsive. I took him for anybody's skeleton, Death's ensign, with his cachinnatory skull, and the numbered ribs, and the extraordinary splay feet—in fact, the whole ungainly and shaky hobbledehoy which man is built on, and by whose image in his weaker moments he is haunted. I had, to be frank, been dancing on a supper with certain of our choicest Wits and Beauties. It is a recipe for conjuring apparitions. Now, then, thinks I, my fine fellow, I will bounce you; and without a salutation I pressed forward. Madam, I give you my word, he behaved to the full pitch as I myself should have done under similar circumstances. Retiring upon an inclination of his structure, he draws up and fetches me a bow of the exact middle nick between dignity and service. I advance, he withdraws, and again

the bow, devoid of obsequiousness, majestically condescending. These, thinks I, be royal manners. I
could have taken him for the Sable King in person,
stripped of his mantle. On my soul, he put me to
the blush."

"And is that all?" asked the duchess, relieving
herself with a sigh.

"Why, madam," quoth the beau, "do you not
see that he could have been none other than mine
own, who could comport himself with that grand
air and gracefulness when wounded by his closest
relative? Upon his opening my door for me, and
accepting the *pas*, which I now right heartily
accorded him, I recognized at once both him and
the reproof he had designedly dealt me—or the
wine supper I had danced on, perhaps I should say ;
and I protest that by such a display of supreme
good breeding he managed to convey the highest
compliment ever received by man, namely the
assurance, that after the withering away of this
mortal garb, I shall still be noted for urbanity and
elegancy. Nay, and more, immortally, without the
slip I was guilty of when I carried the bag of wine."

Duchess Susan fanned herself to assist her
digestion of the anecdote.

"Well, it's not so frightful a story, and I know
you are the great Mr. Beamish," she said.

He questioned her whether the gentleman had
signalled him to her on the hill.

"What can he mean about a gentleman?" she

turned to Chloe. "My duke told me you would meet me, sir. And you are to protect me. And if anything happens, it is to be your fault."

"Entirely," said the beau. "I shall therefore maintain a vigilant guard."

"Except leaving me free. Oof! I've been boxed up so long. I declare, Chloe, I feel like a best dress out for a holiday, and a bit afraid of spoiling. I'm a real child, more than I was when my duke married me. I seemed to go in and grow up again, after I was raised to fortune. And nobody to tell of it! Fancy that! For you can't talk to old gentlemen about what's going on in your heart."

"How of young gentlemen ?" she was asked by the beau.

And she replied, "They find it out."

"Not if you do not assist them," said he.

Duchess Susan let her eyelids and her underlip half drop, as she looked at him with the simple shyness of one of nature's thoughts in her head at peep on the pastures of the world. The melting blue eyes and the cherry lip made an exceedingly quickening picture. "Now, I wonder if that is true ?" she transferred her slyness to speech.

"Beware the middle-aged !" he exclaimed.

She appealed to Chloe. "And I'm sure they're the nicest."

Chloe agreed that they were.

The duchess measured Chloe and the beau together, with a mind swift in apprehending all that it hungered for.

She would have pursued the pleasing theme had she not been directed to gaze below upon the towers and roofs of the Wells, shining sleepily in a siesta of afternoon Summer sunlight.

With a spread of her silken robe, she touched the edifice of her hair, murmuring to Chloe, " I can't abide that powder. You shall see me walk in a hoop. I can. I've done it to slow music till my duke clapped hands. I'm nothing sitting to what I am on my feet. That's because I haven't got fine language yet. I shall. It seems to come last. So, there's the place. And whereabouts do all the great people meet and prommy—? "

" They promenade where you see the trees, madam," said Chloe.

" And where is it where the ladies sit and eat jam tarts with whipped cream on 'em, while the gentlemen stand and pay compliments ? "

Chloe said it was at a shop near the pump room.

Duchess Susan looked out over the house-tops, beyond the dusty hedges.

"Oh, and that powder!" she cried. "I hate to be out of the fashion and a spectacle. But I do love my own hair, and I have such a lot, and I like the colour, and so does my duke. Only, don't let me be fingered at. If once I begin to blush before people, my courage is gone ; my singing inside me is choked ; and I've a real lark going on in me all day long, rain or sunshine—hush, all about love and amusement."

Chloe smiled, and Duchess Susan said, " Just like a bird, for I don't know what it is."

She looked for Chloe to say that she did.

At the moment a pair of mounted squires rode up, and the coach stopped, while Beau Beamish gave orders for the church bells to be set ringing, and the band to meet and precede his equipage at the head of the bath avenue : " in honour of the arrival of her Grace the Duchess of Dewlap."

He delivered these words loudly to his men, and turned an effulgent gaze upon the duchess, so that for a minute she was fascinated and did not consult her hearing ; but presently she fell into an uneasiness; the signs increased, she bit her lip, and after breathing short once or twice, " Was it meaning me, Mr. Beamish ? " she said.

" You, madam, are the person whom we delight to honour," he replied.

" Duchess of what ? " she screwed uneasy features to hear.

" Duchess of Dewlap," said he.

" It's not my title, sir."

" It is your title on my territory, madam."

She made her pretty nose and upper lip ugly with a sneer of " Dew—! And enter that town before all those people as Duchess of . . . . Oh, no, I won't ; I just won't ! Call back those men, now, please ; now, if you please. Pray, Mr.

Beamish! You'll offend me, sir. I'm not going to be a mock. You'll offend my duke, sir. He'd die rather than have my feelings hurt. Here's all my pleasure spoilt. I won't and I sha'n't enter the town as duchess of that stupid name, so call 'em back, call 'em back this instant. I know who I am and what I am, and I know what's due to me, I do."

Beau Beamish rejoined, " I too. Chloe will tell you I am lord here."

" Then I'll go home, I will. I won't be laughed at for a great lady ninny. I'm a real lady of high rank, and such I'll appear. What's a Duchess of Dewlap? One might as well be Duchess of Cowstail, Duchess of Mopsend. And those people! But I won't be that. I won't be played with. I see them staring! No, I can make up my mind, and I beg you to call back your men, or I'll go back home." She muttered, " Be made fun of—made a fool of ! "

" Your Grace's chariot is behind," said the beau.

His despotic coolness provoked her to an outcry and weeping : she repeated, " Dewlap ! Dewlap ! " in sobs ; she shook her shoulders and hid her face.

" You are proud of your title, are you, madam ? " said he.

" I am." She came out of her hands to answer him proudly. " That I am ! " she meant for a stronger affirmation.

" Then mark me," he said impressively ; " I am

your duke's friend, and you are under my charge
here. I am your guardian and you are my ward,
and you can enter the town only on the condition
of obedience to me. Now, mark me, madam ; no
one can rob you of your real name and title saving
yourself. But you are entering a place where you
will encounter a thousand temptations to tarnish,
and haply forfeit it. Be warned : do nothing that
will."

"Then I'm to have my own title ?" said she,
clearing up.

"For the month of your visit you are Duchess
of Dewlap."

"I say I sha'n't ! "

"You shall."

"Never, sir ! "

"I command it."

She flung herself forward, with a wail, upon
Chloe's bosom. "Can't you do something for
me ?" she whimpered.

"It is impossible to move Mr. Beamish," Chloe
said.

Out of a pause, composed of sobs and sighs, the
duchess let loose in a broken voice: "Then I'm
sure I think—I think I'd rather have met—have
met his skeleton ! "

Her sincerity was equal to wit.

Beau Beamish shouted. He cordially applauded
her, and in the genuine kindness of an admiration
that surprised him, he permitted himself the liberty

of taking and saluting her fingers. She fancied there was another chance for her, but he frowned at the mention of it.

Upon these proceedings the exhilarating sound of the band was heard ; simultaneously a festival peal of bells burst forth ; and an admonishment of the necessity for concealing her chagrin and exhibiting both station and a countenance to the people, combined with the excitement of the new scenes and the marching music to banish the acuter sense of disappointment from Duchess Susan's mind ; so she very soon held herself erect, and wore a face open to every wonder, impression-able as the blue lake-surface, crisped here and there by fitful breezes against a level sun.

I T was an axiom with Mr. Beamish, our first, if not our only philosophical beau and a gentleman of some thoughtfulness, that the social English require tyrannical government as much as the political are able to dispense with it : and this he explained by an exposition of the character of a race possessed of the eminent virtue of individual self-assertion, which causes them to insist on good elbow-room wherever they gather together. Society, however, not being tolerable where the smoothness of intercourse is disturbed by a perpetual punching of sides, the merits of the free citizen in them become their demerits when a fraternal circle is established, and they who have shown an example of civilization too notable in one sphere to call for eulogy, are often to be seen elbowing on the ragged edge of barbarism in the other. They must therefore be reduced to accept laws not of their own making, and of an extreme rigidity.

Here too is a further peril ; for the gallant spirits distinguishing them in the state of independence may (he foresaw the melancholy experience of a later age) abandon them utterly in subjection, and the glorious boisterousness befitting the village green forsake them even in their haunts of liberal association, should they once be thoroughly tamed by authority. Our " merrie England " will then be long-faced England, an England of fallen chaps, like a boar's head, bearing for speech a lemon in the mouth : good to feast on, mayhap ; not with !

Mr. Beamish would actually seem to have foreseen the danger of a transition that he could watch over only in his time ; and, as he said, " I go, as I came, on a flash ; " he had neither ancestry nor descendants : he was a genius ; he knew himself a solitary, therefore, in spite of his efforts to create his like. Within his district he did effect something, enough to give him fame as one of the princely fathers of our domestic civilization, though we now appear to have lost by it more than formerly we gained. The chasing of the natural is ever fraught with dubious hazards. If it gallops back, according to the proverb, it will do so at the charge : commonly it gallops off, quite off ; and then for any kind of animation our precarious dependence is upon brains : we have to live on our wits, which are ordinarily less productive than land, and cannot be remitted in entail.

Rightly or wrongly (there are differences of opinion about it) Mr. Beamish repressed the chthonic natural with a rod of iron beneath his rule. The hoyden and the bumpkin had no peace until they had given public imitations of the lady and the gentleman ; nor were the lady and the gentleman privileged to be what he called "free flags." He could be charitable to the passion, but he bellowed the very word itself (hauled up smoking from the brimstone lake) against them that pretended to be shamelessly guilty of the peccadilloes of gallantry. His famous accost of a lady threatening to sink, and already performing like a vessel in that situation—"So, madam, I hear you are preparing to enrol yourself in the very ancient order?" . . . (he named it)—was a piece of insolence that involved him in some discord with the lady's husband and "the rascal steward," as he chose to term the third party in these affairs : yet it is reputed to have saved the lady.

Furthermore, he attacked the vulgarity of persons of quality, and he has told a fashionable dame who was indulging herself in a marked sneer of disdain, not improving to her features, "that he would be pleased to have her assurance it was her face she presented to mankind :" a thing—thanks perhaps to him chiefly—no longer possible of utterance. One of the sex asking him why he addressed his persecutions particularly to women : "Because I fight your battle," says he, "and I find you in the ranks of the enemy." He treated them as traitors.

He was nevertheless well supported by a sex that compensates for dislike of its friend before a certain age by a cordial recognition of him when it has touched the period. A phalanx of great dames gave him the terrors of Olympus for all except the natively audacious, the truculent and the insufferably obtuse ; and from the midst of them he launched decree and bolt to good effect : not, of course, without receiving return missiles, and not without subsequent question whether the work of that man was beneficial to the country, who indeed tamed the bumpkin squire and his brood, but at the cost of their animal spirits and their gift of speech ; viz. by making petrifactions of them. In the surgical operation of tracheotomy, a successful treatment of the patient hangs, we believe, on the promptness and skill of the introduction of the artificial windpipe ; and it may be that our unhappy countrymen when cut off from the source of their breath were not neatly hàndled ; or else that there is a physical opposition in them to anything artificial, and it must be nature or nothing. The dispute shall be left where it stands.

Now, to venture upon parading a beautiful young Duchess of Dewlap, with an odour of the shepherdess about her notwithstanding her acquired art of stepping conformably in a hoop, and to demand full homage of respect for a lady bearing such a title, who had the intoxicating attractions of the ruddy orchard apple on the tree next the roadside wall, when the owner is absent, was bold in Mr. Beamish, passing temerity ; nor would even he have attempted it had he not been assured of the support of his phalanx of great ladies. They

indeed, after being taken into the secret, had stipulated that first they must have an inspection of the
transformed dairymaid ; and the review was not
unfavourable. Duchess Susan came out of it more
scatheless than her duke. She was tongue-tied,
and her tutored walking and really admirable
stature helped her to appease the critics of her sex ;
by whom her too readily blushful innocence was
praised, with a reserve, expressed in the remark,
that she was a monstrous fine toy for a duke's
second childhood, and should never have been let
fly from his nursery. Her milliner was approved.
The duke was a notorious connoisseur of female
charms, and would see, of course, to the decorous
adornment of her person by the best of modistes.
Her smiling was pretty, her eyes were soft ; she
might turn out good, if well guarded for a time ;
but these merits of the woman are not those of the
great lady, and her title was too strong a beam on
her character to give it a fair chance with her
critics. They one and all recommended powder
for her hair and cheeks. That odour of the
shepherdess could be exorcised by no other means,
they declared. Her blushing was indecent.

Truly the critics of the foeman sex behaved in a
way to cause the blushes to swarm rosy as the
troops of young Loves round Cytherea in her sea-
birth, when, some soaring, and sinking some, they
flutter like her loosened zone, and breast the air
thick as flower petals on the summer's breath,

weaving her net for the world. Duchess Susan might protest her inability to keep her blushes down ; the wrong was done by the insolent eyes, and not by her artless cheeks. Ay, but nature, if we are to tame these men, must be swathed and concealed, partly stifled, absolutely stifled upon occasion. The natural woman does not move a foot without striking earth to conjure up the horrid apparition of the natural man, who is not as she, but a cannibal savage. To be the light which leads, it is her business to don the misty vesture of an idea, that she may dwell as an idea in men's minds, very dim, very powerful, but abstruse, unseizable. Much wisdom was imparted to her on the subject, and she understood a little, and echoed hollow to the remainder, willing to show entire docility as far as her intelligence consented to be awake. She was in that stage of the dainty, faintly tinged innocence of the amorousness of themselves when beautiful young women who have not been caught for schooling in infancy deem it a defilement to be made to appear other than the blessed nature has made them, which has made them beautiful, and surely therefore deserves to be worshipped. The lectures of the great ladies and Chloe's counsels failed to persuade her to use the powder puff-ball. Perhaps too, as timidity quitted her, she enjoyed her distinctiveness in their midst.

But the distinctiveness of a Duchess of Dewlap

with the hair and cheeks of our native fields, was
fraught with troubles outrunning Mr. Beamish's
calculations. He had perceived that she would be
attractive ; he had not reckoned on the homo-
geneousness of her particular English charms. A
beauty in red, white, and blue is our goddess
Venus with the apple of Paris in her hand ; and
after two visits to the Pump Room, and one
promenade in the walks about the Assembly
House, she had as completely divided the ordinary
guests of the Wells into male and female in opinion
as her mother Nature had done it in sex. And
the men would not be silenced ; they had gazed
on their divinest, and it was for the women to suc-
cumb to that unwholesome state, so full of thunder.
Knights and squires, military and rural, threw up
their allegiance right and left to devote themselves
to this robust new vision, and in their peculiar
manner, with a general View-halloo, and Yoicks,
Tally-ho, and away we go, pelt ahead ! · Unex-
ampled as it is in England for Beauty to kindle
the ardours of the scent of the fox, Duchess Susan
did more—she turned all her followers into hounds;
they were madmen : within a very few days of her
entrance bets raged about her, and there were
brawls, jolly flings at her character in the form
of lusty encomium, givings of the lie, and upon
one occasion a knock-down blow in public, as
though the place had never known the polishing
touch of Mr. Beamish.

He was thrown into great perplexity by that blow. Discountenancing the duel as much as he could, an affair of the sword was nevertheless more tolerable than the brutal fist : and of all men to be guilty of it, who would have anticipated the young Alonzo, Chloe's quiet, modest lover ! He it was. The case came before Mr. Beamish for his decision ; he had to pronounce an impartial judgment, and for some time, during the examination of evidence, he suffered, as he assures us in his Memoirs, a royal agony. To have to strike with the glaive of Justice them whom we most esteem, is the greatest affliction known to kings. He would have done it : he deserved to reign. Happily the evidence against the gentleman who was tumbled, Mr. Ralph Shepster, excused Mr. Augustus Camwell, otherwise Alonzo, for dealing with him promptly to shut his mouth.

This Shepster, a raw young squire, " recking," Beau Beamish writes of him, " one half of the soil, and t'other half of the town," had involved Chloe in his familiar remarks upon the Duchess of Dewlap ; and the personal respect entertained by Mr. Beamish for Chloe so strongly approved Alonzo's championship of her, that in giving judgement he laid stress on young Alonzo's passion for Chloe, to prove at once the disinterestedness of the assailant, and the judicial nature of the sentence : which was, that Mr. Ralph Shepster should undergo banishment, and had the right to demand reparation. The latter part of this decree assisted in effecting the execution of the former. Shepster declined cold steel, calling it murder, and was effusive of nature's logic on the subject:

"Because a man comes and knocks me down, I'm to go up to him and ask him to run me through!"

His shake of the head signified that he was not such a noodle. Voluble and prolific of illustration, as is no one so much as a son of Nature inspired to speak her words of wisdom, he defied the mandate, and refused himself satisfaction, until in the strangest manner possible flights of white feathers beset him, and he became a mark for persecution too trying for the friendship of his friends. He fled, repeating his tale, that he had seen "Beamish's Duchess," and Chloe attending her, at an assignation in the South Grove, where a gentleman, unknown to the Wells, presented himself to the adventurous ladies, and they walked together—a tale ending with nods.

Shepster's banishment was one of those victories of justice upon which mankind might be congratulated if they left no commotion behind. But, as when a boy has been horsed before his comrades, dread may visit them, yet is there likewise devilry in the school; and everywhere over earth a summary punishment that does not sweep the place clear is likely to infect whom it leaves remaining. The great law-givers, Lycurgus, Draco, Solon, Beamish, sorrowfully acknowledge that they have had recourse to infernal agents, after they have thus purified their circle of an offender. Doctors confess to the same of their physic. The expelling agency has next to be expelled, and it is a subtle poison, affecting our spirits. Duchess Susan had now the incense of a victim to heighten her charms; like the treasure-laden Spanish galleon for whom, on her voyage home from South American waters, our enterprising light-craft privateers lay in wait, she had the double attraction of being desirable and an enemy. To watch above her conscientiously was a harassing business.

Mr. Beamish sent for Chloe, and she came to him at once. Her look was curious ; he studied it while they conversed. So looks one who is watching the sure flight of an arrow, or the happy combinations of an intrigue. Saying, " I am no inquisitor, child," he ventured upon two or three modest inquisitions with regard to her mistress. The title he had disguised Duchess Susan in, he confessed to rueing as the principal cause of the agitation of his principality. " She is courted," he said, " less like a citadel waving a flag than a hostelry where the demand is for sitting room and a tankard ! These be our manners. Yet, I must own, a Duchess of Dewlap is a provocation, and my exclusive desire to protect the name of my lord stands corrected by the perils environing his lady. She is other than I supposed her ; she is, we will hope, an excellent good creature, but too attractive for moat and drawbridge and the customary defences to be neglected."

Chloe met his interrogatory with a ready report of the young duchess's innocence and good nature that pacified Mr. Beamish.

" And you ? " said he.

She smiled for answer.

That smile was not the common smile; it was one of an eager exultingness, producing as he gazed the twitch of an inquisitive reflection of it on his lips. Such a smile bids us guess and quickens us to guess, warns us we burn and speeds our burning, and so, like an angel wafting us to some heaven-feasting promontory, lifts us out of ourselves to see in the universe of colour what the mouth has but pallid speech to tell. That is the very heart's language ; the years are in a look, as mount and vale of the dark land spring up in lightning.

He checked himself : he scarce dared to say it. She nodded.

" You have seen the man, Chloe ? "

Her smiling broke up in the hard lines of an ecstasy neighbouring pain. " He has come ; he is here ; he is faithful ; he has not forgotten me. I was right. I knew ! I knew ! "

" Caseldy has come ? "

" He has come. Do not ask. To have him ! to see him ! Mr. Beamish, he is here."

" At last ! "

"Cruel!"

"Well, Caseldy has come, then! But now, friend Chloe, you should be made aware that the man——"

She stopped her ears. As she did so, Mr. Beamish observed a thick silken skein dangling from one hand. Part of it was plaited, and at the upper end there was a knot. It resembled the commencement of her manufactory of a whip: she swayed it to and fro, allowing him to catch and lift the threads on his fingers for the purpose of examining her work. There was no special compliment to pay, so he dropped it without remark.

Their faces had expressed her wish to hear nothing from him of Caseldy and his submission to say nothing. Her happiness was too big; she appeared to beg to lie down with it on her bosom, in the manner of an outworn young mother who has now first received her infant in her arms from the nurse.

CHAPTER V

HUMOURING Chloe with his usual considerateness, Mr. Beamish forebore to cast a shadow on her new-born joy, and even within himself to doubt the security of its foundation. Caseldy's return to the Wells was at least some assurance of his constancy, seeing that here they appointed to meet when he and Chloe last parted. All might be well, though it was unexplained why he had not presented himself earlier. To the lightest inquiry Chloe's reply was a shiver of happiness.

Moreover, Mr. Beamish calculated that Caseldy would be a serviceable ally in commanding a proper respect for her Grace the Duchess of Dewlap. So he betook himself cheerfully to Caseldy's lodgings to deliver a message of welcome, meeting, on his way thither, Mr. Augustus Camwell, with whom he had a short conversation, greatly to his admiration of the enamoured young gentleman's goodness and self-compression in speaking of Caseldy and Chloe's better fortune. Mr. Camwell seemed hurried.

Caseldy was not at home, and Mr. Beamish proceeded to the lodgings of the duchess. Chloe had found her absent. The two consulted. Mr. Beamish put on a serious air, until Chloe mentioned the pastrycook's shop, for Duchess Susan had a sweet tooth ; she loved a visit to the pastrycook's, whose jam tarts were dearer to her than his more famous hot mutton pies. The pastrycook informed Mr. Beamish that her Grace had been in his shop, earlier than usual, as it happened, and accompanied by a foreign-looking gentleman wearing moustachios. Her Grace, the pastrycook said, had partaken of several tarts, in common with the gentleman, who complimented him upon his excelling the Continental confectioner. Mr. Beamish glanced at Chloe. He pursued his researches down at the Pump Room, while she looked round the ladies' coffee house. Encountering again, they walked back to the duchess's lodgings, where a band stood playing in the road, by order of her Grace ; but the duchess was away, and had not been seen since her morning's departure.

" What sort of character would you give mistress Susan of Dewlap, from your personal acquaintance with it ? " said Mr. Beamish to Chloe, as they stepped from the door.

Chloe mused and said, " I would add 'good' to the unkindest comparison you could find for her."

" But accepting the comparison ! " Mr. Beamish nodded, and revolved upon the circumstance of their being very much in Nature's hands with Duchess

Susan, of whom it might be said that her character was good, yet all the more alive to the temptations besetting the Spring season.   He allied Chloe's adjective to a number of epithets equally applicable to nature and to women, according to current ideas, concluding: "Count, they call your Caseldy at his lodgings. 'The Count he is out for an airing.' He is counted out. Ah! you will make him drop that 'Count' when he takes you from here."

"Do not speak of the time beyond the month," said Chloe, so urgently on a rapid breath as to cause Mr. Beamish to cast an inquiring look at her.

She answered it, "Is not one month of brightness as much as we can ask for?"

The beau clapped his elbows complacently to his sides in philosophical concord with her sentiment.

In the afternoon, on the parade, they were joined by Mr. Camwell, among groups of fashionable ladies and their escorts, pacing serenely, by medical prescription, for an appetite. As he did not comment on the absence of the duchess, Mr. Beamish alluded to it; whereupon he was informed that she was about the meadows, and had been there for some hours.

"Not unguarded," he replied to Mr. Beamish.

"Aha!" quoth the latter; "we have an Argus!" and as the duchess was not on the heights, and the sun's rays were mild in cloud, he agreed to his young friend's proposal that they should advance to meet her. Chloe walked with them, but her face was disdainful; at the stiles she gave her hand to Mr. Beamish; she did not address a word to Mr. Camwell, and he knew the reason. Nevertheless he maintained his air of soldierly resignation to the performance of duty, and held his head like a gentleman unable to conceive the ignominy of having played spy. Chloe shrank from him.

Duchess Susan was distinguished coming across a broad uncut meadow, tirra-lirraing beneath a lark, Caseldy in attendance on her. She stopped short and spoke to him; then came forward, crying ingenuously, "Oh, Mr. Beamish, isn't this just what you wanted me to do?"

"No, madam," said he, "you had my injunctions to the contrary."

"La!" she exclaimed, "I thought I was to run about in the fields now and then to preserve my simplicity. I know I was told so, and who told me!"

Mr. Beamish bowed effusively to the introduction of Caseldy, whose fingers he touched in sign of the renewal of acquaintance, and with a laugh addressed the duchess: "Madam, you remind me of a tale of my infancy. I had a juvenile comrade of the tenderest age, by name Tommy Plumston, and he enjoyed the privilege of intimacy with a component urchin yclept Jimmy Clungeon, with which adventurous roamer, in defiance of his mother's interdict

E

against his leaving the house for a minute during her absence from home, he departed on a tour of the district, resulting, perhaps as a consequence of its completeness, in this, that at a distance computed at four miles from the maternal mansion, he perceived his beloved mama with sufficient clearness to feel sure that she likewise had seen him. Tommy consulted with Jimmy, and then he sprang forward on a run to his frowning mama, and delivered himself in these artless words, which I repeat as they were uttered, to give you the flavour of the innocent babe: he said, 'I frink I frought I hear you call me, ma! and Jimmy Clungeon, he frought he frink so too!' So, you see, the pair of them were under the impression that they were doing right. There is a delicate distinction in the tenses of each frinking where the other frought, enough in itself to stamp sincerity upon the statement."

Caseldy said, "The veracity of a boy possessing a friend named Clungeon is beyond contest."

Duchess Susan opened her eyes. "Four miles from home! And what did his mother do to him?"

"Tommy's mama," said Mr. Beamish, and with the resplendent licence of the period which continued still upon tolerable terms with nature under the compromise of decorous "Oh-fie!" flatly declared the thing she did.

" I fancy, sir, that I caught sight of your figure

on the hill yonder about an hour or so earlier," said Caseldy to Mr. Camwell.

" If it was at the time when you were issuing from that wood, sir, your surmise is correct," said the young gentleman.

" You are long-sighted, sir ! "

" I am, sir."

" And so am I."

" And I," said Chloe.

" Our Chloe will distinguish you accurately at a mile, and has done it," observed Mr. Beamish.

" One guesses tiptoe on a suspicion, and if one is wrong it passes, and if one is right it is a miracle," she said, and raised her voice on a song to quit the subject.

" Ay, ay, Chloe ; so then you had a suspicion, you rogue, the day we had the pleasure of meeting the duchess, had you ? " Mr. Beamish persisted.

Duchess Susan interposed. " Such a pretty song ! and you to stop her, sir ! "

Caseldy took up the air.

" Oh, you two together ! " she cried. " I do love hearing music in the fields ; it is heavenly. Bands in the town and 'voices in the green fields, I say ! Couldn't you join Chloe, Mr. . . . Count, sir, before we come among the people, here where it's all so nice and still. Music ! and my heart does begin so to pit-a-pat. Do you sing, Mr. Alonzo ? "

" Poorly," the young gentleman replied.

" But the Count can sing, and Chloe's a real

angel when she sings; and won't you, dear?" she implored Chloe, to whom Caseldy addressed a prelude with a bow and a flourish of the hand.

Chloe's voice flew forth. Caseldy's rich masculine matched it. The song was gay; he snapped his finger at intervals in foreign style, singing bigchested, with full notes and a fine abandonment, and the quickest susceptibility to his fair companion's cunning modulations, and an eye for Duchess Susan's rapture.

Mr. Beamish and Mr. Camwell applauded them.

"I never can tell what to say when I'm brimming;" the duchess let fall a sigh. "And he can play the flute, Mr. Beamish. He promised me he would go into the orchestra and play a bit at one of your nice evening delicious concerts, and that will be nice—Oh!"

"He promised you, madam, did he so?" said the beau. "Was it on your way to the Wells that he promised you?"

"On my way to the Wells!" she exclaimed softly. "Why, how could anybody promise me a thing before ever he saw me? I call that a strange thing to ask a person. No, to-day, while we were promenading; and I should hear him sing, he said. He does admire his Chloe so. Why, no wonder, is it, now? She can do everything; knit, sew, sing, dance—and talk! She's never uneasy for a word. She makes whole scenes of things go round you, like a picture peep-show, I tell her. And always cheerful. She hasn't a minute of grumps ; and I'm sometimes a dish of stale milk fit only for pigs. With your late hours here, I'm sure I want tickling in the morning, and Chloe carols me one of her songs, and I say, ' There's my bird ! ' "

Mr. Beamish added, " And you will remember she has a heart."

" I should think so ! " said the duchess.

" A heart, madam ! "

" Why, what else ? "

Nothing other, the beau, by his aspect, was constrained to admit.

He appeared puzzled by this daughter of nature in a coronet ; and more on her remarking, " You know about her heart, Mr. Beamish."

He acquiesced, for of course he knew of her life-long devotion to Caseldy ; but there was archness in her tone. However, he did not expect a woman of her education to have the tone perfectly concordant with the circumstances. Speaking tentatively of Caseldy's handsome face and figure, he was pleased to hear the duchess say, " So I tell Chloe."

" Well," said he, " we must consider them united ; they are one."

Duchess Susan replied, " That's what I tell him ; she will do anything you wish."

He repeated these words with an interjection, and decided in his mind that they were merely silly. She was a real shepherdess by birth and

nature, requiring a strong guard over her attractions
on account of her simplicity ; such was his reading
of the problem ; he had conceived it at the first
sight of her, and always recurred to it under the influence of her artless eyes, though his theories upon
men and women were astute, and that cavalier perceived by long-sighted Chloe at Duchess Susan's
coach window perturbed him at whiles. Habitually
to be anticipating the simpleton in a particular person is the sure way of being sometimes the dupe, as
he would not have been the last to warn a neophyte ;
but abstract wisdom is in need of an unappeased
suspicion of much keenness of edge, if we would
have it alive to cope with artless eyes and our prepossessed fancy of their artlessness.

"You talk of Chloe to him ? " he said.

She answered, " Yes, that I do. And he does
love her! I like to hear him. He is one of the
gentlemen who don't make me feel timid with
them."

She received a short lecture on the virtues of
timidity in preserving the sex from danger ; after
which, considering that the lady who does not feel
timid with a particular cavalier has had no sentiment awakened, he relinquished his place to Mr.
Camwell, and proceeded to administer the probe to
Caseldy.

That gentleman was communicatively candid.
Chloe had left him, and he related how, summoned
home to England and compelled to settle a dispute

threatening a lawsuit, he had regretfully to abstain from visiting the Wells for a season, not because of any fear of the attractions of play—he had subdued the frailty of the desire to play — but because he deemed it due to his Chloe to bring her an untroubled face, and he wished first to be the better of the serious annoyances besetting him. For some similar reason he had not written ; he wished to feast on her surprise. "And I had my reward," he said, as if he had been the person principally to suffer through that abstinence. " I found—I may say it to you, Mr. Beamish—love in her eyes. Divine by nature, she is one of the immortals, both in appearance and in stead-fastness."

They referred to Duchess Susan. Caseldy reluctantly owned that it would be an unkindness to remove Chloe from attendance on her during the short remaining term of her stay at the Wells ; and so he had not proposed it, he said, for the duchess was a child, an innocent, not stupid by any means ; but, of course, her transplanting from an inferior to an exalted position put her under disadvantages.

Mr. Beamish spoke of the difficulties of his post as guardian, and also of the strange cavalier seen at her carriage window by Chloe.

Caseldy smiled and said, " If there was one— and Chloe is rather long-sighted—we can hardly expect her to confess it."

" Why not, sir, if she be this piece of innocence ? "
Mr. Beamish was led to inquire.

" She fears you, sir," Caseldy answered. " You
have inspired her with an extraordinary fear of
you."

"I have ? " said the beau : it had been his
endeavour to inspire it, and he swelled somewhat,
rather with relief at the thought of his possessing a
power to control his delicate charge, than with our
vanity ; yet would it be audacious to say that there
was not a dose of the latter. He was a very human
man ; and he had, as we have seen, his ideas of the
effect of the impression of fear upon the hearts of
women. Something, in any case, caused him to
forget the cavalier.

They were drawn to the three preceding them,
by a lively dissension between Chloe and Mr.
Camwell.

Duchess Susan explained it in her blunt style :
" She wants him to go away home, and he says
he will, if she'll give him that double skein of silk
she swings about, and she says she won't, let him
ask as long as he pleases ; so he says he sha'n't
go, and I'm sure I don't see why he should ;
and she says he may stay, but he sha'n't have her
necklace, she calls it. So Mr. Camwell snatches,
and Chloe fires up. Gracious, can't she frown !—
at him. She never frowns at anybody but him."

Caseldy attempted persuasion on Mr. Camwell's
behalf. With his mouth at Chloe's ear, he said

"Give it; let the poor fellow have his memento; despatch him with it."

"I can hear! and that is really kind," exclaimed Duchess Susan.

"Rather a missy-missy schoolgirl sort of necklace," Mr. Beamish observed; "but he might have it, without the dismissal, for I cannot consent to lose Alonzo. No, madam," he nodded at the duchess.

Caseldy continued his whisper: "You can't think of wearing a thing like that about your neck?"

"Indeed," said Chloe, "I think of it."

"Why, what fashion have you over here?"

"It is not yet a fashion," she said.

"A silken circlet will not well become any precious pendant that I know of."

"A bag of dust is not a very precious pendant," she said.

"Oh, a memento mori!" cried he.

And she answered, "Yes."

He rallied her for her superstition, pursuing, "Surely. my love, 'tis a cheap riddance of a pestilent, intrusive jaloux. Whip it into his hands for a mittimus."

"Does his presence distress you?" she asked.

"I will own that to be always having the fellow dogging us, with his dejected leer, is not agreeable. He watches us now, because my lips are close by your cheek. He should be absent; he is one too many. Speed him on his voyage with the souvenir he asks for."

"I keep it for a journey of my own, which I may have to take," said Chloe.

" With me ? "

" You will follow ; you cannot help following me, Caseldy."

He speculated on her front. She was tenderly smiling.

" You are happy, Chloe ? "

" I have never known such happiness," she said. The brilliancy of her eyes confirmed it.

He glanced over at Duchess Susan, who was like a sunflower in the sun. His glance lingered a moment. Her abundant and glowing young charms were the richest fascination an eye like his could dwell on. " That is right," said he. " We will be perfectly happy till the month ends. And after it ? But get us rid of Monsieur le Jeune ; toss him that trifle ; I spare him that. 'Twill be bliss to him, at the cost of a bit of silk thread to us. Besides, if we keep him to cure him of his passion here, might it not be—these boys veer suddenly, like the winds of Albion, from one fair object to t'other—at the cost of the precious and simple lady you are guarding ? I merely hint. These two affect one another, as though it could be. She speaks of him. It shall be as you please ; but a trifle like that, my Chloe, to be rid of a green eye ! "

"You much wish him gone?" she said.

He shrugged. "The fellow is in our way."

"You think him a little perilous for my innocent lady?"

"Candidly, I do."

She stretched the half-plaited silken rope in her two hands to try the strength of it, made a second knot, and consigned it to her pocket.

At once she wore her liveliest playfellow air, in which character no one was so enchanting as Chloe could be, for she became the comrade of men without forfeit of her station among sage sweet ladies, and was like a well-mannered sparkling boy, to whom his admiring seniors have given the lead in sallies, whims, and flights; but pleasanter than a boy, the soft hues of her sex toned her frolic spirit; she seemed her sex's deputy, to tell the coarser where they could meet, as on a bridge above the torrent separating them, gaily for interchange of the best of either, unfired and untempted by fire, yet with all the elements which make fire burn to animate their hearts.

"Lucky the man who wins for himself that lifelong cordial!" Mr. Beamish said to Duchess Susan.

She had small comprehension of metaphorical phrases, but she was quick at reading faces; and comparing the enthusiasm on the face of the beau with Caseldy's look of troubled wonderment and regret, she pitied the lover conscious of not having the larger share of his mistress's affections. When presently he looked at her, the tender-hearted woman could have cried for very compassion, so sensible did he show himself of Chloe's preference of the other.

CHAPTER VI

THAT evening Duchess Susan played at the
Pharaoh table and lost eight hundred pounds,
through desperation at the loss of twenty. After
encouraging her to proceed to this extremity,
Caseldy checked her. He was conducting her out
of the Play room when a couple of young squires
of the Shepster order, and primed with wine, inter-
cepted her to present their condolences, which they
performed with exaggerated gestures, intended for
broad mimicry of the courtliness imported from the
Continent, and a very dulcet harping on the popular
variations of her Christian name, not forgetting her
singular title, "my lovely, lovely Dewlap!"

She was excited and stunned by her immediate
experience in the transfer of money, and she said,
"I'm sure I don't know what you want."

"Yes!" cried they, striking their bosoms as
guitars, and attempting the posture of the thrummer
on the instrument; "she knows. She does know.
Handsome Susie knows what we want." And
one ejaculated, mellifluously, "Oh!" and the other
"Ah!" in flagrant derision of the foreign ways
they produced in boorish burlesque—a self-conso-
latory and a common trick of the boor.

Caseldy was behind. He pushed forward and bowed to them. "Sirs, will you mention to me what you want?"

He said it with a look that meant steel. It cooled them sufficiently to let him place the duchess under the protectorship of Mr. Beamish, then entering from another room with Chloe; whereupon the pair of rustic bucks retired to reinvigorate their valiant blood.

Mr. Beamish had seen that there was cause for gratitude to Caseldy, to whom he said, "She has lost?" and he seemed satisfied on hearing the amount of the loss, and commissioned Caseldy to escort the ladies to their lodgings at once, observing, "Adieu, Count!"

"You will find my foreign title of use to you here, after a bout or two," was the reply.

"No bouts, if possibly to be avoided; though I perceive how the flavour of your countship may spread a wholesome alarm among our rurals, who will readily have at you with fists, but relish not the tricky cold weapon."

Mr. Beamish haughtily bowed the duchess away.

Caseldy seized the opportunity while handing her into her sedan to say, "We will try the fortune-teller for a lucky day to have our revenge."

She answered: "Oh, don't talk to me about playing again ever; I'm nigh on a clean pocket, and never knew such a sinful place as this. I feel I've tumbled into a ditch. And there's Mr. Beamish, all top when he bows to me. You're keeping Chloe waiting, sir."

" Where was she while we were at the table ? "

" Sure she was with Mr. Beamish."

" Ah ! " he groaned.

" The poor soul is in despair over her losses to-night," he turned from the boxed-up duchess to remark to Chloe. " Give her a comfortable cry and a few moral maxims."

" I will," she said. " You love me, Caseldy ? "

" Love you ? I ? Your own ? What assurance would you have ? "

" None, dear friend."

Here was a woman easily deceived.

In the hearts of certain men, owing to an intellectual contempt of easy dupes, compunction in deceiving is diminished by the lightness of their task ; and that soft confidence which will often, if but passingly, bid betrayers reconsider the charms of the fair soul they are abandoning, commends these armoured knights to pursue with redoubled earnest the fruitful ways of treachery. Their feelings are warm for their prey, moreover ; and choosing to judge their victim by the present warmth of their feelings, they can at will be hurt, even to being scandalized, by a coldness that does not waken one suspicion of them. Jealousy would have a chance of arresting, for it is not impossible to tease them back to avowed allegiance ; but sheer indifference also has a stronger hold on them than a dull, blind trustfulness. They hate the burden it imposes ; the blind aspect is only touching enough to remind them of the burden, and they hate it for that, and for the enormous presumption of the belief that they are everlastingly bound to such an imbecile. She walks about with her eyes shut, expecting not to stumble, and when she does, am I to blame? The injured man asks it in the course of his reasoning.

He recurs to his victim's merits, but only compassionately, and the compassion is chilled by the thought that she may in the end start across his path to thwart him. Thereat he is drawn to think of the prize she may rob him of; and when one woman is an obstacle, the other shines desirable as life beyond death ; he must have her ; he sees her in the hue of his desire for her, and the obstacle in that of his repulsion. Cruelty is no more than the man's effort to win the wished object.

She should not leave it to his imagination to conceive that in the end the blind may awaken to thwart him. Better for her to cast him hence, or let him know that she will do battle to keep him. But the pride of a love that has hardened in the faithfulness of love cannot always be wise on trial.

Caseldy walked considerably in the rear of the couple of chairs. He saw on his way what was coming. His two young squires were posted at Duchess Susan's door when she arrived, and he received a blow from one of them in clearing a way for her. She plucked at his hand. "Have they hurt you?" she asked.

"Think of me to-night thanking them and heaven for this, my darling," he replied, with a pressure that lit the flying moment to kindle the after hours.

Chloe had taken help of one of her bearers to jump out. She stretched a finger at the unruly intruders, crying sternly, "There is blood on you—come not nigh me!" The loftiest harangue would not have been so cunning to touch their wits. They stared at one another in the clear moonlight. Which of them had blood on him? As they had not been for blood, but for rough fun, and something to boast of next day, they gesticulated according to the first instructions of the dancing master, by way of gallantry, and were out of Caseldy's path when he placed himself at his liege lady's service. "Take no notice of them, dear," she said.

"No, no," said he; and "What is it?" and his hoarse accent and shaking clasp of her arm sickened her to the sensation of approaching death.

Upstairs Duchess Susan made a show of embracing her. Both were trembling. The duchess ascribed her condition to those dreadful men. "What makes them be at me so?" she said.

And Chloe said, "Because you are beautiful."

"Am I?"

" You are."

" I am ? "

" Very beautiful ; young and beautiful ; beautiful in the bud. You will learn to excuse them, madam."

" But, Chloe——" The duchess shut her mouth. Out of a languid reverie, she sighed: " I suppose I must be! My duke—oh, don't talk of him. Dear man! he's in bed and fast asleep long before this. I wonder how he came to let me come here. I did bother him, I know. Am I very, very beautiful, Chloe, so that men can't help themselves ? "

" Very, madam."

" There, good-night. I want to be in bed, and I can't kiss you because you keep calling me madam, and freeze me to icicles ; but I do love you, Chloe."

" I am sure you do."

" I'm quite certain I do. I know I never mean harm. But how are we women expected to behave, then ? Oh, I'm unhappy, I am."

" You must abstain from playing."

" It's that ! I've lost my money—I forgot. And I shall have to confess it to my duke, though he warned me. Old men hold their fingers up—so! One finger : and you never forget the sight of it, never. It's a round finger, like the handle of a jug, and won't point at you when they're lecturing, and the skin's like an old coat on gaffer's shoulders—

or, Chloe! just like, when you look at the nail, a rumpled counterpane up to the face of a corpse. I declare, it's just like! I feel as if I didn't a bit mind talking of corpses to-night. And my money's gone, and I don't much mind. I'm a wild girl again, handsomer than when that——he is a dear, kind, good old nobleman, with his funny old finger: 'Susan! Susan!' I'm no worse than others. Everybody plays here; everybody superior. Why, you have played, Chloe."

"Never!"

"I've heard you say you played once, and a bigger stake it was, you said, than anybody ever did play."

"Not money."

"What then?"

"My life."

"Goodness—yes! I understand. I understand everything to-night—men too. So you did!— They're not so shamefully wicked, Chloe. Because, I can't see the wrong of human nature—if we're discreet, I mean. Now and then a country dance and a game, and home to bed and dreams. There's no harm in that, I vow.—And that's why you stayed at this place. You like it, Chloe?"

"I am used to it."

"But when you're married to Count Caseldy you'll go?"

"Yes, then."

She uttered it so joylessly that Duchess Susan

added, with intense affectionateness, " You're not obliged to marry him, dear Chloe."

" Nor he me, madam."

The duchess caught at her impulsively to kiss her, and said she would undress herself, as she wished to be alone.

From that night she was a creature inflamed.

THE total disappearance of the pair of heroes who had been the latest in the conspiracy to vex his delicate charge, gave Mr. Beamish a high opinion of Caseldy as an assistant in such an office as he held. They had gone, and nothing more was heard of them. Caseldy confined his observations on the subject to the remark that he had employed the best means to be rid of that kind of worthies ; and whether their souls had fled, or only their bodies, was unknown. But the duchess had quiet promenades with Caseldy to guard her, while Mr. Beamish counted the remaining days of her visit with the impatience of a man having cause to cast eye on a clock. For Duchess Susan was not very manageable now ; she had fits of insurgency, and plainly said that her time was short, and she meant to do as she liked, go where she liked, play when she liked, and be an independent woman—if she was so soon to be taken away and boxed in a castle that was only a bigger sedan.

Caseldy protested he was as helpless as the beau. He described the annoyance of his incessant running about at her heels in all directions amusingly, and suggested that she must be beating the district to recover her " strange cavalier," of whom, or of one that had ridden beside her carriage half a day on her journey to the Wells, he said she had dropped a sort of hint. He complained of the impossibility of his getting an hour in privacy with his Chloe.

" And I, accustomed to consult with her, see too little of her," said Mr. Beamish. " I shall presently be seeing nothing, and already I am sensible of my loss."

He represented his case to Duchess Susan :—that she was for ever driving out long distances and taking Chloe from him, when his occupation precluded his accompanying them ; and as Chloe soon was to be lost to him for good, he deeply felt her absence.

The duchess flung him enigmatical rejoinders : "You can change all that, Mr. Beamish, if you like, and you know you can. Oh, yes, you can. But you like being a butterfly, and when you've made ladies pale you're happy : and there they're to stick and wither for you. Never !—I've that pride. I may be worried, but I'll never sink to green and melancholy for a man."

She bridled at herself in a mirror, wherein not a sign of paleness was reflected.

Mr. Beamish meditated, and he thought it prudent to speak to Caseldy manfully of her childish suspicions, lest she should perchance in like manner perturb the lover's mind.

"Oh, make your mind easy, my dear sir, as far as I am concerned," said Caseldy. "But, to tell you the truth, I think I can interpret her creamy ladyship's innuendos a little differently and quite as clearly. For my part, I prefer the pale to the blowsy, and I stake my right hand on Chloe's fidelity. Whatever harm I may have the senseless cruelty—misfortune, I may rather call it—to do that heavenly-minded woman in our days to come, none shall say of me that I was ever for an instant guilty of the baseness of doubting her purity and constancy. And, sir, I will add that I could perfectly rely also on your honour."

Mr. Beamish bowed. "You do but do me justice. But, say, what interpretation?"

"She began by fearing you," said Caseldy, creating a stare that was followed by a frown. "She fancies you neglect her. Perhaps she has a woman's suspicion that you do it to try her."

Mr. Beamish frenetically cited his many occupations. "How can I be ever dancing attendance on her?" Then he said, "Pooh," and tenderly fingered the ruffles of his wrist. "Tush, tush," said he, "no, no : though if it came to a struggle between us, I might in the interests of my old friend, her lord, whom I have reasons for esteeming, interpose an influence that would make the exercise of my authority agreeable. Hitherto I have seen no actual need of it, and I watch keenly. Her eye has been on Colonel Poltermore once or twice—his on her. The woman is a rose in June, sir, and I forgive the whole world for looking—and for longing too. But I have observed nothing serious."

"He is of our party to the beacon-head to-morrow," said Caseldy. "She insisted that she would have him ; and at least it will grant me furlough for an hour."

"Do me the service to report to me," said Mr. Beamish.

In this fashion he engaged Caseldy to supply him with inventions, and prepared himself to swallow them. It was Poltermore and Poltermore, the Colonel here, the Colonel there, until the chase grew so hot that Mr. Beamish could no longer listen to young Mr. Camwell's fatiguing drone upon his one theme of the double-dealing of Chloe's betrothed. He became of her way of thinking, and treated the young gentleman almost as coldly as she. In time he was ready to guess of his own acuteness that the "strange cavalier" could have been no other than Colonel Poltermore. When Caseldy hinted it, Mr. Beamish said, "I have marked him." He added, in highly self-satisfied style, "With all your foreign training, my friend, you will learn that we English are not so far behind you in the art of unravelling an intrigue in the dark." To which Caseldy replied, that the Continental world had little to teach Mr. Beamish.

Poor Colonel Poltermore, as he came to be called, was clearly a victim of the sudden affability of Duchess Susan. The transformation of a stiff military officer into a nimble Puck, a runner of errands and a sprightly attendant, could not pass without notice. The first effect of her discriminating condescension on this unfortunate gentleman was to make him the champion of her claims to breeding. She had it by nature, she was Nature's great lady, he would protest to the noble dames of the circle he moved in ; and they admitted that she was different in every way from a bourgeoise elevated by marriage to lofty rank : she was not vulgar. But they remained doubtful of the perfect simplicity of a young woman who worked such changes in men as to render one of the famous conquerors of the day her agitated humble servant. By rapid degrees the Colonel had fallen to that. When not by her side, he was ever marching with sharp strides, hurrying through rooms and down alleys and groves until he had discovered and attached himself to her skirts. And, curiously, the object of his jealousy was the devoted Alonzo ! Mr. Beamish laughed when he heard of it. The lady's excitement and giddy mien, however, accused Poltermore of a stage of success requiring to be combated immediately. There was mention of Duchess Susan's mighty wish to pay a visit to the popular fortune-teller of the hut on the heath, and Mr. Beamish put his veto on the expedition. She had obeyed him by abstaining from play of late, so he fully expected that his interdict would be obeyed; and besides the fortune-teller was a rogue of a sham astrologer known to have foretold to certain tender ladies things they were only too desirous to imagine predestined by an extraordinary indication of the course of planets through the zodiac, thus causing them to sin by the example of celestial conjunctions—a piece of wanton impiety. The beau took high ground in his objections to the adventure. Nevertheless, Duchess Susan did go. She drove to the heath at an early hour of the morning, attended by Chloe, Colonel Poltermore, and Caseldy. They subsequently breakfasted at an inn where gipsy repasts were occasionally served to the fashion, and they were back at the Wells as soon as the world was abroad. Their surprise then was prodigious when Mr. Beamish, accosting them in full assembly, inquired whether they were satisfied with the report of their fortunes, and yet more when he positively proved himself acquainted with the fortunes which had been recounted to each of them in privacy.

"You, Colonel Poltermore, are to be in luck's way up to the tenth milestone,—where your chariot will overset and you will be lamed for life."

"Not quite so bad," said the Colonel cheerfully he having been informed of much better.

" And you, Count Caseldy, are to have it all your
own way with good luck, after committing a deed
of slaughter, with the solitary penalty of under-
going a visit every night from the corpse."

"Ghost," Caseldy smilingly corrected him.

" And Chloe would not have her fortune told,
because she knew it ! " Mr. Beamish cast a paternal
glance at her. " And you, madam," he bent his
brows on the duchess, " received the communication that 'All for Love' will sink you as it raised
you, put you down as it took you up, furnish the
feast to the raven gentleman which belongs of right
to the golden eagle—ha ? "

" Nothing of the sort!   And I don't believe in
any of their stories," cried the duchess, with a burning face.

" You deny it, madam ? "

" I do.   There was never a word of a raven or an
eagle, that I'll swear, now."

· " You deny that there was ever a word of ' All for
Love '?   Speak, madam."

"Their conjuror's rigmarole ! " she murmured,
huffing.   " As if I listened to their nonsense ! "

" Does the Duchess of Dewlap dare to give me
the lie ? " said Mr. Beamish.

" That's not my title, and you know it," she
retorted.

" What's this ? " the angry beau sang out.
" What stuff is this you wear ? "   He towered and
laid hand on a border of lace of her morning dress

tore it furiously and swung a length of it round him : and while the duchess panted and trembled at an outrage that won for her the sympathy of every lady present as well as the championship of the gentlemen, he tossed the lace to the floor and trampled on it, making his big voice intelligible over the uproar : " Hear what she does ! 'Tis a felony ! She wears the stuff with Betty Worcester's yellow starch on it for mock antique ! And let who else wears it strip it off before the town shall say we are disgraced—when I tell you that Betty Worcester was hanged at Tyburn yesterday morning for murder ! "

There were shrieks.

Hardly had he finished speaking before the assembly began to melt ; he stood in the centre like a pole unwinding streamers, amid a confusion of hurrying dresses, the sound and whirl and drift whereof was as that of the autumnal strewn leaves on a wind rising in November. The troops of ladies were off to bereave themselves of their fashionable imitation old lace adornment, which denounced them in some sort abettors and associates of the sanguinary loathed wretch, Mrs. Elizabeth Worcester, their benefactress of the previous day, now hanged and dangling on the gallows-tree.

Those ladies who wore not imitation lace or any lace in the morning, were scarcely displeased with the beau for his exposure of them that did. The gentlemen were confounded by his exhibition of audacious power. The two gentlemen nighest upon violently resenting his brutality to Duchess Susan, led her from the room in company with Chloe.

"The woman shall fear me to good purpose," Mr Beamish said to himself.

CHAPTER VIII

MR. CAMWELL was in the ante-room as
Chloe passed out behind the two incensed
supporters of Duchess Susan.

"I shall be by the fir-trees on the Mount at eight
this evening," she said.

"I will be there," he replied.

"Drive Mr. Beamish into the country, that these
gentlemen may have time to cool."

He promised her it should be done.

Close on the hour of her appointment, he stood
under the fir-trees, admiring the sunset along the
western line of hills, and when Chloe joined him he
spoke of the beauty of the scene.

"Though nothing seems more eloquently to say
farewell," he added, with a sinking voice.

"We could say it now, and be friends," she
answered.

"Later than now, you think it unlikely that you
could forgive me, Chloe."

"In truth, sir, you are making it hard for me."

"I have stayed here to keep watch; for no
pleasure of my own," said he.

"Mr. Beamish is an excellent protector of the
duchess."

"Excellent ; and he is cleverly taught to suppose she fears him greatly ; and when she offends him, he makes a display of his Jupiter's awfulness, with the effect on a woman of natural spirit which you have seen, and others had foreseen, that she is exasperated and grows reckless. Tie another knot in your string, Chloe."

She looked away, saying, "Were you not the cause ? You were in collusion with that charlatan of the heath, who told them their fortunes this morning. I see far, both in the dark and in the light."

"But not through a curtain. I was present."

"Hateful, hateful business of the spy! You have worked a great mischief, Mr. Camwell. And how can you reconcile it to your conscience that you should play so base a part ? "

" I have but performed my day, dear madam."

"You pretend that it is your devotion to me! I might be flattered if I saw not so abject a figure in my service. Now have I but four days of my month of happiness remaining, and my request to you is, leave me to enjoy them. I beseech you to go. Very humbly, most earnestly, I beg your departure. Grant it to me, and do not stay to poison my last days here. Leave us to-morrow. I will admit your good intentions. I give you my hand in gratitude. Adieu, Mr. Camwell."

He took her hand. "Adieu. I foresee an early separation, and this dear hand is mine while I have it in mine.   Adieu.   It is a word to be repeated at a parting like ours.   We do not blow out our light with one breath : we let it fade gradually, like yonder sunset."

"Speak so," said she.

"Ah, Chloe, to give one's life!   And it is your happiness I have sought more than your favour."

"I believe it ; but I have not liked the means. You leave us to-morrow?"

" It seems to me that to-morrow is the term."

Her face clouded.   "That tells me a very un-certain promise."

"You looked forth to a month of happiness— meaning a month of delusion.   The delusion ex-pires to-night.   You will awaken to see your end of it in the morning.   You have never looked beyond the month since the day of his arrival."

" Let him not be named, I supplicate you."

" Then you consent that another shall be sacri-ficed for you to enjoy your state of deception an hour longer ? "

" I am not deceived, sir.   I wish for peace, and crave it, and that is all I would have."

" And you make her your peace-offering, whom you have engaged to serve !   Too surely your eyes have been open as well as mine.   Knot by knot— I have watched you—where is it ?—you have marked the points in that silken string where the confirmation of a just suspicion was too strong for you."

"I did it, and still I continued merry?" She subsided from her scornfulness on an involuntary "Ah!" that was a shudder.

"You acted Light Heart, madam, and too well to hoodwink me. Meanwhile you allowed that mischief to proceed, rather than have your crazy lullaby disturbed."

"Indeed, Mr. Camwell, you presume."

"The time, and my knowledge of what it is fraught with, demand it and excuse it. You and I, my dear and one only love on earth, stand outside of ordinary rules. We are between life and death."

"We are so always."

"Listen further to the preacher: We have them close on us, with the question, Which it shall be to-morrow. You are for sleeping on, but I say no; nor shall that iniquity of double treachery be committed because of your desire to be rocked in a cradle. Hear me out. The drug you have swallowed to cheat yourself will not bear the shock awaiting you to-morrow with the first light. Hear these birds! When next they sing, you will be broad awake, and——of me, and the worship and service I would have dedicated to you, I do not . . . it is a spectral sunset of a day that was never to be!—awake, and looking on what? Back from a monstrous villany to the forlorn wretch who winked at it with knots in a string. Count them then, and where will be your answer to heaven? I begged it of you, to save you from those blows of remorse ; yes, terrible ! "

" Oh, no ! "

" Terrible, I say ! "

" You are mistaken, Mr. Camwell. It is my soother. I tell my beads on it."

" See how a persistent residence in this place has made a Pagan of the purest soul among us ! Had you . . . but that day was not to lighten me ! More adorable in your errors that you are than others by their virtues, you have sinned through excess of the qualities men prize. Oh, you have a boundless generosity, unhappily en-wound with a pride as great. There is your fault, that is the cause of your misery. Too generous ! too proud ! You have trusted, and you will not cease to trust ; you have vowed yourself to love, never to remonstrate, never to seem to doubt ; it is too much your religion, rare verily. But bethink you of that inexperienced and most silly good creature who is on the rapids to her destruction. Is she not—you will cry it aloud to-morrow—your victim ? You hear it within you now."

" Friend, my dear, true friend," Chloe said in her deeper voice of melody, " set your mind at ease about to-morrow and her. Her safety is assured. I stake my life on it. She shall not be a victim. At the worst she will but have learnt a lesson. So, then, adieu ! The West hangs like a garland of unwatered flowers, neglected by the mistress they adorned. Remember the scene, and that here we parted, and that Chloe wished you the happiness it was out of her power to bestow, because she was of another world, with her history written out to the last red streak before ever you knew her. Adieu; this time adieu for good!"

Mr. Camwell stood in her path. "Blind eyes, if you like," he said, "but you shall not hear blind language. I forfeit the poor consideration for me that I have treasured; hate me; better hated by you than shun my duty! Your duchess is away at the first dawn this next morning; it has come to that. I speak with full knowledge. Question her."

Chloe threw a faltering scorn of him into her voice, as much as her heart's sharp throbs would allow. "I question you, sir, how you came to this full knowledge you boast of?"

"I have it; let that suffice. Nay, I will be particular; his coach is ordered for the time I name to you; her maid is already at a station on the road of the flight."

"You have their servants in your pay?"

"For the mine—the countermine. We must grub dirt to match deceivers. You, madam, have chosen to be delicate to excess, and have thrown it upon me to be gross, and if you please, abominable, in my means of defending you. It is not too late for you to save the lady, nor too late to bring him to the sense of honour."

"I cannot think Colonel Poltermore so dishonourable."

"Poor Colonel Poltermore! the office he is made to fill is an old one.　Are you not ashamed, Chloe?"

"I have listened too long," she replied.

"Then, if it is your pleasure, depart."

He made way for her.　She passed him.　Taking two hurried steps in the gloom of the twilight, she stopped, held at her heart, and painfully turning to him, threw her arms out, and let herself be seized and kissed.

On his asking pardon of her, which his long habit of respect forced him to do in the thick of rapture and repetitions, she said, "You rob no one."

"Oh," he cried, "there is a reward, then, for faithful love.　But am I the man I was a minute back?　I have you; I embrace you; and I doubt that I am I.　Or is it Chloe's ghost?"

"She has died and visits you."

"And will again?"

Chloe could not speak for languor.

The intensity of the happiness she gave by resting mutely where she was, charmed her senses. But so long had the frost been on them that their awakening to warmth was haunted by speculations on the sweet taste of this reward of faithfulness to him, and the strange taste of her own unfaithfulness to her.　And reflecting on the cold act of speculation while strong arm and glowing mouth were pressing her, she thought her senses might really be dead, and she a ghost visiting the good youth for his comfort. So feel ghosts, she thought, and what we call happiness in love is a match between ecstasy and compliance. Another thought flew through her like a mortal shot: "Not so with those two! with them it will be ecstasy meeting ecstasy; *they* will take and give happiness in equal portions." A pang of jealousy traversed her frame. She made the shrewdness of it help to nerve her fervour in a last strain of him to her bosom, and gently releasing herself, she said, "No one is robbed. And now, dear friend, promise me that you will not disturb Mr. Beamish."

"Chloe," said he, "have you bribed me?"

"I do not wish him to be troubled."

"The duchess, I have told you——"

'I know. But you have Chloe's word that she will watch over the duchess and die to save her. It is an oath. You have heard of some arrangements. I say they shall lead to nothing: it shall not take place. Indeed, my friend, I am awake; I see as much as you see. And those . . . after being where I have been, can you suppose I have a regret? But she is my dear and peculiar charge, and if she runs a risk, trust to me that there shall be no catastrophe; I swear it; so, now, adieu. We sup in company to-night. They will be expecting some of Chloe's verses, and she must sing to herself for a few minutes to stir the bed her songs take wing from ; therefore, we will part, and for her sake avoid her ; do not be present at our table, or in the room, or anywhere there. Yes, you rob no one," she said, in a voice that curled through him deliciously by wavering ; " but I think I may blush at recollections, and I would rather have you absent. Adieu ! I will not ask for obedience from you beyond to-night. Your word ? "

He gave it in a stupor of felicity, and she fled.

CHAPTER IX

CHLOE drew the silken string from her bosom, as she descended the dim pathway through the furzes, and set her fingers travelling along it for the number of the knots. "I have no right to be living," she said. Seven was the number; seven years she had awaited her lover's return; she counted her age and completed it in sevens. Fatalism had sustained her during her lover's absence; it had fast hold of her now. Thereby had she been enabled to say. "He will come;" and saying, "He has come," her touch rested on the first knot in the string. She had no power to displace her fingers, and the cause of the tying of the knot stood across her brain marked in dull red characters, legible neither to her eye nor to her understanding, but a reviving of the hour that brought it on her spirit with human distinctness, except of the light of day: she had a sense of having forfeited light, and of seeing perhaps more clearly. Everything assured her that she saw more clearly than others; she saw too when it was good to cease to live.

Hers was the unhappy lot of one gifted with

poetic imagination to throb with the woman supplanting her, and share the fascination of the man who deceived. At their first meeting, in her presence, she had seen that they were not strangers; she pitied them for speaking falsely, and when she vowed to thwart this course of evil it was to save a younger creature of her sex, not in rivalry. She treated them both with a proud generosity surpassing gentleness. All that there was of selfishness in her bosom resolved to the enjoyment of her one month of strongly willed delusion.

The kiss she had sunk to robbed no one, not even her body's purity, for when this knot was tied she consigned herself to her end, and had become a bag of dust. The other knots in the string pointed to verifications; this first one was a suspicion, and it was the more precious, she felt it to be more a certainty; it had come from the dark world beyond us, where all is known. Her belief that it had come thence was nourished by testimony of the space of blackness wherein she had lived since, exhausting her last vitality in a simulation of infantile happiness, which was nothing other than the carrying on of her emotion of the moment of sharp sour sweet—such as, it may be, the doomed below attain for their knowledge of joy—when, at the first meeting with her lover, the perception of his treachery to the soul confiding in him, told her she had lived, and opened out the cherishable kingdom of insensibility to her for her heritage.

She made her tragic humility speak thankfully to the wound that slew her. "Had it not been so, I should not have seen him," she said :— Her lover would not have come to her but for his pursuit of another woman.

She pardoned him for being attracted by that beautiful transplant of the fields : pardoned her likewise. "He when I saw him first was as beautiful to me. For him I might have done as much."

Far away in a lighted hall of the West, her family raised hands of reproach. They were minute objects, keenly discerned as diminished figures cut in steel. Feeling could not be very warm for them, they were so small, and a sea that had drowned her ran between ; and looking that way she had scarce any warmth of feeling save for a white *rhaiadr* leaping out of broken cloud through branched rocks, where she had climbed and dreamed when a child. The dream was then of the coloured days to come ; now she was more infant in her mind, and she watched the scattered water broaden, and tasted the spray, sat there drinking the scene, untroubled by hopes as a lamb, different only from an infant in knowing that she had thrown off life to travel back to her home and be refreshed. She heard her people talk ; they were unending babblers in the waterfall. Truth was with them, and wisdom.

How, then, could she pretend to any right to live? Already she had no name ; she was less living than a tombstone. For who was Chloe? Her family might pass the grave of Chloe without weeping, without moralizing. They had foreseen her ruin, they had foretold it, they noised it in the waters, and on they sped to the plains, telling the world of their prophecy, and making what was untold as yet a lighter thing to do.

The lamps in an irregularly dotted line underneath the hill beckoned her to her task of appearing as the gayest of them that draw their breath for the day, and have pulses for the morrow.

CHAPTER X

A T midnight the great supper party to cele-
brate the reconciliation of Mr. Beamish and
Duchess Susan broke up, and beneath a soft fair
sky the ladies, with their silvery chatter of gratitude for amusement, caught Chloe in their arms to
kiss her, rendering it natural for their cavaliers to
exclaim that Chloe was blest above mortals. The
duchess preferred to walk. Her spirits were excited, and her language smelt of her origin, but
the superb fleshly beauty of the woman was aglow,
and crying, " I declare I should burst in one of
those boxes—just as if you'd stalled me ! " she
fanned a wind on her face, and sumptuously spread
her spherical skirts, attended by the vanquished
and captive Colonel Poltermore, a gentleman
manifestly bent on insinuating sly slips of speech
to serve for here a pinch of powder, there a match.
" Am I ? " she was heard to say. She blew prodigious deep-chested sighs of a coquette that has
taken to roaring.

Presently her voice tossed out : " As if I would ! "
These vivid illuminations of the Colonel's proceedings were a pasture to the rearward groups,

composed of two very grand ladies, Caseldy, Mr. Beamish, a lord, and Chloe.

"You man! Oh!" sprang from the duchess. "What do I hear? I won't listen; I can't, I mustn't, I oughtn't."

So she said, but her head careened, she gave him her coy reluctant ear, with total abandonment to the seductions of his whispers, and the lord let fly a peal of laughter. It had been a supper of copious wine, and the songs which rise from wine. Nature was excused by our midnight naturalists.

The two great dames, admonished by the violence of the nobleman's laughter, laid claim on Mr. Beamish to accompany them at their parting with Chloe and Duchess Susan.

In the momentary shuffling of couples incident to adieux among a company, the duchess murmured to Caseldy: "Have I done it well?"

He praised her for perfection in her acting. "I am at your door at three, remember."

"My heart's in my mouth," said she.

Colonel Poltermore still had the privilege of conducting her the few farther steps to her lodgings.

Caseldy walked beside Chloe, and silently, until he said, "If I have not yet mentioned the subject——"

"If it is an allusion to money let me not hear it to-night," she replied.

"I can only say that my lawyers have instruc-

tions. But my lawyers cannot pay you in gratitude. Do not think me in your hardest review of
my misconduct ungrateful. I have ever esteemed
you above all women ; I do, and I shall ; you are
too much above me. I am afraid I am a composition of bad stuff; I did not win a very
particularly good name on the Continent ; I begin
to know myself, and in comparison with you, dear
Catherine——'

"You speak to Chloe," she said. "Catherine is
a buried person. She died without pain. She is
by this time dust."

The man heaved his breast. "Women have not
an idea of our temptations."

"You are excused by me for all your errors,
Caseldy. Always remember that."

He sighed profoundly. "Ay, you have a Christian's heart."

She answered, "I have come to the conclusion
that it is a Pagan's."

"As for me," he rejoined, "I am a fatalist.
Through life I have seen my destiny. What is to
be, will be ; we can do nothing."

"I have heard of one who expired of a surfeit
that he anticipated, nay proclaimed, when indulging in the last desired morsel," said Chloe.

"He was driven to it."

"From within."

Caseldy acquiesced ; his wits were clouded, and
an illustration even coarser and more grotesque

would have won a serious nod and a sigh from him. "Yes, we are moved by other hands!"

"It is pleasant to think so: and think it of me to-morrow. Will you?" said Chloe.

He promised it heartily, to induce her to think the same of him.

Their separation was in no way remarkable. The pretty formalities were executed at the door, and the pair of gentlemen departed.

"It's quite dark still," Duchess Susan said, looking up at the sky, and she ran upstairs, and sank, complaining of the weakness of her legs, in a chair of the ante-chamber of her bedroom, where Chloe slept. Then she asked the time of the night. She could not suppress her hushed "Oh!" of heavy throbbing from minute to minute. Suddenly she started off at a quick stride to her own room, saying that it must be sleepiness which affected her so.

Her bedroom had a door to the sitting-room, and thence, as also from Chloe's room, the landing on the stairs was reached, for the room ran parallel with both bed-chambers. She walked in it and threw the window open, but closed it immediately; opened and shut the door, and returned and called for Chloe. She wanted to be read to. Chloe named certain composing books. The duchess chose a book of sermons. "But we're all such dreadful sinners, it's better not to bother ourselves late at night." She dismissed that suggestion. Chloe proposed books of poetry. "Only I don't understand them except about larks, and butter-cups, and hayfields, and that's no comfort to a woman burning," was the answer.

"Are you feverish, madam?" said Chloe. And the duchess was sharp on her: "Yes, madam, I am."

She reproved herself in a change of tone: "No, Chloe, not feverish, only this air of yours here is such an exciting air, as the doctor says; and they made me drink wine, and I played before supper—Oh! my money; I used to say I could get more, but now!" she sighed—"but there's better in the world than money. You know that, don't you, you dear? Tell me. And I want you to be happy; that you'll find. I do wish we could all be!" She wept, and spoke of requiring a little music to compose her.

Chloe stretched a hand for her guitar. Duchess Susan listened to some notes, and cried that it went to her heart and hurt her. "Everything we like a lot has a fence and a board against trespassers, because of such a lot of people in the world," she moaned. "Don't play, put down that thing, please, dear. You're the cleverest creature any-body has ever met; they all say so. I wish I—— Lovely women catch men, and clever women keep them: I've heard that said in this wretched place, and it's a nice prospect for me, next door to a fool! I know I am."

"The duke adores you, madam."

"Poor duke! Do let him be—sleeping so woe-begone with his mouth *so*, and that chin of a baby, like as if he dreamed of a penny whistle. He shouldn't have let me come here. Talk of Mr. Beamish. How he will miss you, Chloe!"

"He will," Chloe said sadly.

"If you go, dear."

"I am going."

"Why should you leave him, Chloe?"

"I must."

"And there, the thought of it makes you miser-able!"

"It does."

"You needn't, I'm sure."

Chloe looked at her.

The duchess turned her head. "Why can't you be gay, as you were at the supper-table, Chloe? You're out to him like a flower when the sun jumps over the hill; you're up like a lark in the dews; as I used to be when I thought of nothing Oh, the early morning; and I'm sleepy. What a beast I feel, with my grandeur, and the time in an hour or two for the birds to sing, and me ready to drop. I must go and undress."

She rushed on Chloe, kissed her hastily, declaring that she was quite dead of fatigue, and dismissed her. "I don't want help, I can undress myself. As if Susan Barley couldn't do that for herself! and you may shut your door—I sha'n't have any frights to-night, I'm so tired out."

" Another kiss," Chloe said tenderly.

" Yes, take it "—the duchess leaned her cheek— " but I'm so tired I don't know what I'm doing."

" It will not be on your conscience," Chloe answered, kissing her warmly.

With those words she withdrew, and the duchess closed the door. She ran a bolt in it immediately.

" I'm too tired to know anything I'm doing " she said to herself, and stood with shut eyes to hug certain thoughts which set her bosom heaving.

There was the bed, there was the clock. She had the option of lying down and floating quietly into the day, all peril past. It seemed sweet for a minute. But it soon seemed an old, a worn, an end-of-autumn life, chill, without aim, like a something that was hungry and toothless. The bed proposing innocent sleep repelled her and drove her to the clock. The clock was awful : the hand at the hour, the finger following the minute, commanded her to stir actively, and drove her to gentle meditations on the bed. She lay down dressed, after setting her light beside the clock, that she might see it at will, and considering it necessary for the bed to appear to have been lain on. Considering also that she ought to be heard moving about in the process of undressing, she rose from the bed to make sure of her reading of the guilty clock. An hour and twenty minutes ! she had no more time than that : and it was not enough for her various preparations, though it was true that her maid had packed and taken a box of the things chiefly needful; but the duchess had to change her shoes and her dress, and run at bo-peep with the changes of her mind, a sedative preface to any fatal step among women of her complexion, for so they invite indecision to exhaust their scruples, and they let the blood have its way. Having so short a space of time, she thought the matter decided, and with some relief she flung despairing on the bed, and lay down for good with her duke. In a little while her head was at work reviewing him sternly, estimating him not less accurately than the male moralist charitable to her sex would do. She quitted the bed, with a spring to escape her imagined lord; and as if she had felt him to be there, she lay down no more. A quiet life like that was flatter to her idea than a handsomely bound big book without any print on the pages, and without a picture. Her contemplation of it, contrasted with the life waved to her view by the timepiece, set her whole system raging; she burned to fly. Providently, nevertheless, she thumped a pillow, and threw the bedclothes into proper disorder, to inform the world that her limbs had warmed them, and that all had been impulse with her. She then proceeded to disrobe, murmuring to herself that she could stop now, and could stop now, at each stage of the advance to a fresh dressing of her person, and moralizing on her singular fate, in the mouth of an observer.

"She was shot up suddenly over everybody's head, and suddenly down she went." Susan whispered to herself: "But it was for love!" Possessed by the rosiness of love, she finished her business, with an attention to everything needed that was equal to perfect serenity of mind. After which there was nothing to do, save to sit humped in a chair, cover her face and count the clock-tickings, that said, Yes—no ; do—don't ; fly—stay ; fly—fly ! It seemed to her she heard a moving. Well she might with that dreadful heart of hers !

Chloe was asleep, at peace by this time, she thought ; and how she envied Chloe ! She might be as happy, if she pleased. Why not ? But what kind of happiness was it ? She likened it to that of the corpse underground, and shrank distastefully.

Susan stood at her glass to have a look at the creature about whom there was all this disturbance, and she threw up her arms high for a languid, not unlovely yawn, that closed in blissful shuddering with the sensation of her lover's arms having wormed round her waist and taken her while she was defenceless. For surely they would. She took a jewelled ring, his gift, from her purse, and kissed it, and drew it on and off her finger, leaving it on. Now she might wear it without fear of inquiries and virtuous eyebrows. O heavenly now —if only it were an hour hence, and going behind galloping horses !

The clock was at the terrible moment. She

hesitated internally and hastened ; once her feet stuck fast, and firmly she said, " No ; " but the clock was her lord. The clock was her lover and her lord ; and obeying it, she managed to get into the sitting-room, on the pretext that she merely wished to see through the front window whether daylight was coming.

How well she knew that half-light of the ebb of the wave of darkness.

Strange enough it was to see it showing houses regaining their solidity of the foregone day, instead of still fields, black hedges, familiar shapes of trees. The houses had no wakefulness, they were but seen to stand, and the light was a revelation of emptiness. Susan's heart was cunning to reproach her duke for the difference of the scene she beheld from that of the innocent open-breasted land. Yes, it was dawn in a wicked place that she never should have been allowed to visit. But where was he whom she looked for ? There ! The cloaked figure of a man was at the corner of the street. It was he. Her heart froze ; but her limbs were strung to throw off the house, and reach air, breathe, and (as her thoughts ran) swoon, well-protected. To her senses the house was a house on fire, and crying to her to escape.

Yet she stepped deliberately, to be sure-footed in a dusky room ; she touched along the wall and came to the door, where a foot-stool nearly tripped her. Here her touch was at fault, for though she knew she must be close by the door, she was met by an obstruction unlike wood, and the door seemed neither shut nor open. She could not find the handle; something hung over it. Thinking coolly, she fancied the thing must be a gown or dressing-gown; it hung heavily. Her fingers were sensible of the touch of silk; she distinguished a depending bulk, and she felt at it very carefully and mechanically, saying within herself, in her anxiety to pass it without noise, "If I should awake poor Chloe, of all people!" Her alarm was that the door might creak. Before any other alarm had struck her brain, the hand she felt with was in a palsy, her mouth gaped, her throat thickened, the dust-ball rose in her throat, and the effort to swallow it down and get breath kept her from acute speculation while she felt again, pinched, plucked at the thing, ready to laugh, ready to shriek. Above her head, all on one side, the thing had a round white top. Could it be a hand that her touch had slid across? An arm too! this was an arm! She clutched it, imagining that it clung to her. She pulled it to release herself from it, desperately she pulled, and a lump descended, and a flash of all the torn nerves of her body told her that a dead human body was upon her.

At a quarter to four o'clock of a midsummer morning, as Mr. Beamish relates of his last share in the Tale of Chloe, a woman's voice, in piercing notes of anguish, rang out three shrieks consecutively, which were heard by him at the instant of his quitting his front doorstep, in obedience to the summons of young Mr. Camwell, delivered ten minutes previously, with great urgency, by that gentleman's lacquey. On his reaching the street of the house inhabited by Duchess Susan, he perceived many night-capped heads at windows, and one window of the house in question lifted but vacant. His first impression accused the pair of gentlemen, whom he saw bearing drawn swords in no friendly attitude, of an ugly brawl that had probably affrighted her Grace, or her personal attendant, a woman capable of screaming, for he was well assured that it could not have been Chloe, the least likely of her sex to abandon herself to the use of their weapons either in terror or in jeopardy. The antagonists were Mr. Camwell and Count Caseldy. On his approaching them, Mr. Camwell sheathed his sword, saying that his work was done. Caseldy was convulsed with wrath, to such a degree as to make the part of an intermediary perilous. There had been passes between them, and Caseldy cried aloud that he would have his enemy's blood. The night-watch was nowhere. Soon, however, certain shopmen and their apprentices assisted Mr. Beamish to preserve the peace, despite the fury of Caseldy and the provocations—" not easy to withstand," says the chronicler—offered by him to young Camwell. The latter said to Mr. Beamish: "I knew I should be no match, so I sent for you," causing his friend astonishment, inasmuch as he was assured of the youth's natural valour.

Mr. Beamish was about to deliver an allocution of reproof to them in equal shares, being entirely unsuspicious of any other reason for the alarum than this palpable outbreak of a rivalry that he would have inclined to attribute to the charms of Chloe, when the house-door swung wide for them to enter, and the landlady of the house, holding clasped hands at full stretch, implored them to run up to the poor lady: "Oh, she's dead; she's dead, dead!"

Caseldy rushed past her.

"How, dead! good woman?" Mr. Beamish questioned her most incredulously, half-smiling.

She answered among her moans: "Dead by the neck; off the door—Oh!"

Young Camwell pressed his forehead, with a call on his Maker's name. As they reached the landing upstairs, Caseldy came out of the sitting-room.

"Which?" said Camwell to the speaking of his face.

"She!" said the other.

"The duchess?" Mr. Beamish exclaimed.

But Camwell walked into the room. He had nothing to ask after that reply.

The figure stretched along the floor was covered

with a sheet. The young man fell at his length beside it, and his face was downward.

Mr. Beamish relates : " To this day, when I write at an interval of fifteen years, I have the tragic ague of that hour in my blood, and I behold the shrouded form of the most admirable of women, whose heart was broken by a faithless man ere she devoted her wreck of life to arrest one weaker than herself on the descent to perdition. Therein it was beneficently granted her to be of the service she prayed to be through her death. She died to save. In a last letter, found upon her pin-cushion, addressed to me under seal of secrecy toward the parties principally concerned, she anticipates the whole confession of the unhappy duchess. Nay, she prophesies : ' The duchess will tell you truly she has had enough of love ! ' Those actual words were reiterated to me by the poor lady daily until her lord arrived to head the funeral procession, and assist in nursing back the shattered health of his wife to a state that should fit her for travelling. To me, at least, she was constant in repeating, ' No more of love ! ' By her behaviour to her duke, I can judge her to have been sincere. She spoke of feeling Chloe's eyes go through her with every word of hers that she recollected. Nor was the end of Chloe less effective upon the traitor. He was in the procession to her grave. He spoke to none. There is a line of the verse bearing the superscription, 'My Reasons for Dying,' that shows her to have been apprehensive to secure the safety of Mr. Camwell:

> I die because my heart is dead :
> To warn a soul from sin I die :
> I die that blood may not be shed, etc.

She feared he would be somewhere on the road to mar the fugitives, and she knew him, as indeed he knew himself, no match for one trained in the foreign tricks of steel, ready though he was to dispute the traitor's way. She remembers Mr. Camwell's petition for the knotted silken string in her request that it shall be cut from her throat and given to him."

Mr. Beamish indulges in verses above the grave of Chloe. They are of a character to cool emotion. But when we find a man who is commonly of the quickest susceptibility to ridicule as well as to what is befitting, careless of exposure, we may reflect on the truthfulness of feeling by which he is drawn to pass his own guard and come forth in his naked-ness ; something of the poet's tongue may breathe to us through his mortal stammering, even if we have to acknowledge that a quotation would scatter pathos.

THE HOUSE ON THE BEACH

THE HOUSE ON THE BEACH

𝔄 Realistic Tale

CHAPTER I

THE experience of great officials who have laid down their dignities before death, or have had the philosophic mind to review themselves while still wielding the deputy sceptre, teaches them that in the exercise of authority over men an eccentric behaviour in trifles has most exposed them to hostile criticism and gone farthest to jeopardize their popularity. It is their Achilles' heel; the place where their mother Nature holds them as she dips them in our waters. The eccentricity of common persons is the entertainment of the multitude, and the maternal hand is perceived or a cherishing and endearing sign upon them; but rarely can this be found suitable for the august in station; only, indeed, when their sceptre is no more fearful than a grandmother's birch; and these must learn from it sooner or later that they are uncomfortably mortal.

When herrings are at auction on a beach, for example, the man of chief distinction in the town should not step in among a poor fraternity to take advantage of an occasion of cheapness, though it be done, as he may protest, to relieve the fishermen of a burden; nor should such a dignitary as the bailiff of a Cinque Port carry home the spoil of victorious bargaining on his arm in a basket. It is not that his conduct is in itself objectionable, so much as that it causes him to be popularly weighed; and during life, until the best of all advocates can plead before our fellow Englishmen that we are out of their way, it is prudent to avoid the process.

Mr. Tinman, however, this high-stepping person in question, happened to have come of a marketing mother. She had started him from a small shop to a big one. He, by the practice of her virtues, had been enabled to start himself as a gentleman. He was a man of this ambition, and prouder behind it. But having started himself precipitately, he took rank among independent incomes, as they are called, only to take fright at the perils of starvation besetting one who has been tempted to abandon the source of fifty per cent. So, if noble imagery were allowable in our time in prose might alarms and partial regrets be assumed to animate the splendid pumpkin cut loose from the suckers. Deprived of that prodigious nourishment of the shop in the fashionable seaport of Helmstone, he retired upon his native town, the Cinque Port of Crikswich, where he rented the cheapest residence he could discover for his habitation, the House on the Beach, and lived imposingly, though not in total disaccord with his old mother's principles. His income, as he observed to his widowed sister and solitary companion almost daily in their privacy, was respectable. The descent from an altitude of fifty to five per cent. cannot but be felt. Nevertheless it was a comforting midnight bolster reflection for a man, turning over to the other side between a dream and a wink, that he was making no bad debts, and one must pay to be addressed as esquire. Once an esquire, you are off the ground in England and on the ladder. An esquire can offer his hand in marriage to a lady in her own right; plain esquires have married duchesses; they marry baronets' daughters every day of the week.

Thoughts of this kind were as the rise and fall of waves in the bosom of the new esquire. How often in his Helmstone shop had he not heard titled ladies disdaining to talk a whit more prettily than ordinary women; and he had been a match for the subtlety of their pride—he understood it. He knew well that at the hint of a proposal from him they would have spoken out in a manner very different to that of ordinary women. The lightning, only to be warded by an esquire, was in them. He quitted business at the age of forty, that he might pretend to espousals with a born lady ; or at least it was one of the ideas in his mind.

And here, I think, is the moment for the epitaph of anticipation over him, and the exclamation, alas !   I would not be premature, but it is necessary to create some interest in him, and no one but a foreigner could feel it at present for the Englishman who is bursting merely to do like the rest of his countrymen, and rise above them to shake them class by class as the dust from his heels.   Alas ! then—and undertaker's pathos is better than none at all—he was not a single-minded aspirant to our social honours.   The old marketing mother, to whom he owed his fortunes, was in his blood to confound his ambition ; and so contradictory was the man's nature that, in revenge for disappointments, there were times when he turned against the saving spirit of parsimony.   Readers deep in Greek dramatic writings will see the fatal Sisters behind the chair of a man who gives frequent and bigger dinners, that he may become important in his neighbourhood, while decreasing the price he pays for his wine, that he may miserably indemnify himself for the outlay.   A sip of his wine fetched the breath, as when men are in the presence of the tremendous elements of nature.   It sounded the constitution more darkly-awful, and with a profounder testimony to stubborn health, than the physician's instruments.   Most of the guests at Mr.

Tinman's table were so constructed that they admired him for its powerful quality the more at his announcement of the price of it ; the combined strength and cheapness probably flattering them, as by another mystic instance of the national energy. It must have been so, since his townsmen rejoiced to hail him as head of their town. Here and there a solitary esquire, fished out of the bathing season to dine at the house on the beach, was guilty of raising one of those clamours concerning subsequent headaches, which spread an evil reputation as a pall. A resident esquire or two, in whom a reminiscence of Tinman's table may be likened to the hook which some old trout has borne away from the angler as the most vivid of warnings to him to beware for the future, caught up the black report and propagated it.

The Lieutenant of the Coastguard hearing the latest conscious victim, or hearing of him, would nod his head and say he had never dined at Tinman's table without a headache ensuing and a visit to the chemist's shop ; which, he was assured, was good for trade, and he acquiesced, as it was right to do in a man devoted to his country. He dined with Tinman again. We try our best to be social. For eight months in our year he had little choice but to dine with Tinman or be a hermit attached to a telescope.

"Where are you going, Lieutenant?" His frank reply to the question was, "I am going to be killed;" and it grew notorious that this meant Tinman's table. We get on together as well as we can. Perhaps if we were an acutely calculating people we should find it preferable both for trade and our physical prosperity to turn and kill Tinman, in contempt of consequences. But we are not, and so he does the business gradually for us. A generous people we must be, for Tinman was not detested. The recollection of "next morning" caused him to be dimly feared.

Tinman, meanwhile, was awake only to the circumstance that he made no progress as an esquire, except on the envelopes of letters, and in his own esteem. That broad region he began to occupy to the exclusion of other inhabitants; and the result of such a state of princely isolation was a plunge of his whole being into deep thoughts. From the hour of his investiture as the town's chief man, thoughts which were long shots took possession of him. He had his wits about him; he was alive to ridicule; he knew he was not popular below, or on easy terms with people above him, and he meditated a surpassing stroke as one of the Band of Esq., that had nothing original about it to perplex and annoy the native mind, yet was dazzling. Few members of the privileged Band of Esq. dare even imagine the thing.

It will hardly be believed, but it is historical fact, that in the act of carrying fresh herrings home on his arm, he entertained the idea of a visit to the First Person and Head of the realm, and was indulging in pleasing visions of the charms of a personal acquaintance. Nay, he had already consulted with brother jurats. For you must know that one of the princesses had recently suffered betrothal in the newspapers, and supposing her to deign to ratify the engagement, what so reasonable on the part of a Cinque Port chieftain as to congratulate his liege mistress, her illustrious mother? These are thoughts and these are deeds which give emotional warmth and colour to the electer members of a population wretchedly befogged. They are our sunlight, and our brighter theme of conversation. They are necessary to the climate and the Saxon mind ; and it would be foolish to put them away, as it is foolish not to do our utmost to be intimate with terrestrial splendours while we have them—as it may be said of wardens, mayors, and bailiffs—at command. Tinman was quite of this opinion. They are there to relieve our dulness. We have them in the place of heavenly ; and he would have argued that we have a right to bother them too. He had a notion, up in the clouds, of a Sailors' Convalescent Hospital at Crikswich to seduce a prince with, hand him the trowel, make him " lay the stone," and then—poor prince ! —refresh him at table. But that was a matter for by and by.

His purchase of herrings completed, Mr. Tinman walked across the mound of shingle to the house on the beach. He was rather a fresh-faced man, of the Saxon colouring, and at a distance looking good-humoured. That he should have been able to make such an appearance while doing daily battle with his wine, was a proof of great physical vigour. His pace was leisurely, as it must needs be over pebbles, where half a step is subtracted from each whole one in passing ; and, besides, he was aware of a general breath at his departure that betokened a censorious assembly. Why should he not market for himself? He threw dignity into his retreating figure in response to the internal interrogation. The moment was one when conscious rectitude requires that man should have a tail for its just display. Philosophers have drawn attention to the power of the human face to express pure virtue, but no sooner has it passed on than the spirit erect within would seem helpless. The breadth of our shoulders is apparently presented for our critics to write on. Poor duty is done by the simple sense of moral worth, to supplant that absence of feature in the plain flat back. We are below the animals in this. How charged with language behind him is a dog! Everybody has noticed it. Let a dog turn away from a hostile circle, and his crisp and wary tail not merely defends him, it menaces ; it is a weapon. Man has no choice but to surge and boil, or stiffen preposterously. Knowing the popular sentiment about his marketing—for men can see behind their backs, though they have nothing to speak with—Tinman resembled those persons of principle who decline to pay for a " Bless your honour ! " from a voluble beggar-woman, and obtain the reverse of it after they have gone by. He was sufficiently sensitive to feel that his back was chalked as on a slate. The only remark following him was, " There he goes !"

He went to the seaward gate of the house on the beach, made practicable in a low flint wall, where he was met by his sister Martha, to whom he handed the basket. Apparently he named the cost of his purchase per dozen. She touched the fish and pressed the bellies of the topmost, it might be to question them tenderly concerning their roes. Then the couple passed out of sight. Herrings were soon after this despatching their odours through the chimneys of all Crikswich, and there was that much of concord and festive union among the inhabitants.

The house on the beach had been posted where it stood, one supposes, for the sake of the sea-view, from which it turned right about to face the town across a patch of grass and salt scurf, looking like a square and scornful corporal engaged in the per-petual review of an awkward squad of. recruits. Sea delighted it not, nor land either. Marine Parade fronting it to the left, shaded sickly eyes, under a worn green verandah, from a sun that rarely appeared, as the traducers of spinsters pre-

tend those virgins are ever keenly on their guard
against him that cometh not. Belle Vue Terrace
stared out of lank glass panes without reserve,
unashamed of its yellow complexion. A gaping
public-house, calling itself newly Hotel, fell backward a step. Villas with the titles of royalty and
bloody battles claimed five feet of garden, and
swelled in bow-windows beside other villas which
drew up firmly, commending to the attention a
decent straightness and unintrusive decorum in
preference. On an elevated meadow to the right
was the Crouch. The Hall of Elba nestled among
weather-beaten dwarf woods further toward the
cliff. Shavenness, featurelessness, emptiness, clam-
miness, scurfiness, formed the outward expression
of a town to which people were reasonably glad to
come from London in summer time, for there was
nothing in Crikswich to distract the naked pursuit
of health. The sea tossed its renovating brine to
the determinedly sniffing animal, who went to his
meals with an appetite that rendered him cordially
eulogistic of the place, in spite of certain frank
whiffs of sewerage coming off an open deposit on
the common to mingle with the brine. Tradition
told of a French lady and gentleman entering the
town to take lodgings for a month, and that on
the morrow they took a boat from the shore, saying
in their faint English to a sailor veteran of the
coastguard, whom they had consulted about the
weather, " It is better *zis* zan *zat*," as they shrugged

between rough sea and corpse-like land. And they were not seen again. Their meaning none knew. Having paid their bill at the lodging-house, their conduct was ascribed to systematic madness. English people came to Crikswich for the pure salt sea air, and they did not expect it to be cooked and dressed and decorated for them. If these things are done to nature, it is nature no longer that you have, but something Frenchified. Those French are for trimming Neptune's beard! Only wait, and you are sure to find variety in nature, more than you may like. You will find it in Neptune. What say you to a breach of the sea-wall, and an inundation of the aromatic grass-flat extending from the house on the beach to the tottering terraces, villas, cottages, and public-house transformed by its ensign to Hotel, along the frontage of the town? Such an event had occurred of old, and had given the house on the beach the serious shaking great Neptune in his wrath alone can give. But many years had intervened. Groins had been run down to intercept him and divert him. He generally did his winter mischief on a mill and salt marshes lower westward. Mr. Tinman had always been extremely zealous in promoting the expenditure of what moneys the town had to spare upon the protection of the shore, as it were for the propitiation or defiance of the sea-god. There was a kindly joke against him on that subject among brother jurats. He retorted

with the joke, that the first thing for Englishmen
to look to was England's defences.

But it will not do to be dwelling too fondly on
our eras of peace, for which we make such splendid
sacrifices.   Peace, saving for the advent of a German
band, which troubled the repose of the town at
intervals, had imparted to the inhabitants of Crikswich, within and without, the likeness to its most
perfect image, together, it must be confessed, with
a degree of nervousness that invested common
events with some of the terrors of the Last Trump,
when one night, just upon the passing of the vernal
equinox, something happened.

CHAPTER II

A CARRIAGE stopped short in the ray of candlelight that was fitfully and feebly capering on the windy blackness outside the open workshop of Crickledon, the carpenter, fronting the sea-beach. Mr. Tinman's house was inquired for. Crickledon left off planing; at half-sprawl over the board, he bawled out, " Turn to the right ; right ahead ; can't mistake it." He nodded to one of the cronies intent on watching his labours: " Not unless they mean to be bait for whiting-pout. Who's that for Tinman, I wonder?" The speculations of Crickledon's friends were lost in the scream of the plane.

One cast an eye through the door and observed that the carriage was there still. " Gentleman's got out and walked," said Crickledon. He was informed that somebody was visible inside. " Gentleman's wife, mayhap," he said. His friends indulged in their privilege of thinking what they liked, and there was the usual silence of tongues in the shop. He furnished them sound and motion for their amusement, and now and then a scrap of conversation ; and the sedater spirits dwelling

in his immediate neighbourhood were accustomed
to step in and see him work up to supper time,
instead of resorting to the more turbid and costly
excitement of the public-house.

Crickledon looked up from the measurement of
a thumb-line.   In the doorway stood a bearded
gentleman, who announced himself with the startling exclamation, " Here's a pretty pickle !" and
bustled to make way for a man well known to
them as Ned Crummins, the upholsterer's man, on
whose back hung an article of furniture, the condition of which, with a condensed brevity of humour
worthy of literary admiration, he displayed by
mutely turning himself about as he entered.

" Smashed !" was the general outcry.

" I ran slap into him," said the gentleman.   " Who
the deuce !—no bones broken, that's one thing.
The fellow . . .   there, look at him : he's like a
glass tortoise."

" It's a chiwal glass," Crickledon remarked, and
laid finger on the star in the centre.

" Gentleman ran slap into me," said Crummins,
depositing the frame on the floor of the shop.

" Never had such a shock in my life," continued
the gentleman.   " Upon my soul, I took him for a
door : I did indeed.   A kind of light flashed from
one of your houses here, and in the pitch dark I
thought I was at the door of old Mart Tinman's
house, and dash me if I didn't go in—crash ! But
what the deuce do you do, carrying that great big

looking-glass at night, man? And, look here: tell me; how was it you happened to be going glass foremost when you'd got the glass on your back?"

" Well, 'tain't my fault, I knows that," rejoined Crummins. " I came along as careful as a man could. I was just going to bawl out to Master Tinman, 'I knows the way, never fear me'; for I thinks I hears 'n call from his house, '*Do* ye see the way?' and into me this gentleman runs all his might, and smash goes the glass. It was just ten steps from Master Tinman's gate, and that careful, I reckoned every foot I put down, that I was; I knows I did, though."

" Why, it was *me* calling, 'I'm sure I can't see the way.' You heard *me*, you donkey!" retorted the bearded gentleman. "What was the good of your turning that glass against me in the very nick when I dashed on you?"

" Well, 'tain't my fault, I swear," said Crummins. " The wind catches voices so on a pitch dark night, you never can tell whether they be on one shoulder or the other. And if I'm to go and lose my place through no fault of mine——"

" Haven't I told you, sir, I'm going to pay the damage? Here," said the gentleman, fumbling at his waistcoat, "here, take this card. Read it."

For the first time during the scene in the carpenter's shop, a certain pomposity swelled the gentleman's tone. His delivery of the card appeared to act on him like the flourish of a trumpet before great men.

"Van Diemen Smith," he proclaimed himself for the assistance of Ned Crummins in his task; the latter's look of sad concern on receiving the card seeming to declare an unscholarly conscience.

An anxious feminine voice was heard close beside Mr. Van Diemen Smith.

"Oh, papa, has there been an accident? Are you hurt?"

"Not a bit, Netty; not a bit. Walked into a big looking-glass in the dark, that's all. A matter of eight or ten pound, and that won't stump us. But these are what I call queer doings in Old England, when you can't take a step in the dark on the seashore without plunging bang into a glass. And it looks like bad luck to my visit to old Mart Tinman. Can you," he addressed the company, "tell me of a clean, wholesome lodging-house? I was thinking of flinging myself, body and baggage, on your mayor, or whatever he is— my old schoolmate; but I don't so much like this beginning. A couple of bed-rooms and sitting-room; clean sheets, well aired; good food, well cooked; payment per week in advance."

The pebble dropped into deep water speaks of its depth by the tardy arrival of bubbles on the surface, and, in like manner, the very simple question put by Mr. Van Diemen Smith pursued its course of penetration in the assembled mind in the carpenter's shop for a considerable period, with no sign to show that it had reached the bottom.

"Surely, papa, we can go to an inn? There must be some hotel," said his daughter.

"There's good accommodation at the Cliff Hotel hard by," said Crickledon.

"But," said one of his friends, "if you don't want to go so far, sir, there's Master Crickledon's own house next door, and his wife lets lodgings, and there's not a better cook along this coast."

"Then why didn't the man mention it? Is he afraid of having me?" asked Mr. Smith, a little thunderingly. "I mayn't be known much yet in England; but I'll tell you, you inquire the route to Mr. Van Diemen Smith over there in Australia ———."

"Yes, papa," interrupted his daughter, "only you must consider that it may not be convenient to take us in at this hour—so late."

"It's not that, miss, begging your pardon," said Crickledon. "I make a point of never recommending my own house. That's where it is. Otherwise you're welcome to try us."

"I *was* thinking of falling bounce on my old schoolmate, and putting Old English hospitality to the proof," Mr. Smith meditated. "But it's late. Yes, and that confounded glass! No, we'll bide with you, Mr. Carpenter. I'll send my card across to Mart Tinman to-morrow, and set him agog at his breakfast."

Mr. Van Diemen Smith waved his hand for Crickledon to lead the way.

Hereupon Ned Crummins looked up from the card he had been turning over and over, more and more like one arriving at a condemnatory judgment of a fish.

" I can't go and gi'e my master a card instead of his glass," he remarked.

"Yes, that reminds me; and I should like to know what you meant by bringing that glass away from Mr. Tinman's house at night," said Mr. Smith. " If I'm to pay for it, I've a right to know. What's the meaning of moving it at night? Eh, let's hear. Night's not the time for moving big glasses like that. I'm not so sure I haven't got a case."

" If you'll step round to my master along o' me, sir," said Crummins, " perhaps he'll explain."

Crummins was requested to state who his master was, and he replied, " Phippun and Company; " but Mr. Smith positively refused to go with him.

" But here," said he, " is a crown for you, for you're a civil fellow. You'll know where to find me in the morning ; and mind, I shall expect Phippun and Company to give me a very good account of their reason for moving a big looking-glass on a night like this. There, be off."

The crown-piece in his hand effected a genial change in Crummins' disposition to communicate.

Crickledon spoke to him about the glass; two or three of the others present jogged him. "What did Mr. Tinman want by having the glass moved so late in the day, Ned? Your master wasn't nervous about his property, was he?"

"Not he," said Crummins, and began to suck down his upper lip and agitate his eyelids and stand uneasily, glimmering signs of the setting in of the tide of narration.

He caught the eye of Mr. Smith, then looked abashed at Miss.

Crickledon saw his dilemma. "Say what's uppermost, Ned; never mind how you says it English is English. Mr. Tinman sent for you to take the glass away, now, didn't he?"

"He did," said Crummins.

"And you went to him."

"Ay, that I did."

"And he fastened the chiwal glass upon your back."

"He did that."

"That's all plain sailing. Had he bought the glass?"

"No, he hadn't bought it. He'd hired it."

As when upon an enforced visit to the dentist, people have had one tooth out, the remaining offenders are more willingly submitted to the operation, insomuch that a poetical license might hazard the statement that they shed them like leaves of the tree, so Crummins, who had shrunk from speech, now volunteered whole sentences in succession and how important they were deemed by his fellow-townsman, Mr. Smith, and especially Miss Annette Smith, could perceive in their ejaculations, before they themselves were drawn into the strong current of interest.

And this was the matter: Tinman had hired the glass for three days. Latish, on the very first day of the hiring, close upon dark, he had despatched imperative orders to Phippun and Company to take the glass out of his house on the spot. And why? Because, as he maintained, there was a fault in the glass causing an incongruous and absurd reflection; and he was at that moment awaiting the arrival of another cheval-glass.

"Cut along, Ned," said Crickledon.

"What the deuce does he want with a cheval-glass at all?" cried Mr. Smith, endangering the flow of the story by suggesting to the narrator that he must "hark back," which to him was equivalent to the jumping of a chasm hindward. Happily his brain had seized a picture:

"Mr. Tinman, he's a-standin' in his best Court suit."

Mr. Tinman's old schoolmate gave a jump; and no wonder.

"Standing?" he cried; and as the act of standing was really not extraordinary, he fixed upon the suit: "Court?"

"So Mrs. Cavely told me, it was what he was

standin' in, and as I found 'n I left 'n," said Crummins.

"He's standing in it now?" said Mr. Van Diemen Smith, with a great gape.

Crummins doggedly repeated the statement. Many would have ornamented it in the repetition, but he was for bare flat truth.

" He must be precious proud of having a Court suit," said Mr. Smith, and gazed at his daughter so glassily that she smiled, though she was impatient to proceed to Mrs. Crickledon's lodgings.

" Oh ! there's where it is ? " interjected the carpenter, with a funny frown at a low word from Ned Crummins. " Practising, is he ? Mr. Tinman's practising before the glass preparatory to his going to the palace in London."

" He gave me a shillin'," said Crummins.

Crickledon comprehended him immediately. " We shan't speak about it, Ned."

What did you see ? was thus cautiously suggested.

The shilling was on Crummins' tongue to check his betrayal of the secret scene. But remembering that he had only witnessed it by accident, and that Mr. Tinman had not completely taken him into his confidence, he thrust his hand down his pocket to finger the crown-piece lying in fellowship with the coin it multiplied five times, and was inspired to think himself at liberty to say : " All I saw was when the door opened. Not the house-door. It was the parlour-door. I saw him walk up to the glass, and walk back from the glass. And when he'd got up *to* the glass he bowed, he did, and he went back'ards just so."

Doubtless the presence of a lady was the active agent that prevented Crummins from doubling his body entirely, and giving more than a rapid indication of the posture of Mr. Tinman in his retreat before the glass. But it was a glimpse of broad burlesque, and though it was received with becoming sobriety by the men in the carpenter's shop, Annette plucked at her father's arm.

She could not get him to depart. That picture of his old schoolmate Martin Tinman practising before a cheval-glass to present himself at the palace in his Court suit, seemed to stupefy his Australian intelligence.

"What right has he got to go to Court?" Mr. Van Diemen Smith inquired, like the foreigner he had become through exile.

" Mr. Tinman's bailiff of the town," said Crickledon.

" And what was his objection to that glass I smashed ? "

" He's rather an irritable gentleman," Crickledon murmured, and turned to Crummins.

Crummins growled : " He said it was misty, and give him a twist."

" What a big fool he must be ! eh ? " Mr. Smith glanced at Crickledon and the other faces for the verdict of Tinman's townsmen upon his character.

They had grounds for thinking differently of Tinman.

" He's no fool," said Crickledon.

Another shook his head. " Sharp at a bargain."

" That he be," said the chorus.

Mr. Smith was informed that Mr. Tinman would probably end by buying up half the town.

" Then," said Mr. Smith, " he can afford to pay half the money for that glass, and pay he shall."

A serious view of the recent catastrophe was presented by his declaration.

In the midst of a colloquy regarding the cost of the glass, during which it began to be seen by Mr. Tinman's townsmen that there was laughing-stuff for a year or so in the scene witnessed by Crummins, if they postponed a bit their right to the laugh and took it in doses, Annette induced her father to signal to Crickledon his readiness to go and see the lodgings. No sooner had he done it than he said, " What on earth made us wait all this time here ? I'm hungry, my dear ; I want supper."

" That is because you have had a disappointment. I know you, papa," said Annette.

" Yes, it's rather a damper about old Mart Tinman," her father assented. " Or else I haven't recovered the shock of smashing that glass, and visit it on him. But, upon my honour, he's my only friend in England, I haven't a single relative that I know of, and to come and find your only friend making a donkey of himself, is enough to make a man think of eating and drinking."

Annette murmured reproachfully: "We can hardly say he is our only friend in England, papa, can we?"

"Do you mean that young fellow? You'll take my appetite away if you talk of him. He's a stranger. I don't believe he's worth a penny. He owns he's what he calls a journalist."

These latter remarks were hurriedly exchanged at the threshold of Crickledon's house.

"It don't look promising," said Mr. Smith.

"I didn't recommend it," said Crickledon.

"Why the deuce do you let your lodgings, then?"

"People who have come once come again."

"Oh! I am in England," Annette sighed joyfully, feeling at home in some trait she had detected in Crickledon.

CHAPTER III

THE story of the shattered cheval-glass and
the visit of Tinman's old schoolmate fresh
from Australia, was at many a breakfast-table
before Tinman heard a word of it, and when he
did he had no time to spare for such incidents, for
he was reading to his widowed sister Martha, in an
impressive tone, at a tolerably high pitch of the
voice, and with a suppressed excitement that
shook away all things external from his mind as
violently as it agitated his body. Not the waves
without but the engine within it is which gives the
shock and tremor to the crazy steamer, forcing it
to cut through the waves and scatter them to
spray ; and so did Martin Tinman make light of
the external attack of the card of VAN DIEMEN
SMITH, and its pencilled line: "*An old chum of
yours, eh, matey ?*" Even the communication of
Phippun & Co. concerning the cheval-glass, failed
to divert him from his particular task. It was
indeed a public duty ; and the cheval-glass, though
pertaining to it, was a private business. He that
has broken the glass, let that man pay for it, he
pronounced : no doubt in simpler fashion, being at
his ease in his home, but with the serenity of one

uplifted. As to the name VAN DIEMEN SMITH, he knew it not, and so he said to himself while accurately recollecting the identity of the old chum who alone of men would have thought of writing : *eh, matey ?*

Mr. Van Diemen Smith did not present the card in person. "*At Crickledon's,*" he wrote, apparently expecting the bailiff of the town to rush over to him before knowing who he was.

Tinman was far too busy. Anybody can read plain penmanship or print, but ask anybody not a Cabinet Minister or a Lord-in-Waiting to read out loud and clear in a Palace, before a Throne.   Oh! the nature of reading is distorted in a trice, and as Tinman said to his worthy sister : " I can do it, but I must lose no time in preparing myself."   Again, at a reperusal, he informed her : " I must habituate myself."   For this purpose he had put on the suit overnight.

The articulation of faultless English was his object.   His sister Martha sat vice-regally to receive his loyal congratulations on the illustrious marriage, and she was pensive, less nervous than her brother from not having to speak continuously, yet somewhat perturbed.   She also had her task, and it was to avoid thinking herself the Person addressed by her suppliant brother, while at the same time she took possession of the scholarly training and perfect knowledge of diction and rules of pronunciation which would infallibly be brought to bear on him in the terrible hour of the delivery of the Address. It was no small task moreover to be compelled to listen right through to the end of the Address, before the very gentlest word of criticism was allowed. She did not exactly complain of the renewal of the rehearsal : a fatigue can be endured when it is a joy. What vexed her was her failing memory for the points of objection, as in her imagined High Seat she conceived them ; for, in painful truth, the instant her brother had finished she entirely lost her acuteness of ear, and with that her recollection : so there was nothing to do but to say : " Excellent ! Quite unobjectionable, dear Martin, quite :" so she said, and emphatically ; but the addition of the word "only" was printed on her contracted brow, and every faculty of Tinman's mind and nature being at strain just then, he asked her testily : " What now ? what's the fault now ? " She assured him with languor that there was not a fault. " It's not your way of talking," said he, and what he said was true. His discernment was extraordinary ; generally he noticed nothing.

Not only were his perceptions quickened by the preparations for the day of great splendour : day of a great furnace to be passed through likewise !— he was learning English at an astonishing rate into the bargain. A pronouncing Dictionary lay open on his table. To this he flew at a hint of a contrary method, and disputes, verifications and triumphs on one side and the other ensued between brother and sister. In his heart the agitated man believed his sister to be a misleading guide. He dared not say it, he thought it, and previous to his African travel through the Dictionary he had thought his sister infallible on these points. He dared not say it, because he knew no one else before whom he could practise, and as it was confidence that he chiefly wanted—above all things, confidence—and confidence comes of practice, he preferred the going on with his practice to an absolute certainty as to correctness.

At midday came another card from Mr. Van Diemen Smith bearing the superscription : *alias Phil R.*

"Can it be possible," Tinman asked his sister, "that Philip *Ribstone* has had the audacity to return to this country? I think," he added, " I am right in treating whoever sends me this card as a counterfeit."

Martha's advice was, that he should take no notice of the card.

" I am seriously engaged," said Tinman. With a " Now, then, dear," he resumed his labours.

Messages had passed between Tinman and Phippun ; and in the afternoon Phippun appeared to broach the question of payment for the cheval-glass. He had seen Mr. Van Diemen Smith, had found him very strange, rather impracticable. He was obliged to tell Tinman that he must hold him responsible for the glass; nor could he send a second until payment was made for the first. It really seemed as if Tinman would be compelled by the force of circumstances, to go and shake his old friend by the hand. Otherwise one could clearly see the man might be off: he might be off at any minute, leaving a legal contention behind him. On the other hand, supposing he had come to Crikswich for assistance in money? Friendship is a good thing, and so is hospitality, which is an essentially English thing, and consequently one that it behoves an Englishman to think it his duty to perform, but we do not extend it to paupers But should a pauper get so close to us as to lay hold of us, vowing he was once our friend, how shake him loose? Tinman foresaw that it might be a matter of five pounds thrown to the dogs, perhaps ten, counting the glass. He put on his hat, full of melancholy presentiments; and it was exactly half-past five o'clock of the spring afternoon when he knocked at Crickledon's door.

Had he looked into Crickledon's shop as he went by, he would have perceived Van Diemen Smith astride a piece of timber, smoking a pipe. Van Diemen saw Tinman. His eyes cocked and watered. It is a disgraceful fact to record of him without periphrasis. In truth, the bearded fellow was almost a woman at heart, and had come from the Antipodes throbbing to slap Martin Tinman on the back, squeeze his hand, run over

England with him, treat him, and talk of old times in the presence of a trotting regiment of champagne. That affair of the cheval-glass had temporarily damped his enthusiasm. The absence of a reply to his double transmission of cards had wounded him; and something in the look of Tinman disgusted his rough taste. But the well-known features recalled the days of youth. Tinman was his one living link to the country he admired as the conqueror of the world, and imaginatively delighted in as the seat of pleasures, and he could not discard the feeling of some love for Tinman without losing his grasp of the reason why he had longed so fervently and travelled so breathlessly to return hither. In the days of their youth, Van Diemen had been Tinman's cordial spirit, at whom he sipped for cheerful visions of life, and a good honest glow of emotion now and then. Whether it was odd or not that the sipper should be oblivious, and the cordial spirit heartily reminiscent of those times, we will not stay to inquire.

Their meeting took place in Crickledon's shop. Tinman was led in by Mrs. Crickledon. His voice made a sound of metal in his throat, and his air was that of a man buttoned up to the palate, as he read from the card, glancing over his eyelids, " A— Mr. Van Diemen Smith, I believe."

" Phil Ribstone, if you like," said the other, without rising.

"Oh, ah, indeed!" Tinman temperately coughed.

"Yes, dear me. So it is. It strikes you as odd?"

"The change of name," said Tinman.

"Not nature, though!"

"Ah! Have you been long in England?"

"Time to run to Helmstone, and on here. You've been lucky in business, I hear."

"Thank you; as things go. Do you think of remaining in England?"

"I've got to settle about a glass I broke last night."

"Ah! I have heard of it. Yes, I fear there will have to be a settlement."

"I shall pay half of the damage. You'll have to stump up your part."

Van Diemen smiled roguishly.

"We must discuss that," said Tinman, smiling too, as a patient in bed may smile at a doctor's joke; for he was, as Crickledon had said of him, no fool on practical points, and Van Diemen's mention of the half-payment reassured him as to his old friend's position in the world, and softly thawed him. "Will you dine with me to-day?"

"I don't mind if I do. I've a girl. You remember little Netty? She's walking out on the beach with a young fellow named Fellingham, whose acquaintance we made on the voyage, and hasn't left us long to ourselves. Will you have

her as well? And I suppose you must ask him.
He's a newspaper man; been round the world;
seen a lot."

Tinman hesitated. An electrical idea of putting
sherry at fifteen shillings per dozen on his table
instead of the ceremonial wine at twenty-five
shillings, assisted him to say hospitably, " Oh! ah!
yes ; any friend of yours."

" And now perhaps you'll shake my fist," said
Van Diemen.

" With pleasure," said Tinman. " It was your
change of name, you know, Philip."

" Look here, Martin. Van Diemen Smith was a
convict, and my benefactor. Why the deuce he
was so fond of that name, I can't tell you ; but his
dying wish was for me to take it and carry it on.
He left me his fortune, for Van Diemen Smith to
enjoy life, as he never did, poor fellow, when he
was alive. The money was got honestly, by hard
labour at a store. He did evil once, and repented
after. But, by Heaven!"—Van Diemen jumped
up and thundered out of a broad chest—" the man
was one of the finest hearts that ever beat. He
was! and I'm proud of him. When he died, I
turned my thoughts home to Old England and
you, Martin."

" Oh!" said Tinman ; and reminded by Van
Diemen's way of speaking, that cordiality was expected of him, he shook his limbs to some brisk-
ness, and continued, " Well, yes, we must all die in

our native land if we can. I hope you're comfortable in your lodgings?"

"I'll give you one of Mrs. Crickledon's dinners to try. You're as good as mayor of this town, I hear?"

"I am the bailiff of the town," said Mr. Tinman.

"You're going to Court, I'm told."

"The appointment," replied Mr. Tinman, "will soon be made. I have not yet an appointed day."

On the great highroad of life there is Expectation, and there is Attainment, and also there is Envy. Mr. Tinman's posture stood for Attainment shadowing Expectation, and sunning itself in the glass of Envy, as he spoke of the appointed day. It was involuntary, and naturally evanescent, a momentary view of the spirit.

He unbent, and begged to be excused for the present, that he might go and apprise his sister of guests coming.

"All right. I daresay we shall see enough of one another," said Van Diemen. And almost before the creak of Tinman's heels was deadened on the road outside the shop, he put the funny question to Crickledon, "Do you box?"

"I make 'em," Crickledon replied.

"Because I should like to have a go in at something, my friend."

Van Diemen stretched and yawned.

Crickledon recommended the taking of a walk.

"I think I will," said the other, and turned back abruptly.　"How long do you work in the day?"

"Generally, all the hours of light," Crickledon replied ; "and always up to supper-time."

"You're healthy and happy?"

"Nothing to complain of."

"Good appetite?"

"Pretty regular."

"You never take a holiday?"

"Except Sundays."

"You'd like to be working then?"

"I won't say that."

"But you're glad to be up Monday morning?"

"It feels cheerfuller in the shop."

"And carpentering's your joy?"

"I think I may say so."

Van Diemen slapped his thigh.　"There's life in Old England yet!"

Crickledon eyed him as he walked away to the beach to look for his daughter, and conceived that there was a touch of the soldier in him.

CHAPTER IV

ANNETTE SMITH'S delight in her native England made her see beauty and kindness everywhere around her; it put a halo about the house on the beach, and thrilled her at Tinman's table when she heard the thunder of the waves hard by. She fancied it had been a most agreeable dinner to her father and Mr. Herbert Fellingham—especially to the latter, who had laughed very much; and she was astonished to hear them at breakfast both complaining of their evening. In answer to which, she exclaimed, "Oh, I think the situation of the house is so romantic!"

"The situation of the host is exceedingly so," said Mr. Fellingham; "but I think his wine the most unromantic liquid I have ever tasted."

"It must be *that!*" cried Van Diemen, puzzled by novel pains in the head. "Old Martin woke up a little like his old self after dinner."

"He drank sparingly," said Mr. Fellingham.

"I am sure you were satirical last night," Annette said reproachfully.

"On the contrary, I told him I thought he was in a romantic situation."

"But I have had a French mademoiselle for my governess, and an Oxford gentleman for my tutor; and I know you accepted French and English from Mr. Tinman and his sister that I should not have approved."

"Netty," said Van Diemen, "has had the best instruction money could procure; and if she says you were satirical, you may depend on it you were."

"Oh, in that case, of course!" Mr. Fellingham rejoined. "Who could help it?"

He thought himself warranted in giving the rein to his wicked satirical spirit, and talked lightly of the accidental character of the letter H in Tinman's pronunciation; of how, like somebody else's hat in a high wind, it descended on somebody else's head, and of how his words walked about asking one another who they were and what they were doing, danced together madly, snapping their fingers at signification; and so forth. He was flippant.

Annette glanced at her father, and dropped her eyelids.

Mr. Fellingham perceived that he was enjoined to be on his guard.

He went one step farther in his fun; upon which Van Diemen said, with a frown, "If you please!"

Nothing could withstand that.

"Hang old Mart Tinman's wine!" Van Diemen

burst out in the dead pause. "My head's a bullet. I'm in a shocking bad temper. I can hardly see. I'm bilious."

Mr. Fellingham counselled his lying down for an hour, and he went grumbling, complaining of Mart Tinman's incredulity about the towering beauty of a place in Australia called Gippsland.

Annette confided to Mr. Fellingham, as soon as they were alone, the chivalrous nature of her father in his friendships, and his indisposition to hear a satirical remark upon his old schoolmate, the moment he understood it to be satire.

Fellingham pleaded : "The man's a perfect burlesque. He's as distinctly made to be laughed at as a mask in a pantomime."

"Papa will not think so," said Annette ; "and papa has been told that he is not to be laughed at as a man of business."

"Do you prize him for that ?"

"I am no judge. I am too happy to be in England to be a judge of anything."

"You did not touch his wine !"

"You men attach so much importance to wine !"

"They do say that powders is a good thing after Mr. Tinman's wine," observed Mrs. Crickledon, who had come into the sitting-room to take away the breakfast things.

Mr. Fellingham gave a peal of laughter ; but Mrs. Crickledon bade him be hushed, for Mr. Van

Diemen Smith had gone to lay down his poor aching head on his pillow. Annette ran upstairs to speak to her father about a doctor.

During her absence, Mr. Fellingham received the popular portrait of Mr. Tinman from the lips of Mrs. Crickledon. He subsequently strolled to the carpenter's shop, and endeavoured to get a confirmation of it.

"My wife talks too much," said Crickledon.

When questioned by a gentleman, however, he was naturally bound to answer to the extent of his knowledge.

"What a funny old country it is!" Mr. Fellingham said to Annette, on their walk to the beach.

She implored him not to laugh at anything English.

"I don't, I assure you," said he. "I love the country, too. But when one comes back from abroad, and plunges into their daily life, it's difficult to retain the real figure of the old country seen from outside, and one has to remember half a dozen great names to right oneself. And Englishmen are so funny! Your father comes here to see his old friend, and begins boasting of the Gippsland he has left behind. Tinman immediately brags of Helvellyn, and they fling mountains at one another till, on their first evening together, there's earthquake and rupture— they were nearly at fisticuffs at one time."

"Oh! surely no," said Annette. "I did not

hear them. They were good friends when you came to the drawing-room. Perhaps the wine did affect poor papa, if it was bad wine. I wish men would never drink any. How much happier they would be."

"But then there would cease to be social meetings in England. What should we do?"

"I know that is a sneer; and you were nearly as enthusiastic as I was on board the vessel," Annette said, sadly.

"Quite true. I was. But see what quaint creatures we have about us! Tinman practising in his Court suit before the cheval-glass! And that good fellow, the carpenter, Crickledon, who has lived with the sea fronting him all his life, and has never been in a boat, and he confesses he has only once gone inland, and has never seen an acorn!"

"I wish I could see one—of a real English oak," said Annette.

"And after being in England a few months you will be sighing for the Continent."

"Never!"

"You think you will be quite contented here?"

"I am sure I shall be. May papa and I never be exiles again! I did not feel it when I was three years old, going out to Australia; but it would be like death to me now. Oh!" Annette shivered with the exile's chill.

"On my honour," said Mr. Fellingham, as softly

as he could with the wind in his teeth, " I love the old country ten times more from your love of it."

" That is not how I want England to be loved," returned Annette.

" The love is in your hands."

She seemed indifferent on hearing it.

He should have seen that the way to woo her was to humour her prepossession by another passion. He could feel that it ennobled her in the abstract, but a latent spite at Tinman on account of his wine, to which he continued angrily to attribute an unwonted dizziness of the head and slight irascibility, made him urgent in his desire that she should separate herself from Tinman and his sister by the sharp division of derision.

Annette declined to laugh at the most risible caricatures of Tinman. In her antagonism she forced her simplicity so far as to say that she did not think him absurd. And supposing Mr. Tinman to have proposed to the titled widow, Lady Ray, as she had heard, and to other ladies young and middle-aged in the neighbourhood, why should he not, if he wished to marry ? If he was economical, surely he had a right to manage his own affairs. Her dread was lest Mr. Tinman and her father should quarrel over the payment for the broken cheval-glass : that she honestly admitted, and Fellingham was so indiscreet as to roar aloud, not so very cordially.

Annette thought him unkindly satirical ; and his

thoughts of her reduced her to the condition of a commonplace girl with expressive eyes.

She had to return to her father. Mr. Fellingham took a walk on the springy turf along the cliffs; and "certainly she is a commonplace girl," he began by reflecting, with a side eye at the fact that his meditations were excited by Tinman's poisoning of his bile. "A girl who can't see the absurdity of Tinman must be destitute of common intelligence." After a while he sniffed the fine sharp air of mingled earth and sea delightedly, and he strode back to the town late in the afternoon, laughing at himself in scorn of his wretched susceptibility to bilious impressions, and really all but hating Tinman as the cause of his weakness—in the manner of the criminal hating the detective, perhaps. He cast it altogether on Tinman that Annette's complexion of character had become discoloured to his mind; for, in spite of the physical freshness with which he returned to her society, he was incapable of throwing off the idea of her being commonplace; and it was with regret that he acknowledged he had gained from his walk only a higher opinion of himself.

Her father was the victim of a sick headache, and lay, a groaning man, on his bed, ministered to by Mrs. Crickledon chiefly. Annette had to conduct the business with Mr. Phippun and Mr. Tinman as to payment for the cheval-glass. She was commissioned to offer half the price for the glass on her father's part ; more he would not pay. Tinman and Phippun sat with her in Crickledon's cottage, and Mrs. Crickledon brought down two messages from her invalid, each positive, to the effect that he would fight with all the arms of English law rather than yield his point.

Tinman declared it to be quite out of the question that he should pay a penny. Phippun vowed that from one or the other of them he would have the money.

Annette naturally was in deep distress, and Fellingham postponed the discussion to the morrow.

Even after such a taste of Tinman as that, Annette could not be induced to join in deriding him privately. She looked pained by Mr. Fellingham's cruel jests. It was monstrous, Fellingham considered, that he should draw on himself a second reprimand from Van Diemen Smith, while they were consulting in entire agreement upon the case of the cheval-glass.

"I must tell you this, mister sir," said Van Diemen, "I like you, but I'll be straightforward and truthful, or I'm not worthy the name of Englishman ; and I do like you, or I shouldn't have given you leave to come down here after us two. You must respect my friend if you care for my respect. That's it. There it is. Now you know my conditions."

" I'm afraid I can't sign the treaty," said Fellingham.

" Here's more," said Van Diemen. " I'm a chilly man myself if I hear a laugh and think I know the aim of it. I'll meet what you like except scorn. I can't stand contempt. So I feel for another. And now you know."

" It puts a stopper on the play of fancy, and checks the throwing off of steam," Fellingham remonstrated. " I promise to do my best, but of all the men I've ever met in my life—Tinman !— the ridiculous ! Pray pardon me ; but the donkey and his looking-glass ! The glass was misty ! He—as particular about his reflection in the glass as a poet with his verses ! Advance, retire, bow ; and such murder of the Queen's English in the very presence ! If I thought he was going to take his wine with him, I'd have him arrested for high treason."

" You've chosen, and you know what you best like," said Van Diemen, pointing his accents—by which is produced the awkward pause, the pitfall of conversation, and sometimes of amity.

Thus it happened that Mr. Herbert Fellingham journeyed back to London a day earlier than he had intended, and without saying what he meant to say.

CHAPTER V

A MONTH later, after a night of sharp frost on the verge of the warmer days of spring, Mr. Fellingham entered Crikswich under a sky of perfect blue that was in brilliant harmony with the green downs, the white cliffs and sparkling sea, and no doubt it was the beauty before his eyes which persuaded him of his delusion in having taken Annette for a commonplace girl. He had come in a merely curious mood to discover whether she was one or not. Who but a commonplace girl would care to reside in Crikswich, he had asked himself; and now he was full sure that no commonplace girl would ever have had the idea. Exquisitely simple, she certainly was; but that may well be a distinction in a young lady whose eyes are expressive.

The sound of sawing attracted him to Crickledon's shop, and the industrious carpenter soon put him on the tide of affairs.

Crickledon pointed to the house on the beach as the place where Mr. Van Diemen Smith and his daughter were staying.

"Dear me! and how does he look?" said Fellingham.

"Our town seems to agree with him, sir."

"Well, I must not say any more, I suppose." Fellingham checked his tongue. "How have they settled that dispute about the cheval-glass?"

"Mr. Tinman had to give way."

"Really!"

"But," Crickledon stopped work, "Mr. Tinman sold him a meadow."

"I see."

"Mr. Smith has been buying a goodish bit of ground here. They tell me he's about purchasing Elba. He has bought the Crouch. He and Mr. Tinman are always out together. They're over at Helmstone now. They've been to London."

"Are they likely to be back to-day?"

"Certain, I should think. Mr. Tinman has to be in London to-morrow."

Crickledon looked. He was not the man to look artful, but there was a lighted corner in his look that revived Fellingham's recollections, and the latter burst out :—

"The Address? I'd half forgotten it. That's not over yet? Has he been practising much?"

"No more glasses ha' been broken."

"And how is your wife, Crickledon?"

"She's at home, sir, ready for a talk, if you've a mind to try her."

Mrs. Crickledon proved to be very ready "That Tinman," was her theme. He had taken away her lodgers, and she knew his objects. Mr.

Smith repented of leaving her, she knew, though he dared not say it in plain words. She knew Miss Smith was tired to death of constant companionship with Mrs. Cavely, Tinman's sister. She generally came once in the day just to escape from Mrs. Cavely, who would not, bless you ! step in to a cottager's house where she was not allowed to patronize. Fortunately Miss Smith had induced her father to get his own wine from the merchants.

"A happy resolution," said Fellingham ; "and a saving one."

He heard further that Mr. Smith would take possession of the Crouch next month, and that Mrs. Cavely hung over Miss Smith like a kite.

"And that old Tinman, old enough to be her father!" said Mrs. Crickledon.

She dealt in the flashes which connect ideas. Fellingham, though a man, and an Englishman, was nervously wakeful enough to see the connection.

"They'll have to consult the young lady first, ma'am."

"If it's her father's nod she'll! bow to it ; now mark me," Mrs. Crickledon said, with emphasis. "She's a young lady who thinks for herself, but she takes her start from her father where it's feeling. And he's gone stone-blind over that Tinman."

While they were speaking, Annette appeared.

" I saw you," she said to Fellingham, gladly and openly, in the most commonplace manner.

" Are you going to give me a walk along the beach ? " said he.

She proposed the country behind the town, and that was quite as much to his taste. But it was not a happy walk. He had decided that he admired her, and the notion of having Tinman for a rival annoyed him. He overflowed with ridicule of Tinman, and this was distressing to Annette because not only did she see that he would not control himself before her father, but he kindled her own satirical spirit in opposition to her father's friendly sentiments toward his old schoolmate.

" Mr. Tinman has been extremely hospitable to us," she said, a little coldly.

" May I ask you, has he consented to receive instruction in deportment and pronunciation ? "

Annette did not answer.

" If practice makes perfect, he must be near the mark by this time."

She continued silent.

" I dare say, in domestic life he's as amiable as he is hospitable, and it must be a daily gratification to see him in his Court suit."

" I have not seen him in his Court suit."

" That is his coyness."

" People talk of those things."

" The common people scandalize the great, about whom they know nothing, you mean ! I am sure that is true, and living in Courts one must be keenly aware of it.   But what a splendid sky and sea!"

"Is it not?"

Annette echoed his false rapture with a candour that melted him.

He was preparing to make up for lost time, when the wild waving of a parasol down a road to the right, coming from the town, caused Annette to stop and say,—

"I think that must be Mrs. Cavely.   We ought to meet her."

Fellingham asked why.

"She is so fond of walks," Annette replied, with a tooth on her lip.

Fellingham thought she seemed fond of runs.

Mrs. Cavely joined them, breathless.   "My dear! the pace you go at!" she shouted.   "I saw you starting.   I followed, I ran, I tore along.   I feared I never should catch you.   And to lose such a morning of English scenery!   Is it not heavenly?"

"One can't say more," Fellingham observed, bowing.

"I am sure I am very glad to see you again, sir. You enjoy Crikswich?"

"Once visited, always desired, like Venice, ma'am.   May I venture to inquire whether Mr. Tinman has presented his Address?"

"The day after to-morrow.   The appointment is made with him," said Mrs. Cavely, more officially in manner, "for the day after to-morrow. He is excited, as you may well believe. But Mr. Smith is an immense relief to him—the very distraction he wanted. We have become one family, you know."

"Indeed, ma'am, I did not know it," said Fellingham.

The communication imparted such satiric venom to his further remarks, that Annette resolved to break her walk and dismiss him for the day.

He called at the house on the beach after the dinner-hour, to see Mr. Van Diemen Smith, when there was literally a duel between him and Tinman ; for Van Diemen's contribution to the table was champagne, and that had been drunk, but Tinman's sherry remained. Tinman would insist on Fellingham's taking a glass. Fellingham parried him with a sedate gravity of irony that was painfully perceptible to Annette. Van Diemen at last backed Tinman's hospitable intent, and, to Fellingham's astonishment, he found that he had been supposed by these two men to be bashfully retreating from a seductive offer all the time that his tricks of fence and transpiercings of one of them had been marvels of skill.

Tinman pushed the glass into his hand.

"You have spilt some," said Fellingham.

"It won't hurt the carpet," said Tinman.

"Won't it ?" Fellingham gazed at the carpet, as if expecting a flame to arise.

He then related the tale of the magnanimous Alexander drinking off the potion, in scorn of the slanderer, to show faith in his friend.

" Alexander—Who was that ? " said Tinman, foiled in his historical recollections by the absence of the surname.

" General Alexander," said Fellingham. " Alexander Philipson, or he declared it was Joveson ; and very fond of wine. But his sherry did for him at last."

" Ah ! he drank too much, then," said Tinman.

" Of his own ! "

Annette admonished the vindictive young gentleman by saying, " How long do you stay in Crikswich, Mr. Fellingham ? "

He had grossly misconducted himself. But an adversary at once offensive and helpless provokes brutality. Annette prudently avoided letting her father understand that satire was in the air ; and neither he nor Tinman was conscious of it exactly : yet both shrank within themselves under the sensation of a devilish blast blowing. Fellingham accompanied them and certain jurats to London next day.

Yes, if you like : when a mayor visits Majesty, it is an important circumstance, and you are at liberty to argue at length that it means more than a desire on his part to show his writing power and his reading power : it is full of comfort to the people, as an exhibition of their majesty likewise ;

and it is an encouragement to men to strive to become mayors, bailiffs, or prime men of any sort ; but a stress in the reporting of it—the making it appear too important a circumstance—will surely breathe the intimation to a politically-minded people that satire is in the air, and however dearly they cherish the privilege of knocking at the first door of the kingdom, and walking ceremoniously in to read their writings, they will, if they are not in one of their moods for prostration, laugh. They will laugh at the report.

All the greater reason is it that we should not indulge them at such periods ; and I say woe's me for any brother of the pen, and one in some esteem, who dressed the report of that presentation of the Address of congratulation by Mr. Bailiff Tinman, of Crikswich! Herbert Fellingham wreaked his personal spite on Tinman. He should have bethought him that it involved another than Tinman —that is to say, an office—which the fitful beast rejoices to paw and play with contemptuously now and then, one may think, as a solace to his pride, and an indemnification for those caprices of abject worship so strongly recalling the days we see through Mr. Darwin's glasses.

He should not have written the report. It sent a titter over England. He was so unwise as to despatch a copy of the newspaper containing it to Van Diemen Smith. Van Diemen perused it with satisfaction. So did Tinman. Both of these praised the able young writer. But they handed the paper to the Coastguard Lieutenant, who asked Tinman how he liked it ; and visitors were beginning to drop in to Crikswich, who made a point of asking for a sight of the chief man ; and then came a comic publication, all in the Republican tone of the time, with Man's Dignity for the standpoint, and the wheezy laughter residing in old puns to back it, in eulogy of the satiric report of the famous Address of congratulation of the Bailiff of Crikswich.

"Annette," Van Diemen said to his daughter, "you'll not encourage that newspaper fellow to come down here any more. He had his warning."

CHAPTER VI

ONE of the most difficult lessons for spirited young men to learn is, that good jokes are not always good policy. They have to be paid for, like good dinners, though dinner and joke shall seem to have been at somebody else's expense. Young Fellingham was treated rudely by Van Diemen Smith, and with some cold reserve by Annette: in consequence of which he thought her more than ever commonplace. He wrote her a letter of playful remonstrance, followed by one that appealed to her sentiments. But she replied to neither of them. So his visits to Crikswich came to an end.

Shall a girl who has no appreciation of fun affect us ?

Her expressive eyes, and her quaint simplicity, and her enthusiasm for England, haunted Mr. Fellingham ; being conjured up by contrast with what he met about him. But shall a girl who would impose upon us the task of holding in our laughter at Tinman · be much regretted ? There could be no companionship between us, Fellingham thought.

On an excursion to the English Lakes he saw the name of Van Diemen Smith in a visitors' book, and changed his ideas on the subject of companionship. Among mountains, or on the sea, or reading history, Annette was one in a thousand. He happened to be at a public ball at Helmstone in the winter season, and who but Annette herself came whirling before him on the arm of an officer! Fellingham did not miss his chance of talking to her. She greeted him gaily, and speaking with the excitement of the dance upon her, appeared a stranger to the serious emotions he was willing to cherish. She had been to the Lakes and to Scotland. Next summer she was going to Wales. All her experiences were delicious. She was insatiable, yet satisfied.

"I wish I had been with you," said Fellingham.

"I wish you had," said she.

Mrs. Cavely was her chaperon at the ball, and he was not permitted to enjoy a lengthened conversation sitting with Annette. What was he to think of a girl who could be submissive to Mrs. Cavely, and danced with any number of officers, and had no idea save of running incessantly over England in the pursuit of pleasure? Her tone of saying, "I wish you had," was that of the most ordinary of wishes, distinctly, if not designedly different from his own melodious depth.

She granted him one waltz, and he talked of her father. Amid his whimsical vagrancies of feeling he had a positive liking for Van Diemen, and he sagaciously said so. Annette's eyes brightened. " Then why do you never go to see him? He has bought Elba. We move into the Hall after Christmas. We are at the Crouch at present. Papa will be sure to make you welcome. Do you not know that he never forgets a friend or breaks a friendship ? "

" I do, and I love him for it," said Fellingham.

If he was not greatly mistaken a gentle pressure on the fingers of his left hand rewarded him.

This determined him. It should here be observed that he was by birth the superior of Annette's parentage, and such is the sentiment of a better blood that the flattery of her warm touch was needed for him to overlook the distinction.

Two of his visits to Crikswich resulted simply in interviews and conversations with Mrs. Crickledon. Van Diemen and his daughter were in London with Tinman and Mrs. Cavely, purchasing furniture for Elba Hall. Mrs. Crickledon had no scruple in saying, that Mrs. Cavely meant her brother to inhabit the Hall, though Mr. Smith had outbid him in the purchase. According to her, Tinman and Mr. Smith had their differences ; for Mr. Smith was a very outspoken gentleman, and had been known to call Tinman names that no man of spirit would bear if he was not scheming.

Fellingham returned to London, where he roamed the streets famous for furniture warehouses, in the vain hope of encountering the new owner of Elba.

Failing in this endeavour, he wrote a love-letter to Annette.

It was her first. She had liked him. Her manner of thinking she might love him was through the reflection that no one stood in the way. The letter opened a world to her, broader than Great Britain.

Fellingham begged her, if she thought favourably of him, to prepare her father for the purport of his visit. If otherwise, she was to interdict the visit with as little delay as possible and cut him adrift.

A decided line of conduct was imperative. Yet you have seen that she was not in love. She was only not unwilling to be in love. And Fellingham was just a trifle warmed. Now mark what events will do to light the fires.

Van Diemen and Tinman, old chums re-united, and both successful in life, had nevertheless, as Mrs. Crickledon said, their differences. They commenced with an opposition to Tinman's views regarding the expenditure of town moneys. Tinman was ever for devoting them to the patriotic defence of "our shores;" whereas Van Diemen, pointing in detestation of the town sewerage reeking across the common under the beach, loudly called on him to preserve our lives, by way of commencement. Then Van Diemen precipitately purchased Elba at a high valuation, and Tinman had expected by waiting to buy it at his own valuation, and sell it out of friendly consideration to his friend afterwards, *for* a friendly consideration. Van Diemen had joined the hunt. Tinman could not mount a horse. They had not quarrelled, but they had snapped about these and other affairs. Van Diemen fancied Tinman was jealous of his wealth. Tinman shrewdly suspected Van Diemen to be contemptuous of his dignity. He suffered a loss in a loan of money ; and instead of pitying him, Van Diemen had laughed him to scorn for expecting security for investments at ten per cent. The bitterness of the pinch to Tinman made him frightfully sensitive to strictures on his discretion. In his anguish he told his sister he was ruined, and she advised him to marry before the crash. She was aware that he exaggerated, but she repeated her advice. She went so far as to name the person. This is known, because she was overheard by her housemaid, a gossip of Mrs. Crickledon's, the subsequently famous " Little Jane."

Now, Annette had shyly intimated to her father the nature of Herbert Fellingham's letter, at the same time professing a perfect readiness to submit to his directions ; and her father's perplexity was very great, for Annette had rather fervently dramatized the young man's words at the ball at Helmstone, which had pleasantly tickled him, and, besides, he liked the young man. On the other hand, he did not at all like the prospect of losing his daughter, and he would have desired her to be a lady of title. He hinted at her right to claim a high position. Annette shrank from the prospect, saying, " Never let me marry one who might be ashamed of my father ! "

" I shouldn't stomach that," said Van Diemen, more disposed in favour of the present suitor.

Annette was now in a tremor. She had a lover ; he was coming. And if he did not come, did it matter ? Not so very much, except to her pride. And if he did, what was she to say to him ? She felt like an actress who may in a few minutes be called on the stage, without knowing her part. This was painfully unlike love, and the poor girl feared it would be her conscientious duty to dismiss him—most gently, of course ; and perhaps, should he be impetuous and picturesque, relent enough to let him hope, and so bring about a happy postponement of the question.

Her father had been to a neighbouring town on business with Mr. Tinman. He knocked at her door at midnight ; and she, in dread of she knew not what—chiefly that the Hour of the Scene had somehow struck—stepped out to him trembling. He was alone. She thought herself the most childish of mortals in supposing that she could have been summoned at midnight to declare her sentiments, and hardly noticed his gloomy depression. He asked her to give him five minutes ; then asked her for a kiss, and told her to go to bed and sleep. But Annette had seen that a great present affliction was on him, and she would not be sent to sleep. She promised to listen patiently, to bear anything, to be brave. "Is it bad news from home ?" she said, speaking of the old home where she had not left her heart, and where his money was invested.

"It's this, my dear Netty," said Van Diemen, suffering her to lead him into her sitting-room ; "we shall have to leave the shores of England."

"Then we are ruined."

"We're not ; the rascal can't do that. We might be off to the Continent, or we might go to America ; we've money. But we can't stay here I'll not live at any man's mercy."

"The Continent! America!" exclaimed the enthusiast for England. "Oh, papa, you love living in England so !"

"Not so much as all that, my dear. You do, that I know. But I don't see how it's to be managed. Mart Tinman and I have been at tooth and claw to-day and half the night ; and he has thrown off the mask, or he's dashed something from my sight, I don't know which. I knocked him down."

"Papa !"

"I picked him up."

"Oh," cried Annette, "has Mr. Tinman been hurt ?"

" He called me a Deserter ! "

Annette shuddered.

She did not know what this thing was, but the name of it opened a cabinet of horrors, and she touched her father timidly, to assure him of her constant love, and a little to reassure herself of his substantial identity.

" And I am one," Van Diemen made the confession at the pitch of his voice. " I am a Deserter ; I'm liable to be branded on the back. And it's in Mart Tinman's power to have me marched away to-morrow morning in the sight of Crikswich, and all I can say for myself, as a man and a Briton, is, I did not desert before the enemy. That I swear I never would have done. Death, if death's in front ; but your poor mother was a handsome woman, my child, and there—I could not go on living in barracks and leaving her unprotected. I can't tell a young woman the tale. A hundred pounds came on me for a legacy, as plump in my hands out of open heaven, and your poor mother and I saw our chance ; we consulted, and we determined to risk it, and I got on board with her and you, and over the seas we went, first to ship-wreck, ultimately to fortune."

Van Diemen laughed miserably. " They noticed in the hunting-field here I had a soldier-like seat. A soldier-like seat it'll be, with a brand on it. I shan't be asked to take a soldier-like seat at any of their tables again. I may at Mart Tinman's, out of pity, after I've undergone my punishment. There's a year still to run out of the twenty of my term of service due. He knows it; he's been reckoning; he has me. But the worst cat-o'-nine-tails for me is the disgrace. To have myself pointed at, 'There goes the Deserter! He was a private in the Cardbineers, and he deserted!' No one'll say, 'Ay, but he clung to the idea of his old schoolmate when abroad, and came back loving him, and trusted him, and was deceived.'"

Van Diemen produced a spasmodic cough with a blow on his chest. Annette was weeping.

"There, now go to bed," said he. "I wish you might have known no more than you did of our flight when I got you on board the ship with your poor mother; but you're a young woman now, and you must help me to think of another cut and run, and what baggage we can scrape together in a jiffy, for I won't live here at Mart Tinman's mercy."

Drying her eyes to weep again, Annette said, when she could speak: "Will nothing quiet him? I was going to bother you with all sorts of silly questions, poor dear papa; but I see I can understand if I try. Will nothing—Is he so very angry? Can we not do something to pacify him? He is fond of money. He—oh, the thought of leaving England! Papa, it will kill you; you set your whole heart on England. We could—I could—could I not, do you not think?—step between you

as a peacemaker. Mr. Tinman is always very courteous to me."

At these words of Annette's, Van Diemen burst
into a short snap of savage laughter. "But that's
far away in the background, Mr. Mart Tinman!"
he said. "You stick to your game, I know that;
but you'll find me flown, though I leave a name to
stink like your common behind me. And," he
added, as a chill reminder, "that name the name
of my benefactor. Poor old Van Diemen! He
thought it a safe bequest to make."

"It was; it is! We will stay; we will not be
exiled," said Annette. "I will do anything. What
was the quarrel about, papa?"

"The fact is, my dear, I just wanted to show
him—and take down his pride—I'm by my Australian education a shrewder hand than his old
country. I bought the house on the beach while
he was chaffering, and then I sold it him at a rise
when the town was looking up—only to make him
see. Then he burst up about something I said of
Australia. I will have the common clean. Let
him live at the Crouch as my tenant if he finds the
house on the beach in danger."

"Papa, I am sure," Annette repeated—"sure I
have influence with Mr. Tinman."

"There are those lips of yours shutting tight,"
said her father. "Just listen, and they'll make a
big O. The donkey! He owns you've got influence, and he offers he'll be silent if you'll pledge

your word to marry him. I'm not sure he didn't say, within the year. I told him to look sharp not to be knocked down again. Mart Tinman for my son-in-law! That's an upside down of my expectations, as good as being at the antipodes without a second voyage back! I let him know you were engaged."

Annette gazed at her father open-mouthed, as he had predicted; now with a little chilly dimple at one corner of the mouth, now at another—as a breeze curves the leaden winter lake here and there. She could not get his meaning into her sight, and she sought, by looking hard, to understand it better; much as when some solitary maiden lady, passing into her bedchamber in the hours of darkness, beholds—tradition telling us she has absolutely beheld—foot of burglar under bed; and lo! she stares, and, cunningly to moderate her horror, doubts, yet cannot but believe that there is a leg, and a trunk, and a head, and two terrible arms bearing pistols, to follow. Sick, she palpitates; she compresses her trepidation; she coughs, perchance she sings a bar or two of an aria. Glancing down again, thrice horrible to her is it to discover that there is *no foot!* For had it remained, it might have been imagined a harmless, empty boot. But the withdrawal has a deadly significance of animal life. . . .

In like manner our stricken Annette perceived the object; so did she gradually apprehend the fact of her being asked for Tinman's bride, and she could not think it credible. She half scented, she devised her plan of escape from another single mention of it. But on her father's remarking, with a shuffle, frightened by her countenance, " Don't listen to what I said, Netty. I won't paint him blacker than he is "—then Annette was sure she had been proposed for by Mr. Tinman, and she fancied her father might have revolved it in his mind that there was this means of keeping Tinman silent, silent for ever, in his own interests.

" It was not true, when you told Mr. Tinman I was engaged, papa," she said.

" No, I know that. Mart Tinman only half— kind of hinted. Come, I say! Where's the un- married man wouldn't like to have a girl like you, Netty! They say he's been rejected all round a circuit of fifteen miles ; and he's not bad-looking, neither—he looks fresh and fair. But I thought it as well to let him know he might get *me* at a dis- advantage, but he couldn't you. Now, don't think about it, my love."

" Not if it is not necessary, papa," said Annette ; and employed her familiar sweetness in persuading him to go to bed, as though he were the afflicted one requiring to be petted.

ROUND under the cliffs by the sea, facing south, are warm seats in winter. The sun that shines there on a day of frost wraps you as in a mantle. Here it was that Mr. Herbert Fellingham found Annette, a chalk-block for her chair, and a mound of chalk-rubble defending her from the keen-tipped breath of the east, now and then shadowing the smooth blue water, faintly, like reflections of a flight of gulls.

Infants are said to have their ideas, and why not young ladies? Those who write of their perplexities in descriptions comical in their length are unkind to them, by making them appear the simplest of the creatures of fiction; and most of us, I am sure, would incline to believe in them if they were only some bit more lightly touched. Those troubled sentiments of our young lady of the comfortable classes are quite worthy of mention. Her poor little eye poring as little fishlike as possible upon the intricate, which she takes for the infinite, has its place in our history, nor should we any of us miss the pathos of it were it not that so large a space is claimed for the exposure. As it is, one

has almost to fight a battle to persuade the world
that she has downright thoughts and feelings, and
really a superhuman delicacy is required in present-
ing her that she may be credible. Even then—so
much being accomplished—the thousands accustomed to chapters of her when she is in the situation of Annette will be disappointed by sentences,
just as of old the Continental eater of oysters would
have been offended at the offer of an exchange of
two live for two dozen dead ones. Annette was in
the grand crucial position of English imaginative
prose. I recognise it, and that to this the stream-
lets flow, thence pours the flood. But what was
the plain truth? She had brought herself to think
she ought to sacrifice herself to Tinman, and her
evasions with Herbert, manifested in tricks of coldness alternating with tones of regret, ended, as they
had commenced, in a mysterious half-sullenness.
She had hardly a word to say. Let me step in
again to observe that she had at the moment no
pointed intention of marrying Tinman. To her
mind the circumstances compelled her to embark
on the idea of doing so, and she saw the extremity
in an extreme distance, as those who are taking
voyages may see death by drowning. Still she
had embarked.

" At all events, I have your word for it that you
don't dislike me ? " said Herbert.

"Oh ! no," she sighed. She liked him as emi-
grants the land they are leaving.

"And you have not promised your hand?"

"No," she said, but sighed in thinking that if she could be induced to promise it, there would not be a word of leaving England.

"Then, as you are not engaged, and don't hate me, I have a chance?" he said, in the semi-wailful interrogative of an organ making a mere windy conclusion.

Ocean sent up a tiny wave at their feet.

"A day like this in winter is rarer than a summer day," Herbert resumed encouragingly.

Annette was replying, "People abuse our climate——" But the thought of having to go out away from this climate in the darkness of exile, with her father to suffer under it worse than herself, overwhelmed her, and fetched the reality of her sorrow in the form of Tinman swimming before her soul with the velocity of a telegraph-pole to the window of the flying train. It was past as soon as seen, but it gave her a desperate sensation of speed.

She began to feel that this was life in earnest.

And Herbert should have been more resolute, fiercer. She needed a strong will.

But he was not on the rapids of the masterful passion. For though going at a certain pace, it was by his own impulsion; and I am afraid I must, with many apologies, compare him to the skater—to the skater on easy, slippery ice, be it understood; but he could perform gyrations as he went, and he rather sailed along than dashed ; he was careful of his figuring. Some lovers, right honest lovers never get beyond this quaint skating-stage ; and some ladies, a right goodly number in a foggy climate, deceived by their occasional runs ahead, take them for vessels on the very torrent of love. Let them take them, and let the race continue. Only we perceive that they are skating ; they are careering over a smooth icy floor, and they can stop at a signal, with just half-a-yard of grating on the heel at the outside. Ice, and not fire nor falling water, has been their medium of progression.

Whether a man should unveil his own sex is quite another question. If we are detected, not solely are we done for, but our love tales too. However, there is not much ground for anxiety on that head. Each member of the other party is blind on her own account.

To Annette the figuring of Herbert was graceful, but it did not catch her up and carry her ; it hardly touched her. He spoke well enough to make her sorry for him, and not warmly enough to make her forget her sorrow for herself.

Herbert could obtain no explanation of the singularity of her conduct from Annette, and he went straight to her father, who was nearly as inexplicable for a time. At last he said—

" If you are ready to quit the country with us, you may have my consent."

"Why quit the country?" Herbert asked, in natural amazement.

Van Diemen declined to tell him.

But seeing the young man look stupefied and wretched, he took a turn about the room, and said : "I haven't robbed," and after more turns, "I haven't murdered." He growled in his menagerie trot within the four walls : "But I'm in a man's power. Will that satisfy you? You'll tell me, because I'm rich, to snap my fingers. I can't. I've got feelings. I'm in his power to hurt me and disgrace me. It's the disgrace—to my disgrace I say it—I dread most. You'd be up to my reason if you had ever served in a regiment. I mean, discipline—if ever you'd known discipline—in the police if you like— anything—anywhere where there's what we used to call spirry de cor. I mean, at school. And I'm," said Van Diemen, "a rank idiot double D. dolt, and flat as a pancake, and transparent as a pane of glass. You see through me. Anybody could. I can't talk of my botheration without betraying myself. What good am I among you sharp fellows in England?"

Language of this kind, by virtue of its unintelligibility, set Mr. Herbert Fellingham's acute speculations at work. He was obliged to lean on Van Diemen's assertion, that he had not robbed and had not murdered, to be comforted by the belief that he was not once a notorious bushranger, or a defaulting manager of mines, or any other thing that is naughtily Australian and kanga-rooly.

He sat at the dinner-table at Elba, eating like the rest of mankind, and looking like a starved beggarman all the while.

Annette, in pity of his bewilderment, would have had her father take him into their confidence. She suggested it covertly, and next she spoke of it to him as a prudent measure, seeing that Mr. Felling-ham might find out his exact degree of liability. Van Diemen shouted; he betrayed himself in his weakness as she could not have imagined him. He was ready to go, he said—go on the spot, give up Elba, fly from Old England : what he could not do was to let his countrymen know what he was, and live among them afterwards. He declared that the fact had eternally been present to his mind, devouring him ; and Annette remembered his kindness to the artillerymen posted along the shore westward of Crikswich, though she could recall no sign of remorse. Van Diemen said : " We have to do with Martin Tinman ; that's one who has a hold on me, and one's enough. Leak out my secret to a second fellow, you double my risks." He would not be taught to see how the second might counter-act the first. The singularity of the action of his character on her position was, that though she knew not a soul to whom she could unburden her wretchedness, and stood far more isolated than in her Australian home, fever and chill struck her blood in contemplation of the necessity of quitting England.

Deep, then, was her gratitude to dear good Mrs. Cavely for stepping in to mediate between her father and Mr. Tinman. And well might she be amazed to hear the origin of their recent dispute.

" It was," Mrs. Cavely said, " that Gippsland ! "

Annette cried : " What ? "

" That Gippsland of yours, my dear. Your father will praise Gippsland whenever my Martin asks him to admire the beauties of our neighbour-hood. Many a time has Martin come home to me complaining of it. We have no doubt on earth that Gippsland is a very fine place ; but my brother has his ideas of dignity, you must know, and I only wish he *had* been more used to contradiction, you may believe me. He is a lamb by nature. And, as he says, ' Why underrate one's own country ? He cannot bear to hear boasting.' Well ! I put it to you, dear Annette, is he so unimportant a person ? He asks to be respected, and especially by his dearest friend. From that to blows ! It's the way with men. They begin about trifles, they drink, they quarrel, and one does what he is sorry for, and one says more than he means. All my Martin desires is to shake your dear father's hand, forgive and forget. To win your esteem, darling Annette, he would humble himself in the dust. Will you not help me to bring these two dear old friends together once more ? It is unreasonable of your dear papa to go on boasting of Gippsland if he is so fond of England, now is it not? My brother is the offended party in the eye of the law. That is quite certain. Do you suppose he dreams of taking advantage of it? He is waiting at home to be told he may call on your father. Rank, dignity, wounded feelings, is nothing to him in comparison with friendship."

Annette thought of the blow which had felled him, and spoke the truth of her heart in saying, " He is very generous."

" *You* understand him." Mrs. Cavely pressed her hand. "We will both go to your dear father. He may," she added, not without a gleam of feminine archness, " praise Gippsland above the Himalayas to me. What my Martin so much objected to was, the speaking of Gippsland at all when there was mention of our Lake scenery. As for me, I know how men love to boast of things nobody else has seen."

The two ladies went in company to Van Diemen, who allowed himself to be melted. He was reserved nevertheless. His reception of Mr. Tinman displeased his daughter. Annette attached the blackest importance to a blow of the fist. In her mind it blazed fiendlike, and the man who forgave it rose a step or two on the sublime. Especially did he do so considering that he had it in his power to dismiss her father and herself from bright beaming England before she had looked on all the cathedrals and churches, the sea-shores and spots named in printed poetry, to say nothing of the nobility.

"Papa, you were not so kind to Mr. Tinman as I could have hoped," said Annette.

"Mart Tinman has me at his mercy, and he'll make me know it," her father returned gloomily. "He may let me off with the Commander-in-chief. He'll blast my reputation some day, though. I shall be hanging my head in society, through him."

Van Diemen imitated the disconsolate appearance of a gallows body, in one of those rapid flashes of spontaneous veri-similitude which spring of an inborn horror painting itself on the outside.

"A Deserter!" he moaned.

He succeeded in impressing the terrible nature of the stigma upon Annette's imagination.

The guest at Elba was busy in adding up the sum of his own impressions, and dividing it by this and that new circumstance; for he was totally in the dark. He was attracted by the mysterious interview of Mrs. Cavely and Annette. Tinman's calling and departing set him upon new calculations. Annette grew cold and visibly distressed by her consciousness of it.

She endeavoured to account for this variation of mood. "We have been invited to dine at the house on the beach to-morrow. I would not have accepted, but papa . . . we seemed to think it a duty. Of course the invitation extends to you.

We fancy you do not greatly enjoy dining there. The table will be laid for you here, if you prefer."

Herbert preferred to try the skill of Mrs. Crickledon.

Now, for positive penetration the head prepossessed by a suspicion is unmatched ; for where there is no daylight, this one at least goes about with a lantern. Herbert begged Mrs. Crickledon to cook a dinner for him, and then to give the right colour to his absence from the table of Mr. Tinman, he started for a winter day's walk over the downs—as sharpening a business as any young fellow, blunt or keen, may undertake ; excellent for men of the pen, whether they be creative, and produce, or slaughtering, and review ; good, then, for the silly sheep of letters and the butchers. He sat down to Mrs. Crickledon's table at half-past six. She was, as she had previously informed him, a forty pound-a-year cook at the period of her courting by Crickledon. That zealous and devoted husband had made his first excursion inland to drop over the downs to the great house, and fetch her away as his bride, on the death of her master. Sir Alfred Pooney, who never would have parted with her in life ; and every day of that man's life he dirtied thirteen plates at dinner, nor more, nor less, but exactly that number, as if he believed there was luck in it. And as Crickledon said, it was odd. But it was always a pleasure to cook for him. Mrs. Crickledon could not abide cooking for a mean eater. And when Crickledon said he had never seen an acorn, he might have seen one had he looked about him in the great park, under the oaks, on the day when he came to be married.

"Then it's a standing compliment to you, Mrs. Crickledon, that he did not," said Herbert.

He remarked with the sententiousness of enforced philosophy, that no wine was better than bad wine.

Mrs. Crickledon spoke of a bottle left by her summer lodgers, who had indeed left two, calling the wine invalid's wine ; and she and her husband had opened one on the anniversary of their marriage day in October. It had the taste of doctor's shop, they both agreed ; and as no friend of theirs could be tempted beyond a sip, they were advised, because it was called a tonic, to mix it with the pig-wash, so that it should not be entirely lost, but benefit the constitution of the pig. Herbert sipped at the remaining bottle, and finding himself in the superior society of an old Manzanilla, refilled his glass.

"Nothing I knows of proves the difference between gentlefolks and poor persons as tastes in wine," said Mrs. Crickledon, admiring him as she brought in a dish of cutlets, with Sir Alfred Pooney's favourite sauce Soubise, wherein rightly onion should be delicate as the idea of love in maidens' thoughts, albeit constituting the element of flavour. Something of such a dictum Sir Alfred Pooney had imparted to his cook, and she repeated it with the fresh elegance of such sweet sayings when transfused through the native mind :

"He said, 'Like as it was what you would call a young gal's blush at a kiss round a corner.'"

The epicurean baronet had the habit of talking in that way.

Herbert drank to his memory. He was well-filled ; he had no work to do, and he was exuberant in spirits, as Mrs. Crickledon knew her countrymen should and would be under those conditions. And suddenly he drew his hand across a forehead so wrinkled and dark, that Mrs. Crickledon exclaimed, "Heart or stomach ?"

"Oh, no," said he. "I'm sound enough in both, I hope."

"That old Tinman's up to one of his games," she observed.

"Do you think so ?"

"He's circumventing Miss Annette Smith."

"Pooh ! Crickledon. A man of his age can't be seriously thinking of proposing for a young lady."

"He's a well-kept man. He's never racketed. He hadn't the rackets in him. And she mayn't care for him. But we hear things drop."

"What things have you heard drop, Crickledon ? In a profound silence you may hear pins ; in a hubbub you may hear cannon-balls. But I never believe in eavesdropping gossip."

"He was heard to say to Mr. Smith," Crickledon pursued, and she lowered her voice, "he was heard to say, it was when they were quarrelling over that chewal, and they went at one another pretty hard before Mr. Smith beat him and he sold Mr. Smith that meadow ; he was heard to say, there was worse than transportation for Mr. Smith if he but lifted his finger. They Tinmans have awful tempers. His old mother died malignant, though she was a saving woman, and never owed a penny to a Christian a hour longer than it took to pay the money. And old Tinman's just such another."

"Transportation!" Herbert ejaculated, "that's sheer nonsense, Crickledon. I'm sure your husband would tell you so."

"It was my husband brought me the words," Mrs. Crickledon rejoined with some triumph. "He did tell me, I own, to keep it shut ; but my speaking to you, a friend of Mr. Smith's, won't do no harm. He heard them under the battery, over that chewal glass ; 'And you shall pay,' says Mr. Smith, and 'I shan't,' says old Tinman. Mr. Smith said he would have it if he had to squeeze a death-bed confession from a sinner. Then old Tinman fires out, 'You!' he says, 'you——' and he stammered. 'Mr. Smith,' my husband said—and you never saw a man so shocked as my husband at being obliged to hear them at one another—'Mr. Smith used the word damn.' You may laugh, sir."

"You say it so capitally, Crickledon."

"And then old Tinman said, 'And a D. to you ; and if I lift my finger, it's Big D. on your back.'"

" And what did Mr. Smith say, then ? "

" He said, like a man shot, my husband says he said, ' My God ! ' "

Herbert Fellingham jumped away from the table.

" You tell me, Crickledon, your husband actually heard that—just those words ?—the tones ? "

" My husband says he heard him say, ' My God ! ' just like a poor man shot or stabbed. You may speak to Crickledon, if you speaks to him alone, sir. I say you ought to know. For I've noticed Mr. Smith since that day has never looked to me the same easy-minded happy gentleman he was when we first knew him. He would have had me go to cook for him at Elba, but Crickledon thought I'd better be independent, and Mr. Smith said to me, ' Perhaps you're right, Crickledon, for who knows how long I may be among you ? ' "

Herbert took the solace of tobacco in Crickledon's shop. Thence, with the story confirmed to him, he sauntered round the house on the beach.

CHAPTER VIII

THE moon was over sea. Coasting vessels that had run into the bay for shelter from the North wind lay with their shadows thrown shoreward on the cold smooth water, almost to the verge of the beach, where there was neither breath nor sound of wind, only the lisp at the pebbles.

Mrs. Crickledon's dinner and the state of his heart made young Fellingham indifferent to a wintry atmosphere. It sufficed him that the night was fair. He stretched himself on the shingle, thinking of the Manzanilla, and Annette, and the fine flavour given to tobacco by a dry still air in moonlight—thinking of his work, too, in the background, as far as mental lassitude would allow of it. The idea of taking Annette to see his first play at the theatre—when it should be performed —was very soothing. The beach rather looked like a stage, and the sea like a ghostly audience, with, if you will, the broadside bulks of black sailing craft at anchor for representatives of the newspaper press. Annette was a nice girl ; if a little commonplace and low-born, yet sweet. What a subject he could make of her father ! " The Deserter " offered a new complication. Fellingham rapidly sketched it in fancy—Van Diemen, as a Member of the Parliament of Great Britain, led away from the House of Commons to be branded on the back! What a magnificent fall! We have so few intensely dramatic positions in English real life that the meditative author grew enamoured of this one, and laughed out a royal " Ha !" like a monarch reviewing his well-appointed soldiery.

" There you are," said Van Diemen's voice ; " I smelt your pipe. You're a rum fellow, to be lying out on the beach on a cold night. Lord! I don't like you the worse for it. I was for the romance of the moon in my young days."

" Where is Annette ? " said Fellingham, jumping to his feet.

" My daughter ? She's taking leave of her intended."

" What's that ?" Fellingham gasped. " Good heavens, Mr. Smith, what do you mean ? "

" Pick up your pipe, my lad. Girls choose as they please, I suppose."

" Her *intended*, did you say, sir ? What can that mean ? "

" My dear good young fellow, don't make a fuss. We're all going to stay here, and very glad to see you from time to time. The fact is, I oughtn't to have quarrelled with Mart Tinman as I've done ; I'm too peppery by nature. The fact is, I struck him, and he forgave it. I couldn't have done that myself. And I believe I'm in for a headache to-morrow; upon my soul, I do. Mart Tinman would champagne us; but, poor old boy, I struck him, and I couldn't make amends—didn't see my way; and we joined hands over the glass—to the deuce with the glass!—and the end of it is, Netty—she didn't propose it, but as I'm in his—I say, as I had struck him, she—it was rather solemn, if you had seen us—she burst into tears, and there was Mrs. Cavely, and old Mart, and me as big a fool— if I'm not a villain!"

Fellingham perceived a more than common effect of Tinman's wine. He touched Van Diemen on the shoulder. "May I beg to hear exactly what has happened?"

"Upon my soul, we're all going to live comfortably in Old England, and no more quarrelling and decamping," was the stupid rejoinder. "Except that I didn't exactly—I think you said 'exactly'? —I didn't bargain for old Mart as my—but he's a sound man; Mart's my junior; he's rich. He's eco . . he's eco . . . you know — my Lord! where's my brains?—but he's upright—'nomical!"

"An economical man," said Fellingham, with sedate impatience.

"My dear sir, I'm heartily obliged to you for your assistance," returned Van Diemen. "Here she is."

Annette had come out of the gate in the flint wall. She started slightly on seeing Herbert, whom she had taken for a coastguard, she said.

He bowed. He kept his head bent, peering at her intrusively.

"It's the air on champagne," Van Diemen said, calling on his lungs to clear themselves and right him. "I wasn't a bit queer in the house."

"The air on Tinman's champagne!" said Fellingham. "It must be like the contact of two hostile chemical elements."

Annette walked faster.

They descended from the shingle to the scant-bladed grass-sweep running round the salted town-refuse on toward Elba. Van Diemen sniffed, ejaculating, "I'll be best man with Mart Tinman about this business! You'll stop with us, Mr.—what's your Christian name? Stop with us as long as you like. Old friends for me! The joke of it is that Nelson was my man, and yet I went and enlisted in the cavalry. If you talk of chemical substances, old Mart Tinman was a sneak who never cared a dump for his country; and I'm not to speak a single syllable about that . .. . over there . . Australia . . . Gippsland! So down he went, clean over. Very sorry for what we have done. Contrite. Penitent."

"Now we feel the wind a little," said Annette.

Fellingham murmured, "Allow me; your shawl is flying loose."

He laid his hands on her arms, and, pressing her in a tremble, said, "One sign! It's not true? A word! Do you hate me?"

"Thank you very much, but I am not cold," she replied, and linked herself to her father.

Van Diemen immediately shouted, "For we are jolly boys! for we are jolly boys! It's the air on the champagne. And hang me," said he, as they entered the grounds of Elba, "if I don't walk over my property."

Annette interposed ; she stood like a reed in his way.

"No! my Lord! I'll see what I sold you for!" he cried. "I'm an' owner of the soil of Old England, and care no more for the title of squire than Napoleon Bonaparty. But I'll tell you what, Mr. Hubbard : your mother was never so astonished at her dog as old Van Diemen would be to hear himself called squire in Old England. And a convict he was, for he did wrong once, but he worked his redemption. And the smell of my own property makes me feel my legs again. And I'll tell you what, Mr. Hubbard, as Netty calls you when she speaks of you in private : Mart Tinman's ideas of wine are pretty much like his ideas of healthy smells, and when I'm bailiff of Crikswich, mind, he'll find two to one against him in our town-council. I love my country, but hang me if I don't purify it!"

Saying this, with the excitement of a high resolve upon him, Van Diemen bored through a shrubbery-brake, and Fellingham said to Annette : "Have I lost you?"

"I belong to my father," said she, contracting and disengaging her feminine garments to step after him in the cold silver-spotted dusk of the winter woods.

Van Diemen came out on a fish-pond.

"Here you are, young ones!" he said to the pair. "This way, Fellowman. I'm clearer now, and it's my belief I've been talking nonsense. I'm puffed up with money, and haven't the heart I once had. I say, Fellowman, Fellowbird, Hubbard—what's your right name?—fancy an old carp fished out of that pond and flung into the sea. That's exile! And if the girl don't mind, what does it matter?"

"Mr. Herbert Fellingham, I think, would like to go to bed, papa," said Annette.

"Miss Smith must be getting cold," Fellingham hinted.

"Bounce away indoors," replied Van Diemen, and he led them like a bull.

Annette was disinclined to leave them together in the smoking-room, and under the pretext of wishing to see her father to bed she remained with them, though there was a novel directness and heat of tone in Herbert that alarmed her, and with reason. He divined in hideous outlines what had happened. He was no longer figuring on easy ice, but desperate at the prospect of a loss to himself, and a fate for Annette, that tossed him from repulsion to incredulity, and so back.

Van Diemen begged him to light his pipe.

" I'm off to London to-morrow," said Fellingham. " I don't want to go, for very particular reasons ; I may be of more use there. I have a cousin who's a General officer in the army, and if I have your permission—you see, anything's better, as it seems to me, than that you should depend for peace and comfort on one man's tongue not wagging, especially when he is not the best of tempers—if I have your permission—without mentioning names, of course—I'll consult him."

There was a dead silence.

" You know you may trust me, sir. I love your daughter with all my heart. Your honour and your interests are mine."

Van Diemen struggled for composure.

" Netty, what have you been at ? " he said.

" It is untrue, papa ! " she answered the unworded accusation.

" Annette has told me nothing, sir. I have heard it. You must brace your mind to the fact that it is known. What is known to Mr. Tinman is pretty sure to be known generally at the next disagreement."

" That scoundrel Mart ! " Van Diemen muttered.

" I am positive Mr. Tinman did not speak of you, papa," said Annette, and turned her eyes from the half-paralysed figure of her father on Herbert to put him to proof.

" No, but he made himself heard when it was

being discussed. At any rate, it's known; and the thing to do is to meet it."

"I'm off. I'll not stop a day. I'd rather live on the Continent," said Van Diemen, shaking himself, as to prepare for the step into that desert.

"Mr. Tinman has been most generous!" Annette protested tearfully.

"I won't say no: I think you are deceived and lend him your own generosity," said Herbert. "Can you suppose it generous, that even in the extremest case, he should speak of the matter to your father, and talk of denouncing him? He did it."

"He was provoked."

"A gentleman is distinguished by his not allowing himself to be provoked."

"I am engaged to him, and I cannot hear it said that he is not a gentleman."

The first part of her sentence Annette uttered bravely; at the conclusion she broke down. She wished Herbert to be aware of the truth, that he might stay his attacks on Mr. Tinman; and she believed he had only been guessing the circumstances in which her father was placed; but the comparison between her two suitors forced itself on her now, when the younger one spoke in a manner so self-contained, brief, and full of feeling.

She had to leave the room weeping.

"Has your daughter engaged herself, sir?" said Herbert.

"Talk to me to-morrow ; don't give us up if she has—we were trapped, it's my opinion," said Van Diemen. " There's the devil in that wine of Mart Tinman's. I feel it still, and in the morning it'll be worse. What can she see in him ? I must quit the country ; carry her off. How he did it, I don't know. It was that woman, the widow, the fellow's sister. She talked till she piped her eye—talked about our lasting union. On my soul, I believe I egged Netty on ! I was in a mollified way with that wine ; all of a sudden the woman joins their hands ! And I—a man of spirit will despise me ! —what I thought of was, ' now my secret's safe ! ' You've sobered me, young sir. I see myself, if that's being sober. I don't ask your opinion of men ; I am a deserter, false to my colours, a breaker of his oath. Only mark this : I was married, and a common trooper, married to a hand-some young woman, true as steel ; but she was handsome, and we were starvation poor, and she had to endure persecution from an officer day by day. Bear that situation in your mind. Provi-dence dropped me a hundred pounds out of the sky. Properly speaking, it popped up out of the earth, for I reaped it, you may say, from a relative's grave. Rich and poor's all right, if I'm rich and you're poor ; and you may be happy though you're poor ; but where there are many poor young women, lots of rich men are a terrible temptation to them. That's my dear good wife speaking, and had she been spared to me I never should have come back to Old England, and heart's delight and heartache I should not have known. She was my backbone, she was my breast-comforter too. Why did she stick to me? Because I had faith in her when appearances were against her. But she never forgave this country the hurt to her woman's pride. You'll have noticed a squarish jaw in Netty. That's her mother. And I shall have to encounter it, supposing I find Mart Tinman has been playing me false. I'm blown on somehow. I'll think of what course I'll take 'twixt now and morning. Good night, young gentleman."

"Good night, sir," said Herbert, adding, "I will get information from the Horse Guards ; as for the people knowing it about here, you're not living much in society——"

"It's not other people's feelings, it's my own," Van Diemen silenced him. "I feel it, if it's in the wind ; ever since Mart Tinman spoke the thing out, I've felt on my skin cold and hot."

He flourished his lighted candle and went to bed, manifestly solaced by the idea that he was the victim of his own feelings.

Herbert could not sleep. Annette's monstrous choice of Tinman in preference to himself constantly assailed and shook his understanding. There was the "squarish jaw" mentioned by her father to think of. It filled him with a vague apprehension, but he was unable to imagine that a

young girl, and an English girl, and an enthusiastic young English girl, could be devoid of
sentiment ; and presuming her to have it, as one
must, there was no fear that she would persist in
her loathsome choice when she knew her father
was against it.

CHAPTER IX

ANNETTE did not shun him next morning. She did not shun the subject, either. But she had been exact in arranging that she should not be more than a few minutes downstairs before her father. Herbert found that, compared with her, girls of sentiment are commonplace indeed. She had conceived an insane idea of nobility in Tinman that blinded her to his face, figure, and character—his manners, likewise. He had forgiven a blow !

Silly as the delusion might be, it clothed her in whimsical attractiveness.

It was a beauty in her to dwell so firmly upon moral quality. Overthrown and stunned as he was, and reduced to helplessness by her brief and positive replies, Herbert was obliged to admire the singular young lady, who spoke, without much shyness, of her incongruous, destined mate, though his admiration had an edge cutting like irony. While in the turn for candour, she ought to have told him that, previous to her decision, she had weighed the case of the diverse claims of himself and Tinman, and resolved them according to her predilection for the peaceful residence of her father and herself in England. This she had done a little regretfully, because of the natural sympathy of the young girl for the younger man. But the younger man had seemed to her seriously-straightforward mind too light and airy in his wooing, like one of her waltzing officers—very well so long as she stepped the measure with him, and not forcible enough to take her off her feet. He had changed, and now that he had become persuasive, she feared he would disturb the serenity with which she desired and strove to contemplate her decision. Tinman's magnanimity was present in her imagination to sustain her, though she was aware that Mrs. Cavely had surprised her will, and caused it to surrender unconsulted by her wiser intelligence.

"I cannot listen to you," she said to Herbert, after listening longer than was prudent. "If what you say of papa is true, I do not think he will remain in Crikswich, or even in England. But I am sure the old friend we used to speak of so much in Australia has not wilfully betrayed him."

Herbert would have had to say, "Look on us two!" to proceed in his baffled wooing; and the very ludicrousness of the contrast led him to see the folly and shame of proposing it.

Van Diemen came down to breakfast looking haggard and restless. "I haven't had my morning's walk—I can't go out to be hooted," he said, calling to his daughter for tea, and strong tea;

and explaining to Herbert that he knew it to be
bad for the nerves, but it was an antidote to bad
champagne.

Mr. Herbert Fellingham had previously received
an invitation on behalf of a sister of his to Crikswich. A dull sense of genuine sagacity inspired
him to remind Annette of it. She wrote prettily
to Miss Mary Fellingham, and Herbert had some
faint joy in carrying away the letter of her hand-
writing.

"Fetch her soon, for we shan't be here long,"
Van Diemen said to him at parting. He ex-
pressed a certain dread of his next meeting with
Mart Tinman.

Herbert speedily brought Mary Fellingham to
Elba, and left her there. The situation was apparently unaltered. Van Diemen looked worn,
like a man who has been feeding mainly on his
reflections, which was manifest in his few melancholy bits of speech. He said to Herbert : "How
you feel a thing when you are found out!" and,
"It doesn't do for a man with a heart to do
wrong!" He designated the two principal roads
by which poor sinners come to a conscience. His
own would have slumbered but for discovery ; and,
as he remarked, if it had not been for his heart
leading him to Tinman, he would not have fallen
into that man's power.

The arrival of a young lady of fashionable appearance at Elba was matter of cogitation to Mrs.

Cavely. She was disposed to suspect that it meant something, and Van Diemen's behaviour to her brother would of itself have fortified any suspicion. He did not call at the house on the beach, he did not invite Martin to dinner, he was rarely seen, and when he appeared at the Town Council he once or twice violently opposed his friend Martin, who came home ruffled, deeply offended in his interests and his dignity.

"Have you noticed any difference in Annette's treatment of you, dear?" Mrs. Cavely inquired.

"No," said Tinman; "none. She shakes hands. She asks after my health. She offers me my cup of tea."

"I have seen all that. But does she avoid privacy with you?"

"Dear me, no! Why should she? I hope, Martha, I am a man who may be confided in by any young lady in England."

"I am sure you may, dear Martin."

"She has an objection to name the . . . the day," said Martin. "I have informed her that I have an objection to long engagements. I don't like her new companion. She says she has been presented at Court. I greatly doubt it."

"It's to give herself a style, you may depend. I don't believe her!" exclaimed Mrs. Cavely, with sharp personal asperity.

Brother and sister examined together the Court Guide they had purchased on the occasion at once

of their largest outlay and most thrilling gratification; in it they certainly found the name of
General Fellingham. "But he can't be related to
a newspaper-writer," said Mrs. Cavely.

To which her brother rejoined, "Unless the
young man turned scamp. I hate unproductive
professions."

"I hate *him*, Martin." Mrs. Cavely laughed in
scorn. "I should say, I pity him. It's as clear to
me as the sun at noonday, he wanted Annette.
That's why I was in a hurry. How I dreaded he
would come that evening to our dinner! When I
saw him absent, I could have cried out it was
Providence! And so be careful—we have had
everything done for us from on High as yet—but
be careful of your temper, dear Martin. I will
hasten on the union; for it's a shame of a girl to
drag a man behind her till he's old at the altar.
Temper, dear, if you will only think of it, is the
weak point."

"Now he has begun boasting to me of his
Australian wines!" Tinman ejaculated.

"Bear it. Bear it as you do Gippsland. My
dear, you have the retort in your heart:—Yes! but
have you a Court in Australia?"

"Ha! and his Australian wines cost twice the
amount I pay for mine!"

"Quite true. We are not obliged to buy them,
I should hope. I would, though—a dozen—if I
thought it necessary, to keep him quiet."

Tinman continued muttering angrily over the Australian wines, with a word of irritation at Gippsland, while promising to be watchful of his temper.

"What good is Australia to us," he asked, "if it doesn't bring us money?"

"It's going to, my dear," said Mrs. Cavely. "Think of that when he begins boasting his Australia. And though it's convict's money, as he confesses——"

"With his convict's money!" Tinman interjected tremblingly. "How long am I expected to wait?"

"Rely on me to hurry on the day," said Mrs. Cavely. "There is no other annoyance?"

"Wherever I am going to buy, that man outbids me!—and then says it's the old country's want of pluck and dash, and doing things large-handed! A man who'd go on his knees to stop in England!" Tinman vociferated in a breath; and fairly reddened by the effort: "He may have to do it yet. I can't stand insult."

"You are less able to stand insult after Honours," his sister said, in obedience to what she had observed of him since his famous visit to London. "It must be so, in nature. But temper is everything just now. Remember, it was by command of temper, and letting her father put himself in the wrong, you got hold of Annette. And I would abstain even from wine. For some-

times after it, you have owned it disagreed.   And
I have noticed these eruptions between you and
Mr. Smith—as he calls himself—generally after
wine."

"Always the poor! the poor! money for the
poor!"   Tinman   harped   on   further   grievances
against Van Diemen.   "I say doctors have said
the drain on the common is healthy ; it's a healthy
smell, nourishing.   We've always had it and been
a healthy town.   But the sea encroaches, and I say
my house and my property is in danger.   He
buys my house over my head, and offers me the
Crouch to live in at an advanced rent.   And then
he sells me my house at an advanced price, and I
buy, and then he votes against a penny for the
protection of the shore!   And we're in winter
again !   As if he was not in my power !"

"My dear Martin, to Elba we go, and soon, if
you will govern your temper," said Mrs. Cavely.
"You're an angel to let me speak of it so, and
it's only that man that irritates you.   I call him
sinfully ostentatious."

"I could blow him from a gun if I spoke out,
and he knows it !   He's wanting in common
gratitude, let alone respect," Tinman snorted.

"But he has a daughter, my dear."

Tinman slowly and crackingly subsided.

His main grievance against Van Diemen was
the non-recognition of his importance by that
uncultured Australian, who did not seem to be

conscious of the dignities and distinctions we come to in our country. The moneyed daughter, the prospective marriage, for an economical man rejected by every lady surrounding him, advised him to lock up his temper in submission to Martha.

"Bring Annette to dine with us," he said, on Martha's proposing a visit to the dear young creature.

Martha drank a glass of her brother's wine at lunch, and departed on the mission.

Annette declined to be brought. Her excuse was her guest, Miss Fellingham.

"Bring her too, by all means—if you'll condescend, I am sure," Mrs. Cavely said to Mary.

"I am much obliged to you ; I do not dine out at present," said the London lady.

"Dear me ! are you ill ? "

" No."

" Nothing in the family, I hope ? "

" My family ? "

"I am sure, I beg pardon," said Mrs. Cavely, bridling with a spite pardonable by the severest moralist.

"Can I speak to you alone ? " she addressed Annette.

Miss Fellingham rose.

Mrs. Cavely confronted her. "I can't allow it; I can't think of it. I'm only taking a little liberty with one I may call my future sister-in-law."

"Shall I come out with you?" said Annette, in sheer lassitude assisting Mary Fellingham in her scheme to show the distastefulness of this lady and her brother.

"Not if you don't wish to."

"I have no objection."

"Another time will do."

"Will you write?"

"By post indeed!"

Mrs. Cavely delivered a laugh supposed to be peculiar to the English stage.

"It would be a penny thrown away," said Annette. "I thought you could send a messenger."

Intercommunication with Miss Fellingham had done mischief to her high moral conception of the pair inhabiting the house on the beach.

Mrs. Cavely saw it, and could not conceal that she smarted.

Her counsel to her brother, after recounting the offensive scene to him in animated dialogue, was, to give Van Diemen a fright.

"I wish I had not drunk that glass of sherry before starting," she exclaimed, both savagely and sagely. "It's best after business. And these gentlemen's habits of yours of taking to dining late upset me. I'm afraid I showed temper; but you, Martin, would not have borne one-tenth of what I did."

"How dare you say so!" her brother rebuked

her indignantly ; and the house on the beach enclosed with difficulty a storm between brother and sister, happily not heard outside, because of loud winds raging.

Nevertheless Tinman pondered on Martha's idea of the wisdom of giving Van Diemen a fright.

CHAPTER X

THE English have been called a bad-tempered
people, but this is to judge of them by their
manifestations; whereas an examination into
causes might prove them to be no worse tempered
than that man is a bad sleeper who lies in a biting
bed. If a sagacious instinct directs them to dis-
countenance realistic tales, the realistic tale should
justify its appearance by the discovery of an
apology for the tormented souls. Once they
sang madrigals, once they danced on the green,
they revelled in their lusty humours, without
having recourse to the pun for fun, an exhibition
of hundreds of bare legs for jollity, a sentimental
wailing all in the throat for music. Evidence is
procurable that they have been an artificially-
reared people, feeding on the genius of inventors,
transposers, adulterators, instead of the products
of nature, for the last half century; and it is unfair
to affirm of them that they are positively this or
that. They are experiments. They are the sons
and victims of a desperate Energy, alluring by
cheapness, satiating with quantity, that it may
mount in the social scale, at the expense of their

tissues. The land is in a state of fermentation to mount, and the shop, which has shot half their stars to their social zenith, is what verily they would scald themselves to wash themselves free of. Nor is it in any degree a reprehensible sign that they should fly as from hue and cry the title of tradesman. It is on the contrary the spot of sanity, which bids us right cordially hope. Energy transferred to the moral sense, may clear them yet.

Meanwhile this beer, this wine, both are of a character to have killed more than the tempers of a less gifted people. Martin Tinman invited Van Diemen Smith to try the flavour of a wine that, as he said, he thought of "laying down."

It has been hinted before of a strange effect upon the minds of men who knew what they were going to, when they received an invitation to dine with Tinman. For the sake of a little social meeting at any cost, they accepted it; accepted it with a sigh, midway as by engineering measurement between prospective and retrospective; as nearly mechanical as things human may be, like the Mussulman's accustomed cry of Kismet. Has it not been related of the little Jew babe sucking at its mother's breast in Jerusalem, that this innocent, long after the Captivity, would start convulsively, relinquishing its feast, and indulging in the purest Hebrew lamentation of the most tenacious of races, at the passing sound of a Baby-

Ionian or a Ninevite voice?   In some such manner did men, unable to refuse, deep in what remained to them of nature, listen to Tinman; and so did Van Diemen, sighing heavily under the operation of simple animal instinct.

"You seem miserable," said Tinman, not oblivious of his design to give his friend a fright.

"Do I? No, I'm all right," Van Diemen replied. "I'm thinking of alterations at the hall before Summer, to accommodate guests — if I stay here."

"I suppose you would not like to be separated from Annette."

"Separated?   No, I should think I shouldn't. Who'd do it?"

"Because I should not like to leave my good sister Martha all to herself in a house so near the sea."

"Why not go to the Crouch, man?"

"Thank you."

"No thanks needed if you don't take advantage of the offer."

They were at the entrance to Elba, whither Mr. Tinman was betaking himself to see his intended. He asked if Annette was at home, and to his great stupefaction heard that she had gone to London for a week.

Dissembling the spite aroused within him, he postponed his very strongly fortified design, and said, "You must be lonely."

Van Diemen informed him that it would be for a night only, as young Fellingham was coming down to keep him company.

" At six o'clock this evening, then," said Tinman. " We're not fashionable in winter."

" Hang me, if I know when ever we were ! " Van Diemen rejoined.

" Come, though, you'd like to be. You've got your ambition, Philip, like other men."

" Respectable and respected—that's my ambition, Mr. Mart."

Tinman simpered : " With your wealth ! "

" Ay, I'm rich—for a contented mind."

" I'm pretty sure you'll approve my new vintage," said Tinman. " It's direct from Oporto, my wine-merchant tells me, on his word."

" What's the price ? "

" No, no, no. Try it first. It's rather a stiff price."

Van Diemen was partially reassured by the announcement. " What do you call a stiff price ? "

" Well!—over thirty."

" Double that, and you may have a chance."

" Now," cried Tinman, exasperated, " how can a man from Australia know anything about prices for port ? You can't divest your ideas of diggers' prices. You're like an intoxicating drink yourself on the tradesmen of our town. You think it fine —ha ! ha ! I daresay, Philip, I should be doing the same if I were up to your mark at my banker's.   We can't all of us be lords, nor baronets."

Catching up his temper thus cleverly, he curbed that habitual runaway, and retired from his old friend's presence to explode in the society of the solitary Martha.

Annette's behaviour was as bitterly criticised by the sister as by the brother.

"She has gone to those Fellingham people; and she may be thinking of jilting us," Mrs. Cavely said.

"In that case, I have no mercy," cried her brother. "I have borne"—he bowed with a professional spiritual humility—"as I should, but it may get past endurance. I say I have borne enough; and if the worst comes to the worst, and I hand him over to the authorities—I say I mean him no harm, but he has struck me. He beat me as a boy and he has struck me as a man, and I say I have no thought of revenge, but I cannot have him here; and I say if I drive him out of the country back to his Gippsland—— "

Martin Tinman quivered for speech, probably for that which feedeth speech, as is the way with angry men.

"And what? what then?" said Martha, with the tender mellifluousness of sisterly reproach. "What good can you expect of letting temper get the better of you, dear?"

Tinman did not enjoy her recent turn for

usurping the lead in their consultations, and he said, tartly, "This good, Martha. We shall get the Hall at my price, and be Head People here. Which," he raised his note, "which he, a Deserter, has no right to pretend to give himself out to be. What your feelings may be as an old inhabitant, I don't know, but I have always looked up to the people at Elba Hall, and I say I don't like to have a Deserter squandering convict's money there—with his forty-pound-a-year cook, and his champagne at seventy a' dozen. It's the luxury of Sodom and Gomorrah."

"That does not prevent its being very nice to dine there," said Mrs. Cavely ; "and it shall be our table for good if I have any management."

"You mean me, ma'am," bellowed Tinman.

"Not at all," she breathed, in dulcet contrast. "You are good-looking, Martin, but you have not half such pretty eyes as the person I mean. I never ventured to dream of managing you, Martin. I am thinking of the people at Elba."

"But why this extraordinary treatment of me, Martha ? "

"She's a child, having her head turned by those Fellinghams. But she's honourable ; she has sworn to me she *would* be honourable."

"You do think I may as well give him a fright ? " Tinman inquired hungrily.

"A sort of hint ; but very gentle, Martin. Do be gentle—casual like—as if you didn't want to say it. Get him on his Gippsland. Then if he brings you to words, you can always laugh back, and say you will go to Kew and see the Fernery, and fancy all that, so high, on Helvellyn or the Downs. *Why* "—Mrs. Cavely, at the end of her astute advices and cautionings, as usual, gave loose to her natural character—" *Why* that man came back to England at all, with his boastings of Gippsland, I can't for the life of me find out. It's a perfect mystery."

" It is," Tinman sounded his voice at a great depth, reflectively. Glad of taking the part she was perpetually assuming of late, he put out his hand and said : " But it may have been ordained for our good, Martha."

" True, dear," said she, with an earnest sentiment of thankfulness to the Power which had led him round to her way of thinking and feeling.

CHAPTER XI

ANNETTE had gone to the big metropolis, which burns in colonial imaginations as the sun of cities, and was about to see something of London, under the excellent auspices of her new friend, Mary Fellingham, and a dense fog. She was alarmed by the darkness, a little in fear, too, of Herbert ; and these feelings caused her to chide herself for leaving her father.

Hearing her speak of her father sadly, Herbert kindly proposed to go down to Crikswich on the very day of her coming. She thanked him, and gave him a taste of bitterness by smiling favourably on his offer ; but as he wished her to discern and take to heart the difference between one man and another, in the light of a suitor, he let her perceive that it cost him heavy pangs to depart immediately, and left her to brood on his example. Mary Fellingham liked Annette. She thought her a sensible girl of uncultivated sensibilities, the reverse of thousands ; not commonplace, therefore ; and that the sensibilities were expanding was to be seen in her gradual unreadiness to talk of her engagement to Mr. Tinman, though her intimacy with Mary warmed daily. She considered she was bound to marry the man at some distant date, and did not feel unhappiness yet. She had only felt uneasy when she had to greet and converse with her intended ; especially when the London young lady had been present. Herbert's departure relieved her of the pressing sense of contrast. She praised him to Mary for his extreme kindness to her father, and down in her unsounded heart desired that her father might appreciate it even more than she did.

Herbert drove into Crikswich at night, and stopped at Crickledon's, where he heard that Van Diemen was dining with Tinman.

Crickledon the carpenter permitted certain dry curves to play round his lips like miniature shavings at the name of Tinman ; but Herbert asked, "What is it now?" in vain, and he went to Crickledon the cook.

This union of the two Crickledons, male and female, was an ideal one, such as poor women dream of ; and men would do the same, if they knew how poor they are. Each had a profession, each was independent of the other, each supported the fabric. Consequently there was mutual respect, as between two pillars of a house. Each saw the other's faults with a sly wink to the world, and an occasional interchange of sarcasm that was tonic, very strengthening to the wits without endangering the habit of affection. Crickledon the cook stood for her own opinions, and directed the public conduct of Crickledon the carpenter ; and if he went astray from the line she marked out, she put it down to human nature, to which she was tolerant. He, when she had not followed his advice, ascribed it to the nature of women. She never said she was the equal of her husband ; but the carpenter proudly acknowledged that she was as good as a man, and he bore with foibles rather derogatory to such high stature, by teaching himself to observe a neatness of domestic and general management that told him he certainly was not as good as a woman. Herbert delighted in them. The cook regaled the carpenter with skilful, tasty, and economic dishes ; and the carpenter, obedient to her supplications, had promised, in the event of his outliving her, that no hands but his should have the making of her coffin. " It is so nice," she said, " to think one's own husband will put together the box you are to lie in, of his own make ! " Had they been even a doubtfully united pair, the cook's anticipation of a comfortable coffin, the work of the best carpenter in England, would have kept them together ; and that which fine cookery does for the cementing of couples needs not to be recounted to those who have read a chapter or two of the natural history of the male sex.

" Crickledon, my dear soul, your husband is labouring with a bit of fun," Herbert said to her.

"He wouldn't laugh loud at Punch, for fear of an action," she replied. "He never laughs out till he gets to bed, and has locked the door; and when he does, he says 'Hush!' to me. Tinman isn't bailiff again just yet, and where he has his bailiff's best Court suit from, you may ask. He exercises in it off and on all the week, at night, and sometimes in the middle of the day."

Herbert rallied her for her gossip's credulity.

"It's truth," she declared. "I have it from the maid of the house, little Jane, whom he pays four pound a year for all the work of the house: a clever little thing with her hands and her head she is; and can read and write beautiful; and she's a mind to leave 'em if they don't advance her. She knocked and went in while he was full blaze, and bowing his poll to his glass. And now he turns the key, and a child might know he was at it."

"He can't be such a donkey!"

"And he's been seen at the window on the seaside. 'Who's your Admiral staying at the house on the beach?' men have inquired as they come ashore. My husband has heard it. Tinman's got it on his brain. He might be cured by marriage to a sound-headed woman, but he'll soon be wanting to walk about in silk legs if he stops a bachelor. They tell me his old mother here had a dress value twenty pound; and pomp's inherited. Save as he may, there's his leak."

Herbert's contempt for Tinman was intense; it

was that of the young and ignorant who live in their imaginations like spendthrifts, unaware of the importance of them as the food of life, and of how necessary it is to seize upon the solider one among them for perpetual sustenance when the unsubstantial are vanishing. The great event of his bailiff's term of office had become the sun of Tinman's system. He basked in its rays. He meant to be again the proud official, royally distinguished ; meantime, though he knew not that his days were dull, he groaned under the dulness ; and, as cart or cab horses, uncomplaining as a rule, show their view of the nature of harness when they have release to frisk in a field, it is possible that existence was made tolerable to the jogging man by some minutes of excitement in his bailiff's Court suit. Really to pasture on our recollections we ought to dramatize them. There is, however, only the testimony of a maid and a mariner to show that Tinman did it, and those are witnesses coming of particularly long-bow classes, given to magnify small items of fact.

On reaching the hall Herbert found the fire alight in the smoking-room, and soon after settling himself there he heard Van Diemen's voice at the hall-door saying good night to Tinman.

"Thank the Lord ! there you are," said Van Diemen, entering the room. "I couldn't have hoped so much. That rascal !" he turned round to the door. "He has been threatening me, and

then smoothing me. Hang his oil ! It's com-
bustible. And hang the port he's for laying down,
as he calls it. 'Leave it to posterity,' says I.
'Why?' says he. 'Because the young ones 'll be
better able to take care of themselves,' says I, and
he insists on an explanation. I gave it to him.
Out he bursts like a wasp's nest. He may have
said what he did say in temper. He seemed
sorry afterwards—poor old Mart ! The scoundrel
talked of Horse Guards and telegraph wires."

"Scoundrel, but more ninny," said Herbert, full
of his contempt. "Dare him to do his worst.
The General tells me they'd be glad to overlook it
at the Guards, even if they had all the facts.
Branding's out of the question."

"I swear it was done in my time," cried Van
Diemen, all on fire.

"It's out of the question. You might be advised to leave England for a few months. As for
the society here——"

"If I leave, I leave for good. My heart's
broken. I'm disappointed. I'm deceived in my
friend. He and I in the old days ! What's come
to him ? What on earth is it changes men who
stop in England so ? It can't be the climate.
And did you mention my name to General
Fellingham ? "

"Certainly not," said Herbert. "But listen to
me, sir, a moment. Why not get together half-a-
dozen friends of the neighbourhood, and make a

clean breast of it. Englishmen like that kind of manliness, and they are sure to ring sound to it."

" I couldn't!" Van Diemen sighed. "It's not a natural feeling I have about it—I've brooded on the word. If I have a nightmare, I see Deserter written in sulphur on the black wall."

"You can't remain at his mercy, and be bullied as you are. He makes you ill, sir. He won't do anything, but he'll go on worrying you. I'd stop him at once. I'd take the train to-morrow and get an introduction to the Commander-in-Chief. He's the very man to be kind to you in a situation like this. The General would get you the introduction."

"That's more to my taste ; but no, I couldn't," Van Diemen moaned in his weakness. "Money has unmanned me. I wasn't this kind of man formerly ; nor more was Mart Tinman, the traitor! All the world seems changeing for the worse, and England isn't what she used to be."

"You let that man spoil it for you, sir." Herbert related Mrs. Crickledon's tale of Mr. Tinman adding, "He's an utter donkey. I should defy him. What I should do would be to let him know to-morrow morning that you don't intend to see him again. Blow for blow, is the thing he requires. He'll be cringing to you in a week."

"And you'd like to marry Annette," said Van Diemen, relishing, nevertheless, the advice, whose origin and object he perceived so plainly.

"Of course I should," said Herbert, franker still in his colour than his speech.

"I don't *see* him my girl's husband." Van Diemen eyed the red hollow in the falling coals. "When I came first, and found him a healthy man, good-looking enough for a trifle over forty, I'd have given her gladly, she nodding Yes. Now all my fear is she's in earnest. Upon my soul, I had the notion old Mart was a sort of a boy still; playing man, you know. But how can you understand? I fancied his airs and stiffness were put on; thought I saw him burning true behind it. Who can tell? He seems to be jealous of my buying property in his native town. Something frets him. I ought never to have struck him! There's my error, and I repent it. Strike a friend! I wonder he didn't go off to the Horse Guards at once. I might have done it in his place, if I found I couldn't lick him. I should have tried kicking first."

"Yes, shinning before peaching," said Herbert, astonished almost as much as he was disgusted by the inveterate sentimental attachment of Van Diemen to his old friend.

Martin Tinman anticipated good things of the fright he had given the man after dinner. He had, undoubtedly, yielded to temper, forgetting pure policy, which it is so exceeding difficult to practise. But he had soothed the startled beast; they had shaken hands at parting, and Tinman hoped that the week of Annette's absence would enable him to mould her father. Young Fellingham's appointment to come to Elba had slipped Mr. Tinman's memory. It was annoying to see this intruder. "At all events, he's not with Annette," said Mrs. Cavely. "How long has her father to run on?"

"Five months," Tinman replied. "He would have completed his term of service in five months."

"And to think of his being a rich man *because* he deserted," Mrs. Cavely interjected. "Oh! I do call it immoral. He ought to be apprehended and punished, to be an example for the good of society. If you lose time, my dear Martin, your chance is gone. He's wriggling now. And if I could believe he talked us over to that young impudent, who hasn't a penny that he doesn't get from his pen, I'd say, denounce him to-morrow. I long for Elba. I hate this house. It will be swallowed up some day; I know it; I have dreamt it. Elba at any cost. Depend upon it, Martin, you have been foiled in your suits on account of the mean house you inhabit. Enter Elba as that girl's husband, or go there to own it, and girls will crawl to you."

"You are a ridiculous woman, Martha," said Tinman, not dissenting.

The mixture of an idea of public duty with a feeling of personal rancour is a strong incentive to the pursuit of a stern line of conduct; and the glimmer of self-interest superadded does not check the steps of the moralist. Nevertheless, Tinman held himself in. He loved peace. He preached it, he disseminated it. At a meeting in the town he strove to win Van Diemen's voice in favour of a vote for further moneys to protect " our shores." Van Diemen laughed at him, telling him he wanted a battery. " No," said Tinman, " I've had enough to do with soldiers."

" How's that ? "

" They might be more cautious. I say, they might learn to know their friends from their enemies."

" That's it, that's it," said Van Diemen. " If you say much more, my hearty, you'll find me bidding against you next week for Marine Parade and Belle Vue Terrace. I've a cute eye for property, and this town's looking up."

" You look about you before you speculate in land and house property here," retorted Tinman.

Van Diemen bore so much from him that he asked himself whether he could be an Englishman. The title of Deserter was his raw wound. He attempted to form the habit of stigmatizing himself with it in the privacy of his chamber, and he succeeded in establishing the habit of talking to himself, so that he was heard by the household, and Annette, on her return, was obliged to warn him of his indiscretion. This development of a new weakness exasperated him. Rather to prove his courage by defiance than to baffle Tinman's ambition to become the principal owner of houses in Crikswich, by outbidding him at the auction for the sale of Marine Parade and Belle Vue Terrace, Van Diemen ran the houses up at the auction, and ultimately had Belle Vue knocked down to him. So fierce was the quarrel that Annette, in conjunction with Mrs. Cavely, was called on to interpose with her sweetest grace. "My native place," Tinman said to her; "it is my native place. I have a pride in it; I desire to own property in it, and your father opposes me. He opposes me. Then says I may have it back at auction price, after he has gone far to double the price! I have borne— I say I have borne too much."

"Aren't your properties to be equal to one?" said Mrs. Cavely, smiling mother-like from Tinman to Annette.

He sought to produce a fondling eye in a wry face, and said, "Yes, I will remember that."

"Annette will bless you with her dear hand in a month or two at the outside," Mrs. Cavely murmured, cherishingly.

"She will?" Tinman cracked his body to bend to her.

"Oh, I cannot say; do not distress me. Be friendly with papa," the girl resumed, moving to escape.

"That is the essential," said Mrs. Cavely; and

continued, when Annette had gone, " The essential is to get over the next few months, miss, and then to snap your fingers at us. Martin, I would force that man to sell you Belle Vue *under* the price he paid for it, just to try your power."

Tinman was not quite so forcible. He obtained Belle Vue at auction price, and his passion for revenge was tipped with fire by having it accorded as a friend's favour.

The poisoned state of his mind was increased by a December high wind that rattled his casements, and warned him of his accession of property exposed to the elements. Both he and his sister attributed their nervousness to the sinister behaviour of Van Diemen. For the house on the beach had only, in most distant times, been threatened by the sea, and no house on earth was better protected from man,—Neptune, in the shape of a coastguard, being paid by Government to patrol about it during the hours of darkness. They had never had any fears before Van Diemen arrived, and caused them to give thrice their ordinary number of dinners to guests per annum. In fact, before Van Diemen came, the house on the beach looked on Crikswich without a rival to challenge its anticipated lordship over the place, and for some inexplicable reason it seemed to its inhabitants to have been a safer as well as a happier residence.

They were consoled by Tinman's performance

of a clever stroke in privately purchasing the cottages west of the town, and including Crickledon's shop, abutting on Marine Parade. Then from the house on the beach they looked at an entire frontage of their property.

They entered the month of February. No further time was to be lost, "or we shall wake up to find that man has fooled us," Mrs. Cavely said. Tinman appeared at Elba to demand a private interview with Annette. His hat was blown into the hall as the door opened to him, and he himself was glad to be sheltered by the door, so violent was the gale. Annette and her father were sitting together. They kept the betrothed gentleman waiting a very long time. At last Van Diemen went to him, and said, "Netty'll see you, if you must. I suppose you have no business with me?"

"Not to-day," Tinman replied.

Van Diemen strode round the drawing-room with his hands in his pockets. "There's a disparity of ages," he said, abruptly, as if desirous to pour out his lesson while he remembered it. "A man upwards of forty marries a girl under twenty, he's over sixty before she's forty; he's decaying when she's only mellow. I ought never to have struck you, I know. And you're such an infernal bad temper at times, and age doesn't improve that, they say; and she's been educated tip-top. She's sharp on grammar, and a man mayn't like that much when he's a husband. See her, if you must.

But she doesn't take to the idea; there's the truth. Disparity of ages and unsuitableness of dispositions—what was it Fellingham said?—like two barrel-organs grinding different tunes all day in a house."

"I don't want to hear Mr. Fellingham's comparisons," Tinman snapped.

"Oh! he's nothing to the girl," said Van Diemen. "She doesn't stomach leaving me."

"My dear Philip! why should she leave you? When we have interests in common as one household——"

"She says you're such a damned bad temper."

Tinman was pursuing amicably, "When we are united——" But the frightful charge brought against his temper drew him up. "Fiery I may be. Annette has seen I am forgiving. I am a Christian. You have provoked me; you have struck me."

"I'll give you a couple of thousand pounds in hard money to be off the bargain, and not bother the girl," said Van Diemen.

"Now," rejoined Tinman, "I am offended. I like money, like most men who have made it. You do, Philip. But I don't come courting like a pauper. Not for ten thousand; not for twenty. Money cannot be a compensation to me for the loss of Annette. I say I love Annette."

"Because," Van Diemen continued his speech, "you trapped us into that engagement, Mart. You dosed me with the stuff you buy for wine, while

your sister sat sugaring and mollifying my girl ;
and she did the trick in a minute, taking Netty by
surprise when I was all heart and no head ; and
since that you may have seen the girl turn her
head from marriage like my woods from the
wind."

"Mr. Van Diemen Smith!" Tinman panted ;
he mastered himself. "You shall not provoke me.
My introductions of you in this neighbourhood, my
patronage, prove my friendship."

"You'll be a good old fellow, Mart, when you
get over your hopes of being knighted."

"Mr. Fellingham may set you against my wine,
Philip. Let me tell you, I know you—you would
not object to have your daughter called Lady."

"With a spindle-shanked husband capering in a
Court suit before he goes to bed every night, that
he mayn't forget what a fine fellow he was one day
bygone! You're growing lean on it, Mart, like a
recollection fifty years old."

"You have never forgiven me that day, Philip!"

"Jealous, am I? Take the money, give up the
girl, and see what friends we'll be. I'll back your
buyings, I'll advertise your sellings. I'll pay a
painter to paint you in your Court suit, and hang
up a copy of you in my dining-room."

"Here is Annette," said Tinman, who had been
showing Ætna's tokens of insurgency.

He admired Annette. Not till latterly had
Herbert Fellingham been so true an admirer of

Annette as Tinman was. She looked sincere and she dressed inexpensively. For these reasons she was the best example of womankind that he knew, and her enthusiasm for England had the sympathetic effect on him of obscuring the rest of the world, and thrilling him with the reassuring belief that he was blest in his blood and his birthplace—points which her father, with his boastings of Gippsland, and other people talking of scenes on the Continent, sometimes disturbed in his mind.

"Annette," said he, "I come requesting to converse with you in private."

"If you wish it—I would rather not," she answered.

Tinman raised his head, as often at Helmstone when some offending shopwoman was to hear her doom.

He bent to her. "I see. Before your father, then!"

"It isn't an agreeable bit of business to me," Van Diemen grumbled, frowning and shrugging.

"I have come, Annette, to ask you, to beg you, entreat—before a third person—laughing, Philip?"

"The wrong side of my mouth, my friend. And I'll tell you what : we're in for heavy seas, and I'm not sorry you've taken the house on the beach off my hands."

"Pray, Mr. Tinman, speak at once, if you please, and I will do my best. Papa vexes you."

"No, no," replied Tinman.

He renewed his commencement. Van Diemen interrupted him again.

"Hang your power over me, as you call it. Eh, old Mart? I'm a Deserter. I'll pay a thousand pounds to the British army, whether they punish me or not. March me off to-morrow."

"Papa, you are unjust, unkind." Annette turned to him in tears.

"No, no," said Tinman, "I do not feel it. Your father has misunderstood me, Annette."

"I am sure he has," she said fervently. "And, Mr. Tinman, I will faithfully promise that so long as you are good to my dear father, I will not be untrue to my engagement, only do not wish me to name any day. We shall be such very good dear friends if you consent to this. Will you?"

Pausing for a space, the enamoured man unrolled his voice in lamentation: "Oh! Annette, how long will you keep me?"

"There, you'll set her crying!" said Van Diemen. "Now you can run upstairs, Netty. By jingo! Mart Tinman, you've got a bass voice for love affairs."

"Annette," Tinman called to her, and made her turn round as she was retiring. "I must know the day before the end of winter. Please. In kind consideration. My arrangements demand it."

"Do let the girl go," said Van Diemen. "Dine with me to-night, and I'll give you a wine to brisk your spirits, old boy."

"Thank you. When I have ordered dinner at home, I —— and my wine agrees with *me*," Tinman replied.

"I doubt it."

"You shall not provoke me, Philip."

They parted stiffly.

Mrs. Cavely had unpleasant domestic news to communicate to her brother, in return for his tale of affliction and wrath. It concerned the ungrateful conduct of their little housemaid Jane, who, as Mrs. Cavely said, "egged on by that woman Crickledon," had been hinting at an advance of wages.

"She didn't dare speak, but I saw what was in her when she broke a plate, and wouldn't say she was sorry. I know she goes to Crickledon and talks us over. She's a willing worker, but she has no heart."

Tinman had been accustomed in his shop at Helmstone—where heaven had blessed him with the patronage of the rich, as visibly as rays of supernal light are seen selecting from above the heads of prophets in the illustrations to cheap holy books—to deal with willing workers that have no hearts. Before the application for an advance of wages—and he knew the signs of it coming—his method was to calculate how much he might be asked for, and divide the estimated sum by the figure 4 ; which, as it seemed to come from a generous impulse, and had been unsolicited, was often humbly accepted, and the willing worker pursued her lean and hungry course in his service. The treatment did not always agree with his males. Women it suited, because they do not like to lift up their voices unless they are in a passion ; and if you take from them the grounds of temper, you take their words away—you make chickens of them. And as Tinman said, "Gratitude I *never* expect!" Why not? For the reason that he knew human nature. He could record shocking instances of the ingratitude of human nature, as revealed to him in the term of his tenure of the shop at Helmstone. Blest from above, human nature's wickedness had from below too frequently besulphured and suffumigated him for his memory to be dim ; and though he was ever ready to own himself an example that heaven prevaileth, he could cite instances of scandalmongering shop-women dismissed and working him mischief in the town, which pointed to him in person for a proof that the Powers of Good and Evil were still engaged in unhappy contention. Witness Strikes ! witness Revolutions !

"Tell her, when she lays the cloth, that I advance her, on account of general good conduct, five shillings per annum. Add," said Tinman, "that I wish no thanks. It is for her merits—to reward her ; you understand me, Martha ?"

"Quite ; if you think it prudent, Martin."

"I do. She is not to breathe a syllable to cook."

"She will."

"Then keep your eye on cook."

Mrs. Cavely promised she would do so. She felt sure she was paying five shillings for ingratitude ; and, therefore, it was with humility that she owned her error when, while her brother sipped his sugared acrid liquor after dinner (in devotion to the doctor's decree, that he should take a couple of glasses, rigorously as body-lashing friar), she imparted to him the singular effect of the advance of wages upon little Jane—"Oh, ma'am ! and me never asked you for it !" She informed her brother how little Jane had confided to her that they were called "close," and how little Jane had vowed she would—the willing little thing !—go about letting everybody know their kindness.

"Yes ! Ah !" Tinman inhaled the praise. "No, no ; I don't want to be puffed," he said. "Remember cook. I have," he continued, meditatively, "rarely found my plan fail. But mind, I give the Crickledons notice to quit to-morrow. They are a pest. Besides, I shall probably think of erecting villas."

"How dreadful the wind is !" Mrs. Cavely exclaimed. "I would give that girl Annette one chance more. Try her by letter."

Tinman despatched a business letter to Annette, which brought back a vague, unbusiness-like reply. Two days afterward Mrs. Cavely reported to her brother the presence of Mr. Fellingham and Miss

Mary Fellingham in Crikswich. At her dictation he wrote a second letter. This time the reply came from Van Diemen :—

" MY DEAR MARTIN,—Please do not go on bothering my girl. She does not like the idea of leaving me, and my experience tells me I could not live in the house with you. So there it is. Take it friendly. I have always wanted to be, and am,   " Your friend,

                                                " PHIL."

Tinman proceeded straight to Elba ; that is, as nearly straight as the wind would allow his legs to walk. Van Diemen was announced to be out ; Miss Annette begged to be excused, under the pretext that she was unwell ; and Tinman heard of a dinner-party at Elba that night.

He met Mr. Fellingham on the carriage drive. The young Londoner presumed to touch upon Tinman's private affairs by pleading on behalf of the Crickledons, who were, he said, much dejected by the notice they had received to quit house and shop.

" Another time," bawled Tinman. " I can't hear you in this wind."

" Come in," said Fellingham.

" The master of the house is absent," was the smart retort roared at him ; and Tinman staggered away, enjoying it as he did his wine.

His house rocked. He was backed by his sister in the assurance that he had been duped.

The process he supposed to be thinking, which was the castigation of his brains with every sting wherewith a native touchiness could ply immediate recollection, led him to conclude that he must bring Van Diemen to his senses, and Annette running to him for mercy.

He sat down that night amid the howling of the storm, wind whistling, water crashing, casements rattling, beach desperately dragging, as by the wide-stretched star-fish fingers of the half-engulphed.

He hardly knew what he wrote. The man was in a state of personal terror, burning with indignation at Van Diemen as the main cause of his jeopardy. For, in order to prosecute his pursuit of Annette, he had abstained from going to Helmstone to pay moneys into his bank there, and what was precious to life as well as life itself, was imperilled by those two—Annette and her father—who, had they been true, had they been honest, to say nothing of honourable, would by this time have opened Elba to him as a fast and safe abode.

His letter was addressed, on a large envelope,

"To the Adjutant-General,
"Horse Guards."

But if ever consigned to the Post, that post-office must be in London ; and Tinman left the letter on his desk till the morning should bring counsel to him as to the London friend to whom he might despatch it under cover for posting, if he pushed it so far.

Sleep was impossible. Black night favoured the tearing fiends of shipwreck, and looking through a back window over sea, Tinman saw with dismay huge towering ghost-white wreaths, that travelled up swiftly on his level, and lit the dark as they flung themselves in ruin, with a gasp, across the mound of shingle at his feet.

He undressed. His sister called to him to know if they were in danger. Clothed in his dressing-gown, he slipped along to her door, to vociferate to her hoarsely that she must not frighten the servants; and one fine quality in the training of the couple, which had helped them to prosper, a form of self-command, kept her quiet in her shivering fears.

For a distraction Tinman pulled open the drawers of his wardrobe. His glittering suit lay in one. And he thought, " What wonderful changes there are in the world ! " meaning, between a man exposed to the wrath of the elements, and the same individual reading from vellum, in that suit, in a palace, to the Head of all of us !

The presumption is, that he must have often done it before. The fact is established, that he did it that night. The conclusion drawn from it is, that it must have given him a sense of stability and safety.

At any rate, that he put on the suit is quite certain.

Probably it was a work of ingratiation and degrees ; a feeling of the silk, a trying on to one leg, then a matching of the fellow with it. O you Revolutionists ! who would have no state, no ceremonial, and but one order of galligaskins ! This man must have been wooed away in spirit to forgetfulness of the tempest scourging his mighty neighbour to a bigger and a farther leap ; he must have obtained from the contemplation of himself in his suit that which would be the saving of all men, in especial, of his countrymen—imagination, namely.

Certain it is, as I have said, that he attired himself in the suit. He covered it with his dressing-gown, and he lay down on his bed so garbed, to await the morrow's light, being probably surprised by sleep acting upon fatigue and nerves appeased and soothed.

CHAPTER XII

ELBA lay more sheltered from South-east winds under the slopes of down than any other house in Crikswich. The South-easter struck off the cliff to a martello tower and the house on the beach, leaving Elba to repose, so that the worst wind for that coast was one of the most comfortable for the owner of the hall, and he looked from his upper window on a sea of crumbling grey chalk, lashed unremittingly by the featureless piping gale, without fear that his elevated grounds and walls would be open at high tide to the ravage of water. Van Diemen had no idea of calamity being at work on land when he sat down to breakfast. He told Herbert that he had prayed for poor fellows at sea last night. Mary Fellingham and Annette were anxious to finish breakfast and mount the down to gaze on the sea, and receiving a caution from Van Diemen not to go too near the cliff, they were inclined to think he was needlessly timorous on their account.

Before they were half way through the meal, word was brought in of great breaches in the shingle, and water covering the common. Van

Diemen sent for his head gardener, whose report of the state of things outside took the comprehensive form of prophecy; he predicted the fall of the town.

"Nonsense; what do you mean, John Scott?" said Van Diemen, eyeing his orderly breakfast table and the man in turns. "It doesn't seem like that, yet, does it?"

"The house on the beach won't stand an hour longer, sir."

"Who says so?"

"It's cut off from land now, and waves mast-high all about it."

"Mart Tinman!" cried Van Diemen.

All started; all jumped up; and there was a scampering for hats and cloaks. Maids and men of the house ran in and out confirming the news of inundation. Some in terror for the fate of relatives, others pleasantly excited, glad of catastrophe if it but killed monotony, for at any rate it was a change of demons.

The view from the outer bank of Elba was of water covering the space of the common up to the stones of Marine Parade and Belle Vue. But at a distance it had not the appearance of angry water; the ladies thought it picturesque, and the house on the beach was seen standing firm. A second look showed the house completely isolated; and as the party led by Van Diemen circled hurriedly toward the town, they discerned heavy cataracts of foam pouring down the wrecked mound of shingle on either side of the house.

"Why, the outer wall's washed away," said Van Diemen.

" Are they in real danger ? " asked Annette, her teeth chattering, and the cold and other matters at her heart precluding for the moment such warmth of sympathy as she hoped soon to feel for them. She was glad to hear her father say :

"Oh ! they're high and dry by this time. We shall find them in the town. And we'll take them in and comfort them. Ten to one they haven't breakfasted. They shan't go to an inn while I'm handy."

He dashed ahead, followed closely by Herbert. The ladies beheld them talking to townsfolk as they passed along the upper streets, and did not augur well of their increase of speed. At the head of the town water was visible, part of the way up the main street, and crossing it, the ladies went swiftly under the old church, on the tower of which were spectators, through the churchyard to a high meadow that dropped to a stone wall fixed between the meadow and a grass bank above the level of the road, where now salt water beat and cast some spray. Not less than a hundred people were in this field, among them Crickledon and his wife. All were in silent watch of the house on the beach, which was to east of the field, at a distance of perhaps three stonethrows. The scene was wild.

Continuously the torrents poured through the shingle-clefts, and momently a thunder sounded, and high leapt a billow that topped the house and folded it weltering.

"They tell me Mart Tinman's *in* the house," Van Diemen roared to Herbert. He listened to further information, and bellowed : "There's no boat !"

Herbert answered : "It must be a mistake, I think ; here's Crickledon says he had a warning before dawn and managed to move most of his things, and the people over there must have been awakened by the row in time to get off."

"I can't hear a word you say ; " Van Diemen tried to pitch his voice higher than the wind. "Did you say a boat ? But where ? "

Crickledon the carpenter made signal to Herbert. They stepped rapidly up the field.

"Women feels their weakness in times like these, my dear," Mrs. Crickledon said to Annette. "What with our clothes and our cowardice it do seem we're not the equals of men when winds is high."

Annette expressed the hope to her that she had not lost much property. Mrs. Crickledon said she was glad to let her know she was insured in an Accident Company. "But," said she, " I do grieve for that poor man Tinman, if alive he be, and comes ashore to find his property wrecked by water. Bless ye! he wouldn't insure against anything less common than fire ; and my house and

Crickledon's shop are floating timbers by this time; and Marine Parade and Belle Vue are safe to go. And it'll be a pretty welcome for him, poor man, from his investments."

A cry at a tremendous blow of a wave on the doomed house, rose from the field. Back and front door were broken down, and the force of water drove a round volume through the channel, shaking the walls.

" I can't stand this," Van Diemen cried.

Annette was too late to hold him back. He ran up the field. She was preparing to run after when Mrs. Crickledon touched her arm and implored her : " Interfere not with men, but let them follow their judgments when it's seasons of mighty peril, my dear. If any one's guilty it's me, for minding my husband of a boat that was launched for a life-boat here, and wouldn't answer, and is at the shed by the Crouch—left lying there, I've often said, as if it was a-sulking. My goodness ! "

A linen sheet had been flung out from one of the windows of the house on the beach, and flew loose and flapping in sign of distress.

" It looks as if they had gone mad in that house, to have waited so long for to declare theirselves, poor souls," Mrs. Crickledon said, sighing.

She was assured right and left that signals had been seen before, and some one stated that the cook of Mr. Tinman, and also Mrs. Cavely, were on shore.

"It's his furniture, poor man, he sticks to: and nothing gets round the heart so!" resumed Mrs. Crickledon. "There goes his bed-linen."

The sheet was whirled and snapped away by the wind; distended, doubled, like a flock of winter geese changing alphabetical letters on the clouds, darted this way and that, and finally outspread on the waters breaking against Marine Parade.

"They cannot have thought there was positive danger in remaining," said Annette.

"Mr. Tinman was waiting for the cheapest Insurance office," a man remarked to Mrs. Crickledon.

"The least to pay is to the undertaker," she replied, standing on tiptoe. "And it's to be hoped he'll pay more to-day. If only those walls don't fall and stop the chance of the boat to save him for more outlay, poor man! What boats was on the beach last night, high up and over the ridge as they was, are planks by this time and only good for carpenters."

"Half our town's done for," one old man said; and another followed him in a pious tone: "From water we came and to water we go."

They talked of ancient inroads of the sea, none so serious as this threatened to be for them. The gallant solidity of the house on the beach had withstood heavy gales: it was a brave house. Heaven be thanked, no fishing boats were out. Chiefly well-to-do people would be the sufferers — an exceptional case. For it is the mysterious and unexplained dispensation that: "Mostly heaven chastises we."

A knot of excited gazers drew the rest of the field to them. Mrs. Crickledon, on the edge of the crowd, reported what was doing to Annette and Miss Fellingham. A boat had been launched from the town. "Praise the Lord, there's none but coastguard in it!" she exclaimed, and excused herself for having her heart on her husband.

Annette was as deeply thankful that her father was not in the boat.

They looked round and saw Herbert beside them. Van Diemen was in the rear, panting, and straining his neck to catch sight of the boat now pulling fast across a tumbled sea to where Tinman himself was perceived, beckoning them wildly, half out of one of the windows.

"A pound apiece to those fellows, and two if they land Mart Tinman dry; I've promised it, and they'll earn it. Look at that! Quick, you rascals!"

To the east a portion of the house had fallen, melted away. Where it stood, just below the line of shingle, it was now like a structure wasting on a tormented submerged reef. The whole line was given over to the waves.

"Where is his sister?" Annette shrieked to her father.

"Safe ashore; and one of the women with her. But Mart Tinman would stop, the fool! to—poor old boy !—save his papers and things ; and hasn't a head to do it, Martha Cavely tells me. They're at him now ! They've got him in ! There's another ? Oh ! it's a girl, who wouldn't go and leave him. They'll pull to the field here. Brave lads ! By jingo, why ain't Englishmen always in danger !—eh ? if you want to see them shine ! "

" It's little Jane," said Mrs. Crickledon, who had been joined by her husband, and now that she knew him to be no longer in peril, kept her hand on him to restrain him, just for comfort's sake.

The boat held under the lee of the house-wreck a minute ; then, as if shooting a small rapid, came down on a wave crowned with foam, to hurrahs from the townsmen.

" They're all right," said Van Diemen, puffing as at a mist before his eyes. " They'll pull westward, with the wind, and land him among us. I remember when old Mart and I were bathing once, he was younger than me, and couldn't swim much, and I saw him going down. It'd have been hard to see him washed off before one's eyes thirty years afterwards. Here they come. He's all right. He's in his dressing-gown ! "

The crowd made way for Mr. Van Diemen Smith to welcome his friend. Two of the coastguard jumped out and handed him to the dry bank, while Herbert, Van Diemen, and Crickledon took him by hand and arm, and hoisted him on to the flint wall, preparatory to his descent into the field. In this exposed situation the wind, whose pranks are endless when it is once up, seized and blew Martin Tinman's dressing-gown wide as two violently flapping wings on each side of him, and finally over his head.

Van Diemen turned a pair of stupefied flat eyes on Herbert, who cast a sly look at the ladies. Tinman had sprung down. But not before the world, in one tempestuous glimpse, had caught sight of the Court suit.

Perfect gravity greeted him from the crowd.

"Safe, old Mart! and glad to be able to say it," said Van Diemen.

"We are so happy," said Annette.

"House, furniture, property, everything I possess!" ejaculated Tinman, shivering.

"Fiddle, man; you want some hot breakfast in you. Your sister has gone on to Elba. Come you too, old Mart; and where's that plucky little girl who stood by you?"

"Was there a girl?" said Tinman.

"Yes, and there was a boy wanted to help." Van Diemen pointed at Herbert.

Tinman looked, and piteously asked, "Have you examined Marine Parade and Belle Vue? It depends on the tide!"

"Here is little Jane, sir," said Mrs. Crickledon.

"Fall in," Van Diemen said to little Jane.

The girl was bobbing curtseys to Annette, on her introduction by Mrs. Crickledon.

"Martin, you stay at my house; you stay at Elba till you get things comfortable about you, and then you shall have the Crouch for a year, rent free. Eh, Netty?"

Annette chimed in: "Anything we can do, anything. Nothing can be too much."

Van Diemen was praising little Jane for her devotion to her master.

"Master have been so kind to me," said little Jane.

"Now, march; it is cold," Van Diemen gave the word, and Herbert stood by Mary rather dejectedly, foreseeing that his prospects at Elba were darkened.

"Now then, Mart, left leg forward," Van Diemen linked his arm in his friend's.

"I must have a look," Tinman broke from him, and cast a forlorn look of farewell on the last of the house on the beach.

"You've got me left to you, old Mart; don't forget that," said Van Diemen.

Tinman's chest fell. "Yes, yes," he responded. He was touched.

"And I told those fellows if they landed you dry they should have—I'd give them double pay; and I do believe they've earned their money."

"I don't think I'm very wet, I'm cold," said Tinman.

"You can't help being cold, so come along."

"But, Philip!" Tinman lifted his voice; "I've

lost everything. I tried to save a little. I worked hard, I exposed my life, and all in vain."

The voice of little Jane was heard.

"What's the matter with the child?" said Van Diemen.

Annette went up to her quietly.

But little Jane was addressing her master.

"Oh! if you please, I did manage to save something the last thing when the boat was at the window, and if you please, sir, all the bundles is lost, but I saved you a paper-cutter, and your letter to the Horse Guards, and here they are, sir."

The grateful little creature drew the letter and paper-cutter from her bosom, and held them out to Mr. Tinman.

"What!" cried he, not clearly comprehending how much her devotion had accomplished for him.

"A letter to the Horse Guards!" cried Van Diemen.

"Here, give it me," said little Jane's master, and grasped it nervously.

"What's in that letter?" Van Diemen asked. "Let me look at that letter. Don't tell me it's private correspondence."

"My dear Philip, dear friend, kind thanks ; it's not a letter," said Tinman.

"Not a letter! why, I read the address, 'Horse Guards.' I read it as it passed into your hands. Now, my man, one look at that letter, or take the consequences."

"Kind thanks for your assistance, dear Philip, indeed! Oh! this? Oh! it's nothing." He tore it in halves.

His face was of the winter sea-colour, with the chalk-wash on it.

"Tear again, and I shall know what to think of the contents," Van Diemen frowned. "Let me see what you've said. You've sworn you would do it, and there it is at last, by miracle; but let me see it and I'll overlook it, and you shall be my house-mate still. If not!——"

Tinman tore away.

"You mistake, you mistake, you're entirely wrong," he said, as he pursued with desperation his task of rendering a single word unreadable.

Van Diemen stood fronting him; the accumulation of stores of petty injuries and meannesses which he had endured from this man, swelled under the whip of the conclusive exhibition of treachery. He looked so black that Annette called "Papa!"

"Philip," said Tinman. "Philip! my best friend!"

"Pooh, you're a poor creature. Come along and breakfast at Elba, and you can sleep at the Crouch, and good-night to you. Crickledon," he called to the houseless couple, "you stop at Elba till I build you a shop."

With these words, Van Diemen led the way, walking alone. Herbert was compelled to walk with Tinman.

Mary and Annette came behind, and Mary pinched Annette's arm so sharply that she must have cried out aloud had it been possible for her to feel pain at that moment, instead of a personal exultation, flying wildly over the clash of astonishment and horror, like a sea-bird over the foam.

In the first silent place they came to, Mary murmured the words: "Little Jane."

Annette looked round at Mrs. Crickledon, who wound up the procession, taking little Jane by the hand. Little Jane was walking demurely, with a placid face. Annette glanced at Tinman. Her excited feelings nearly rose to a scream of laughter. For hours after, Mary had only to say to her: "Little Jane," to produce the same convulsion. It rolled her heart and senses in a headlong surge, shook her to burning tears, and seemed to her ideas the most wonderful running together of opposite things ever known on this earth. The young lady was ashamed of her laughter; but she was deeply indebted to it, for never was mind made so clear by that beneficent exercise.

THE CASE OF GENERAL OPLE AND
LADY CAMPER

THE CASE OF GENERAL OPLE AND LADY CAMPER

CHAPTER I

AN excursion beyond the immediate suburbs of London, projected long before his pony-carriage was hired to conduct him, in fact ever since his retirement from active service, led General Ople across a famous common, with which he fell in love at once, to a lofty highway along the borders of a park, for which he promptly exchanged his heart, and so gradually within a stone's-throw or so of the river-side, where he determined not solely to bestow his affections but to settle for life. It may be seen that he was of an adventurous temperament, though he had thought fit to loosen his sword-belt. The pony-carriage, however, had been hired for the very special purpose of helping him to pass in review the lines of what he called country houses, cottages, or even sites for building, not too remote from sweet London : and as when Cœlebs goes forth intending to pursue and obtain, there is no doubt of his bringing home a wife, the circumstance that there stood a house to let, in an airy situation, at a certain distance in hail of the metropolis he worshipped, was enough to kindle the General's enthusiasm. He would have taken the first he saw, had it not been for his daughter, who accompanied him, and at the age of eighteen was about to undertake the management of his house. Fortune, under Elizabeth Ople's guiding restraint, directed him to an epitome of the comforts. The place he fell upon is only to be described in the tongue of auctioneers, and for the first week after taking it he modestly followed them by terming it bijou. In time, when his own imagination, instigated by a state of something more than mere contentment, had been at work on it, he chose the happy phrase, "a gentlemanly residence." For it was, he declared, a small estate. There was a lodge to it, resembling two sentry-boxes forced into union, where in one half an old couple sat bent, in the other half lay compressed; there was a back-drive to discoverable stables; there was a bit of grass that would have appeared a meadow if magnified; and there was a wall round the kitchen-garden and a strip of wood round the flower-garden. The prying of the outside world was impossible. Comfort, fortification, and gentlemanliness made the place, as the General said, an ideal English home.

The compass of the estate was half an acre, and perhaps a perch or two, just the size for the hugging love General Ople was happiest in giving.

He wisely decided to retain the old couple at the lodge, whose members were used to restriction, and also not to purchase a cow, that would have wanted pasture. With the old man, while the old woman attended to the bell at the handsome front entrance with its gilt-spiked gates, he undertook to do the gardening ; a business he delighted in, so long as he could perform it in a gentlemanly man-ner, that is to say, so long as he was not over-looked. He was perfectly concealed from the road. Only one house, and curiously indeed, only one window of the house, and further to show the protection extended to Douro Lodge, that window an attic, overlooked him. And the house was empty.

The house (for who can hope, and who should desire a commodious house, with conservatories, aviaries, pond and boat-shed, and other joys of wealth, to remain unoccupied) was taken two sea-sons later by a lady, of whom Fame, rolling like a dust-cloud from the place she had left, reported that she was eccentric. The word is uninstructive: it does not frighten. In a lady of a certain age, it is rather a characteristic of aristocracy, in retire-ment. And at least it implies wealth.

General Ople was very anxious to see her. He had the sentiment of humble respectfulness toward aristocracy, and there was that in riches which aroused his admiration. London, for instance, he was not afraid to say he thought the wonder of the

world.   He remarked, in addition, that the sacking
of London would suffice to make every common
soldier of the foreign army of occupation an independent gentleman for the term of his natural
days.   But this is a nightmare! said he, startling
himself with an abhorrent dream of envy of those
enriched invading officers : for Booty is the one
lovely thing which the military mind can contemplate in the abstract.   His habit was to go off in
an explosion of heavy sighs when he had delivered
himself so far, like a man at war with himself.

The lady arrived in time : she received the cards
of the neighbourhood, and signalized her eccentricity by paying no attention to them, excepting
the card of a Mrs. Baerens, who had audience of
her at once.   By express arrangement, the card
of General Wilson Ople, as her nearest neighbour,
·followed the card of the rector, the social head of
the district ; and the rector was granted an interview, but Lady Camper was not at home to General Ople.   She is of superior station to me, and
may not wish to associate with me, the General
modestly said.   Nevertheless he was wounded :
for in spite of himself, and without the slightest
wish to obtrude his own person, as he explained
the meaning that he had in him, his rank in the
British army forced him to be the representative
of it, in the absence of any one of a superior rank.
So that he was professionally hurt, and his heart
being in his profession, it may be honestly stated

that he was wounded in his feelings, though he said no, and insisted on the distinction. Once a day his walk for constitutional exercise compelled him to pass before Lady Camper's windows, which were not bashfully withdrawn, as he said humorously of Douro Lodge, in the seclusion of half-pay, but bowed out imperiously, militarily, like a generalissimo on horseback, and had full command of the road and levels up to the swelling park-foliage. He went by at a smart stride, with a delicate depression of his upright bearing, as though hastening to greet a friend in view, whose hand was getting ready for the shake. This much would have been observed by a housemaid ; and considering his fine figure and the peculiar shining silveriness of his hair, the acceleration of his gait was noticeable. When he drove by, the pony's right ear was flicked, to the extreme indignation of a mettlesome little animal. It ensued in consequence that the General was borne flying under the eyes of Lady Camper, and such pace displeasing him, he reduced it invariably at a step or two beyond the corner of her grounds.

But neither he nor his daughter Elizabeth attached importance to so trivial a circumstance. The General punctiliously avoided glancing at the windows during the passage past them, whether in his wild career or on foot. Elizabeth took a side-shot, as one looks at a wayside tree. Their speech concerning Lady Camper was an exchange of

commonplaces over her loneliness : and this condition of hers was the more perplexing to General
Ople on his hearing from his daughter that the
lady was very fine-looking, and not so very old, as
he had fancied eccentric ladies must be. The
rector's account of her, too, excited the mind.
She had informed him bluntly, that she now and
then went to church to save appearances, but was
not a church-goer, finding it impossible to support
the length of the service ; might, however, be
reckoned in subscriptions for all the charities, and
left her pew open to poor people, and none but the
poor. She had travelled over Europe, and knew
the East. Sketches in water-colours of the scenes
she had visited adorned her walls, and a pair of
pistols, that she had found useful, she affirmed, lay
on the writing-desk in her drawing-room. General
Ople gathered from the rector that she had a
great contempt for men : yet it was curiously
varied with lamentations over the weakness of
women. "Really she cannot possibly be an example of that," said the General, thinking of the
pistols.

Now, we learn from those who have studied
women on the chess-board, and know what ebony
or ivory will do along particular lines, or hopping,
that men much talked about will take possession
of their thoughts ; and certainly the fact may be
accepted for one of their moves. But the whole
fabric of our knowledge of them, which we are

taught to build on this originally acute perception, is shattered when we hear, that it is exactly the same, in the same degree, in proportion to the amount of work they have to do, exactly the same with men and their thoughts in the case of women much talked about. So it was with General Ople, and nothing is left for me to say except, that there is broader ground than the chess-board. I am earnest in protesting the similarity of the singular couples on common earth, because otherwise the General is in peril of the accusation that he is a feminine character ; and not simply was he a gallant officer, and a veteran in gunpowder strife, he was also (and it is an extraordinary thing that a genuine humility did not prevent it, and did survive it) a lord and conqueror of the sex. He had done his pretty bit of mischief, all in the way of honour, of course, but hearts had knocked. And now, with his bright white hair, his close-brushed white whiskers on a face burnt brown, his clear-cut features, and a winning droop of his eyelids, there was powder in him still, if not shot.

There was a lamentable susceptibility to ladies' charms. On the other hand, for the protection of the sex, a remainder of shyness kept him from active enterprise and in the state of suffering, so long as indications of encouragement were wanting. He had killed the soft ones, who came to him, attracted by the softness in him, to be killed : but clever women alarmed and paralyzed him. Their aptness to question and require immediate sparkling answers ; their demand for fresh wit, of a kind that is not furnished by publications which strike it into heads with a hammer, and supply it wholesale ; their various reading ; their power of ridicule too ; made them awful in his contemplation.

Supposing (for the inflammable officer was now thinking, and deeply thinking, of a clever woman), supposing that Lady Camper's pistols were needed in her defence one night : at the first report proclaiming her extremity, valour might gain an introduction to her upon easy terms, and would not be expected to be witty. She would, perhaps, after the excitement, admit his masculine superiority, in the beautiful old fashion, by fainting in his arms. Such was the reverie he passingly indulged, and only so could he venture to hope for an acquaintance with the formidable lady who was his next neighbour. But the proud society of the burglarious denied him opportunity.

Meanwhile, he learnt that Lady Camper had a nephew, and the young gentleman was in a cavalry regiment. General Ople met him outside his gates, received and returned a polite salute, liked his appearance and manners, and talked of him to Elizabeth, asking her if by chance she had seen him. She replied that she believed she had, and praised his horsemanship. The General discovered that he was an excellent sculler. His daughter was rowing him up the river when the young gentleman shot by, with a splendid stroke, in an outrigger, backed, and floating alongside presumed to enter into conversation, during which he managed to express regrets at his aunt's ·turn for solitariness. As they belonged to sister branches of the same Service, the General and Mr. Reginald Rolles had a theme in common, and a passion. Elizabeth told her father that nothing afforded her so much pleasure as to hear him talk with Mr. Rolles on military matters. General Ople assured her that it pleased him likewise. He began to spy about for Mr. Rolles, and it sometimes occurred that they conversed across the wall; it could hardly be avoided. A hint or two, an undefinable flying allusion, gave the General to understand that Lady Camper had not been happy in her marriage. He was pained to think of her misfortune; but as she was not over forty, the disaster was, perhaps, not irremediable; that is to say, if she could be taught to extend her forgiveness to men, and abandon her solitude. " If," he said to his daughter, "Lady Camper should by any chance be induced to contract a second alliance, she would, one might expect, be humanized, and we should have highly agreeable neighbours." Elizabeth artlessly hoped for such an event to take place.

She rarely differed with her father, up to whom, taking example from the world around him, she looked as the pattern of a man of wise conduct.

And he was one ; and though modest, he was in good humour with himself, approved himself, and could say that, without boasting of success, he was a satisfied man, until he met his touchstone in Lady Camper.

CHAPTER II

THIS is the pathetic matter of my story, and it requires pointing out, because he never could explain what it was that seemed to him so cruel in it, for he was no brilliant son of fortune, he was no great pretender, none of those who are logically displaced from the heights they have been raised to, manifestly created to show the moral in Providence. He was modest, retiring, humbly contented; a gentlemanly residence appeased his ambition. Popular, he could own that he was, but not meteorically; rather by reason of his willingness to receive light than to shed it. Why, then, was the terrible test brought to bear upon him, of all men? He was one of us; no worse, and not strikingly or perilously better; and he could not but feel, in the bitterness of his reflections upon an inexplicable destiny, that the punishment befalling him, unmerited as it was, looked like absence of Design in the scheme of things Above. It looked as if the blow had been dealt him by reckless chance. And to believe that, was for the mind of General Ople the having to return to his alphabet and recommence the ascent of the laborious mountain of understanding.

To proceed, the General's introduction to Lady Camper was owing to a message she sent him by her gardener, with a request that he would cut down a branch of a wych-elm, obscuring her view across his grounds toward the river. The General consulted with his daughter, and came to the conclusion that, as he could hardly despatch a written reply to a verbal message, yet greatly wished to subscribe to the wishes of Lady Camper, the best thing for him to do was to apply for an interview. He sent word that he would wait on Lady Camper immediately, and betook himself forthwith to his toilette. She was the niece of an earl.

Elizabeth commended his appearance, " passed him," as he would have said ; and well she might, for his hat, surtout, trousers and boots, were worthy of an introduction to Royalty. A touch of scarlet silk round the neck gave him bloom, and better than that, the blooming consciousness of it.

" You are not to be nervous, papa," Elizabeth said.

" Not at all," replied the General. " I say, not at all, my dear," he repeated, and so betrayed that he had fallen into the nervous mood. " I was saying, I have known worse mornings than this." He turned to her and smiled brightly, nodded, and set his face to meet the future.

He was absent an hour and a half.

He came back with his radiance a little subdued, by no means eclipsed ; as, when experience has afforded us matter for thought, we cease to shine dazzlingly, yet are not clouded ; the rays have merely grown serener. The sum of his impressions was conveyed in the reflective utterance— "It only shows, my dear, how different the reality is from our anticipation of it!"

Lady Camper had been charming ; full of condescension, neighbourly, friendly, willing to be satisfied with the sacrifice of the smallest branch of the wych-elm, and only requiring that much for complimentary reasons.

Elizabeth wished to hear what they were, and she thought the request rather singular ; but the General begged her to bear in mind, that they were dealing with a very extraordinary woman ; " highly accomplished, really exceedingly handsome," he said to himself, aloud.

The reasons were, her liking for air and view, and desire to see into her neighbour's grounds without having to mount to the attic.

Elizabeth gave a slight exclamation, and blushed.

" So, my dear, we are objects of interest to her ladyship," said the General.

He assured her that Lady Camper's manners were delightful. Strange to tell, she knew a great deal of his antecedent history, things he had not supposed were known ; " little matters," he remarked, by which his daughter faintly conceived a reference to the conquests of his dashing days. Lady Camper had deigned to impart some of her own, incidentally; that she was of Welsh blood, and born among the mountains. "She has a romantic look," was the General's comment; and that her husband had been an insatiable traveller before he became an invalid, and had never cared for Art. "Quite an extraordinary circumstance, with such a wife!" the General said.

He fell upon the wych-elm with his own hands, under cover of the leafage, and the next day he paid his respects to Lady Camper, to inquire if her ladyship saw any further obstruction to the view.

"None," she replied. "And now we shall see what the two birds will do."

Apparently, then, she entertained an animosity to a pair of birds in the tree.

"Yes, yes; I say they chirp early in the morning," said General Ople.

"At all hours."

"The song of birds? . . ." he pleaded softly for nature.

"If the nest is provided for them; but I don't like vagabond chirping."

The General perfectly acquiesced. This, in an engagement with a clever woman, is what you should do, or else you are likely to find yourself planted unawares in a high wind, your hat blown off, and your coat-tails anywhere ; in other words, you will stand ridiculous in your bewilderment ; and General Ople ever footed with the utmost caution to avoid that quagmire of the ridiculous. The extremer quags he had hitherto escaped ; the smaller, into which he fell in his agile evasions of the big, he had hitherto been blest in finding none to notice.

He requested her ladyship's permission to present his daughter. Lady Camper sent in her card.

Elizabeth Ople beheld a tall, handsomely-mannered lady, with good features and penetrating dark eyes, an easy carriage of her person and an agreeable voice, but (the vision of her age flashed out under the compelling eyes of youth) fifty if a day. The rich colouring confessed to it. But she was very pleasing, and Elizabeth's perception dwelt on it only because her father's manly chivalry had defended the lady against one year more than forty.

The richness of the colouring, Elizabeth feared, was artificial, and it caused her ingenuous young blood a shudder. For we are so devoted to nature when the dame is flattering us with her gifts, that we loathe the substitute, omitting to think how much less it is an imposition than a form of practical adoration of the genuine.

Our young detective, however, concealed her emotion of childish horror.

Lady Camper remarked of her, "She seems honest, and that is the most we can hope of girls."

"She is a jewel for an honest man," the General sighed, "some day!"

"Let us hope it will be a distant day."

"Yet," said the General, "girls expect to marry."

Lady Camper fixed her black eyes on him, but did not speak.

He told Elizabeth that her ladyship's eyes were exceedingly searching: "Only," said he, "as I have nothing to hide, I am able to submit to inspection;" and he laughed slightly up to an arresting cough, and made the mantelpiece ornaments pass muster.

General Ople was the hero to champion a lady whose airs of haughtiness caused her to be somewhat backbitten. He assured everybody, that Lady Camper was much misunderstood; she was a most remarkable woman; she was a most affable and highly intelligent lady. Building up her attributes on a splendid climax, he declared she was pious, charitable, witty, and really an extraordinary artist. He laid particular stress on her artistic qualities, describing her power with the brush, her water-colour sketches, and also some immensely clever caricatures. As he talked of no one else, his friends heard enough of Lady Camper, who was anything but a favourite. The Pollingtons, the Wilders, the Wardens, the Baerens, the Goslings, and others of his acquaintance, talked of Lady Camper and General Ople rather maliciously. They were all City people, and they admired the General, but mourned that he should so abjectly have fallen at the feet of a lady as red with rouge as a railway bill. His not seeing it showed the state he was in. The sister of Mrs. Pollington, an amiable widow, relict of a large City warehouse, named Barcop, was chilled by a falling off in his attentions. His apology for not appearing at garden parties was, that he was engaged to wait on Lady Camper.

And at one time, her not condescending to exchange visits with the obsequious General was a topic fertile in irony. But she did condescend.

Lady Camper came to his gate unexpectedly, rang the bell, and was let in like an ordinary visitor. It happened that the General was gardening—not the pretty occupation of pruning, he was digging—and of necessity his coat was off, and he was hot, dusty, unpresentable. From adoring earth as the mother of roses, you may pass into a lady's presence without purification ; you cannot (or so the General thought) when you are caught in the act of adoring the mother of cabbages. And though he himself loved the cabbage equally with the rose, in his heart respected the vegetable yet more than he esteemed the flower, for he gloried in his kitchen garden, this was not a secret for the world to know, and he almost heeled over on his beam ends when word was brought of the extreme honour Lady Camper had done him. He worked his arms hurriedly into his fatigue jacket, trusting to get away to the house and spend a couple of minutes on his adornment ; and with any other visitor it might have been accomplished, but Lady Camper disliked sitting alone in a room. She was on the square of lawn as the General stole along the walk. Had she kept her back to him, he might have rounded her like the shadow of a dial, undetected. She was frightfully acute of hearing. She turned while he was in the agony of hesitation, in a queer attitude, one leg on the march, projected by a frenzied tip-toe of the hinder leg, the very fatallest moment she could possibly have selected for unveiling him.

Of course there was no choice but to surrender on the spot.

He began to squander his dizzy wits in profuse apologies. Lady Camper simply spoke of the nice little nest of a garden, smelt the flowers, accepted a Niel rose and a Rohan, a Céline, a Falcot, and La France.

" A beautiful rose indeed," she said of the latter, "only it smells of macassar oil."

" Really, it never struck me, I say it never struck me before," rejoined the General, smelling it as at a pinch of snuff. " I was saying, I always . . . " And he tacitly, with the absurdest of smiles, begged permission to leave unterminated a sentence not in itself particularly difficult.

" I have a nose," observed Lady Camper.

Like the nobly-bred person she was, according to General Ople's version of the interview on his estate, when he stood before her in his gardening costume, she put him at his ease, or she exerted herself to do so ; and if he underwent considerable anguish, it was the fault of his excessive scrupulousness regarding dress, propriety, appearance.

He conducted her at her request to the kitchen garden and the handful of paddock, the stables and coach-house, then back to the lawn.

" It is the home for a young couple," she said.

" I am no longer young," the General bowed, with the sigh peculiar to this confession. " I say, I am no longer young, but I call the place a gentlemanly residence. I was saying, I . . ."

" Yes, yes!" Lady Camper tossed her head, half closing her eyes, with a contraction of the brows, as if in pain.

He perceived a similar expression whenever he spoke of his residence.

Perhaps it recalled happier days to enter such a nest. Perhaps it had been such a home for a young couple that she had entered on her marriage with Sir Scrope Camper, before he inherited his title and estates.

The General was at a loss to conceive what it was.

T

It recurred at another mention of his idea of the nature of the residence. It was almost a paroxysm. He determined not to vex her reminiscences again ; and as this resolution directed his mind to his residence, thinking it pre-eminently gentlemanly, his tongue committed the error of repeating it, with "gentlemanlike" for a variation.

Elizabeth was out—he knew not where. The housemaid informed him, that Miss Elizabeth was out rowing on the water.

"Is she alone ? " Lady Camper inquired of him.

" I fancy so," the General replied.

"The poor child has no mother."

"It has been a sad loss to us both, Lady Camper."

" No doubt. She is too pretty to go out alone."

"I can trust her."

"Girls ! "

"She has the spirit of a man."

"That is well. She has a spirit ; it will be tried."

The General modestly furnished an instance or two of her spiritedness.

Lady Camper seemed to like this theme; she looked graciously interested.

"Still, you should not suffer her to go out alone," she said.

"I place implicit confidence in her," said the General ; and Lady Camper gave it up.

She proposed to walk down the lanes to the river-side, to meet Elizabeth returning.

The General manifested alacrity checked by reluctance. Lady Camper had told him she objected to sit in a strange room by herself; after that, he could hardly leave her to dash upstairs to change his clothes; yet how, attired as he was, in a fatigue jacket, that warned him not to imagine his back view, and held him constantly a little to the rear of Lady Camper, lest she should be troubled by it;—and he knew the habit of the second rank to criticise the front—how consent to face the outer world in such style side by side with the lady he admired?

"Come," said she; and he shot forward a step, looking as if he had missed fire.

"Are you not coming, General?"

He advanced mechanically.

Not a soul met them down the lanes, except a little one, to whom Lady Camper gave a small silver-piece, because she was a picture.

The act of charity sank into the General's heart, as any pretty performance will do upon a warm waxen bed.

Lady Camper surprised him by answering his thoughts. "No; it's for my own pleasure."

Presently she said, "Here they are."

General Ople beheld his daughter by the riverside at the end of the lane, under escort of Mr. Reginald Rolles.

It was another picture, and a pleasing one. The young lady and the young gentleman wore boating hats, and were both dressed in white, and standing by or just turning from the outrigger and light skiff they were about to leave in charge of a waterman. Elizabeth stretched a finger at arm's-length, issuing directions, which Mr. Rolles took up and worded further to the man, for the sake of emphasis; and he, rather than Elizabeth, was guilty of the half-start at sight of the persons who were approaching.

" My nephew, you should know, is intended for a working soldier," said Lady Camper; " I like that sort of soldier best."

General Ople drooped his shoulders at the personal compliment.

She resumed. " His pay is a matter of importance to him. You are aware of the smallness of a subaltern's pay."

" I," said the General, " I say I feel my poor half-pay, having always been a working soldier myself, very important, I was saying, very important to me."

" Why did you retire ? "

Her interest in him seemed promising. He replied conscientiously, " Beyond the duties of General of Brigade, I could not, I say I could not, dare to aspire; I can accept and execute orders; I shrink from responsibility."

" It is a pity," said she, " that you were not, like my nephew Reginald, entirely dependent on your profession."

She laid such stress on her remark, that the General, who had just expressed a very modest estimate of his abilities, was unable to reject the flattery of her assuming him to be a man of some fortune. He coughed, and said, "Very little." The thought came to him that he might have to make a statement to her in time, and he emphasized, "Very little indeed. Sufficient," he assured her, "for a gentlemanly appearance."

"I have given you your warning," was her inscrutable rejoinder, uttered within earshot of the young people, to whom, especially to Elizabeth, she was gracious. The damsel's boating uniform was praised, and her sunny flush of exercise and exposure.

Lady Camper regretted that she could not abandon her parasol: "I freckle so easily."

The General, puzzling over her strange words about a warning, gazed at the red rose of art on her cheek with an air of profound abstraction.

"I freckle so easily," she repeated, dropping her parasol to defend her face from the calculating scrutiny.

"I burn brown," said Elizabeth.

Lady Camper laid the bud of a Falcot rose against the young girl's cheek, but fetched streams of colour, that overwhelmed the momentary comparison of the sun-swarthed skin with the rich dusky yellow of the rose in its deepening inward to soft brown.

Reginald stretched his hand for the privileged
flower, and she let him take it ; then she looked
at the General ; but the General was looking, with
his usual air of satisfaction, nowhere.

CHAPTER III

" LADY CAMPER is no common enigma,"
General Ople observed to his daughter.

Elizabeth inclined to be pleased with her, for at
her suggestion the General had bought a couple of
horses, that she might ride in the park, accompanied by her father or the little groom.   Still,
the great lady was hard to read.   She tested the
resources of his income by all sorts of instigation
to expenditure, which his gallantry could not
withstand ; she encouraged him to talk of his
deeds in arms ; she was friendly, almost affec-
tionate, and most bountiful in the presents of
fruit, peaches, nectarines, grapes, and hot-house
wonders, that she showered on his table ; but she
was an enigma in her evident dissatisfaction with
him for something he seemed to have left unsaid.
And what could that be ?

At their last interview she had asked him, " Are
you sure, General, you have nothing more to tell
me ? "

And as he remarked, when relating it to Elizabeth, " One might really be tempted to misappre-
hend her ladyship's . . . I say one might

commit oneself beyond recovery. Now, my dear, what do you think she intended?"

Elizabeth was "burning brown," or darkly blushing, as her manner was.

She answered, "I am certain you know of nothing that would interest her; nothing, unless . . . "

"Well?" the General urged her.

"How can I speak it, papa?"

"You really can't mean . . . "

"Papa, what could I mean?"

"If I were fool enough!" he murmured. "No, no, I am an old man. I was saying, I am past the age of folly."

One day Elizabeth came home from her ride in a thoughtful mood. She had not, further than has been mentioned, incited her father to think of the age of folly; but voluntarily or not, Lady Camper had, by an excess of graciousness amounting to downright invitation; as thus, "Will you persist in withholding your confidence from me, General?" She added, "I am not so difficult a person." These prompting speeches occurred on the morning of the day when Elizabeth sat at his table, after a long ride into the country, profoundly meditative.

A note was handed to General Ople, with the request that he would step in to speak with Lady Camper in the course of the evening, or next morning. Elizabeth waited till his hat was on, then said, " Papa, on my ride to-day, I met Mr. Rolles."

" I am glad you had an agreeable escort, my dear."

" I could not refuse his company."

" Certainly not.   And where did you ride ? "

" To a beautiful valley ; and there we met . . . "

" Her ladyship ? "

" Yes."

" She always admires you on horseback."

" So you know it, papa, if she should speak of it."

" And I am bound to tell you, my child," said the General, " that this morning Lady Camper's manner to me was . . . if I were a fool . . . I say, this morning I beat a retreat, but apparently she . .   I see no way out of it, supposing she . . . "

" I am sure she esteems you, dear papa," said Elizabeth.

" You take to her, my dear ? " the General inquired, anxiously ; " a little ? A little afraid of her ? "

" A little," Elizabeth replied, " only a little."

" Don't be agitated about me."

" No, papa ; you are sure to do right."

" But you are trembling."

" Oh ! no.   I wish you success."

General Ople was overjoyed to be reinforced by his daughter's good wishes.   He kissed her to thank her. He turned back to her to kiss her again. She had greatly lightened the difficulty at least of a delicate position.

It was just like the imperious nature of Lady Camper to summon him in the evening to terminate the conversation of the morning, from the visible pitfall of which he had beaten a rather precipitate retreat. But if his daughter cordially wished him success, and Lady Camper offered him the crown of it, why then he had only to pluck up spirit, like a good commander who has to pass a fordable river in the enemy's presence ; a dash, a splash, a rattling volley or two, and you are over, established on the opposite bank. But you must be positive of victory, otherwise, with the river behind you, your new position is likely to be ticklish. So the General entered Lady Camper's drawing-room warily, watching the fair enemy. He knew he was captivating, his old conquests whispered in his ears, and her reception of him all but pointed to a footstool at her feet. He might have fallen there at once, had he not remembered a hint that Mr. Reginald Rolles had dropped concerning Lady Camper's amazing variability.

Lady Camper began.

"General, you ran away from me this morning. Let me speak. And, by the way, I must reproach you ; you should not have left it to me. Things have now gone so far that I cannot pretend to be blind. I know your feelings as a father. Your daughter's happiness . . . "

" My lady," the General interposed, " I have her distinct assurance that it is, I say it is wrapt up in mine."

" Let me speak. Young people will say anything. Well, they have a certain excuse for selfishness ; we have not. I am in some degree bound to my nephew ; he is my sister's son."

" Assuredly, my lady. I would not stand in his light, be quite assured. If I am, I was saying if I am not mistaken, I . . . and he is, or has the making of an excellent soldier in him, and is likely to be a distinguished cavalry officer."

" He has to carve his own way in the world, General."

" All good soldiers have, my lady. And if my position is not, after a considerable term of service, I say if . . ."

" To continue," said Lady Camper : " I never have liked early marriages. I was married in my teens before I knew men. Now I do know them, and now . . ."

The General plunged forward : " The honour you do us now :—a mature experience is worth :— my dear Lady Camper, I have admired you :— and your objection to early marriages cannot apply to . . . indeed, madam, vigour, they say . . . though youth, of course . . . yet young people, as you observe . . . and I have, though perhaps my reputation is against it, I was saying I have a natural timidity with your sex, and I am grey-headed, white-headed, but happily without a single malady."

Lady Camper's brows showed a trifling bewilderment. "I am speaking of these young people, General Ople."

"I consent to everything beforehand, my dear lady. He should be, I say Mr. Rolles should be provided for."

"So should she, General, so should Elizabeth."

"She shall be, she will, dear madam. What I have, with your permission, if—good heaven! Lady Camper, I scarcely know where I am. She would . . . I shall not like to lose her : you would not wish it. In time she will . . . she has every quality of a good wife."

"There, stay there, and be intelligible," said Lady Camper. "She has every quality. Money should be one of them. Has she money?"

"Oh! my lady," the General exclaimed, "we shall not come upon your purse when her time comes."

"Has she ten thousand pounds?"

"Elizabeth? She will have, at her father's death . . . but as for my income, it is moderate, and only sufficient to maintain a gentlemanly appearance in proper self-respect. I make no show. I say I make no show. A wealthy marriage is the last thing on earth I should have aimed at. I prefer quiet and retirement. Personally, I mean. That is my personal taste. But if the lady : I say if it should happen that the lady . . . and indeed I am not one to press a suit : but if she who distinguishes and honours me should chance to be wealthy, all I can do is to leave her wealth at her disposal, and that I do : I do that unreservedly. I feel I am very confused, alarmingly confused. Your ladyship merits a superior . . . I trust I have not . . . I am entirely at your ladyship's mercy."

"Are you prepared, if your daughter is asked in marriage, to settle ten thousand pounds on her, General Ople ? "

The General collected himself. In his heart he thoroughly appreciated the moral beauty of Lady Camper's extreme solicitude on behalf of his daughter's provision ; but he would have desired a postponement of that and other material questions belonging to a distant future until his own fate was decided.

So he said : " Your ladyship's generosity is very marked. I say it is very marked."

" How, my good General Ople ! how is it marked in any degree ? " cried Lady Camper. " I am not generous. I don't pretend to be ; and certainly I don't want the young people to think me so. I want to be just. I have assumed that you intend to be the same. Then will you do me the favour to reply to me ? "

The General smiled winningly and intently, to

show her that he prized her, and would not let her
escape his eulogies.

"Marked, in this way, dear madam, that you
think of my daughter's future more than I. I
say more than her father himself does. I know
I ought to speak more warmly, I feel warmly. I
was never an eloquent man, and if you take me as
a soldier, I am, as I have ever been in the service,
I was saying I am Wilson Ople, of the grade of
General, to be relied on for executing orders ; and,
madam, you are Lady Camper, and you command
me. I cannot be more precise. In fact, it is the
feeling of the necessity for keeping close to the
business that destroys what I would say. I am
in fact lamentably incompetent to conduct my own
case."

Lady Camper left her chair.

"Dear me, this is very strange, unless I am
singularly in error," she said.

The General now faintly guessed that he might
be in error, for his part.

But he had burned his ships, blown up his
bridges ; retreat could not be thought of.

He stood, his head bent and appealing to her
side-face, like one pleadingly in pursuit, and very
deferentially, with a courteous vehemence, he
entreated first her ladyship's pardon for his presumption, and then the gift of her ladyship's
hand.

As for his language, it was the tongue of

General Ople. But his bearing was fine. If his clipped white silken hair spoke of age, his figure breathed manliness. He was a picture, and she loved pictures.

For his own sake, she begged him to cease. She dreaded to hear of something "gentlemanly."

"This is a new idea to me, my dear General," she said. "You must give me time. People at our age have to think of fitness. Of course, in a sense, we are both free to do as we like. Perhaps I may be of some aid to you. My preference is for absolute independence. And I wished to talk of a different affair. Come to me to-morrow. Do not be hurt if I decide that we had better remain as we are."

The General bowed. His efforts, and the wavering of the fair enemy's flag, had inspired him with a positive re-awakening of masculine passion to gain this fortress. He said well : " I have, then, the happiness, madam, of being allowed to hope until to-morrow ? "

She replied, " I would not deprive you of a moment of happiness. Bring good sense with you when you do come."

The General asked eagerly, " I have your lady-ship's permission to come early ? "

" Consult your happiness," she answered ; and if to his mind she seemed returning to the state of enigma, it was on the whole deliciously. She restored him his youth. He told Elizabeth that night, he really must begin to think of marrying her to some worthy young fellow. "Though," said he, with an air of frank intoxication, "my opinion is, the young ones are not so lively as the old in these days, or I should have been besieged before now."

The exact substance of the interview he forbore to relate to his inquisitive daughter, with a very honourable discretion.

CHAPTER IV

ELIZABETH came riding home to breakfast from a gallop round the park, and passing Lady Camper's gates, received the salutation of her parasol. Lady Camper talked with her through the bars. There was not a sign to tell of a change or twist in her neighbourly affability. She remarked simply enough, that it was her nephew's habit to take early gallops, and possibly Elizabeth might have seen him, for his quarters were proximate; but she did not demand an answer. She had passed a rather restless night, she said. "How is the General?"

"Papa must have slept soundly, for he usually calls to me through his door when he hears I am up," said Elizabeth.

Lady Camper nodded kindly and walked on.

Early in the morning General Ople was ready for battle. His forces were, the anticipation of victory, a carefully arranged toilette, and an unaccustomed spirit of enterprise in the realms of speech; for he was no longer in such awe of Lady Camper.

"You have slept well?" she inquired.

"Excellently, my lady."

"Yes, your daughter tells me she heard you, as she went by your door in the morning for a ride to meet my nephew. You are, I shall assume, prepared for business."

"Elizabeth? . . . to meet? . . . ." General Ople's impression of anything extraneous to his emotion was feeble and passed instantly. "Prepared! Oh, certainly;" and he struck in a compliment on her ladyship's fresh morning bloom.

"It can hardly be visible," she responded ; "I have not painted yet."

"Does your ladyship proceed to your painting in the very early morning ? "

"Rouge. I rouge."

"Dear me! I should not have supposed it."

"You have speculated on it very openly, General. I remember your trying to see a freckle through the rouge ; but the truth is, I am of a supernatural paleness if I do not rouge, so I do. You understand, therefore, I have a false complexion. Now to business."

"If your ladyship insists on calling it business. I have little to offer—myself ! "

"You have a gentlemanly residence."

"It is, my lady, it is. It is a bijou."

"Ah ! " Lady Camper sighed dejectedly.

"It is a perfect bijou ! "

"Oblige me, General, by not pronouncing the French word as if you were swearing by something in English, like a trooper."

General Ople started, admitted that the word was French, and apologized for his pronunciation. Her variability was now visible over a corner of the battlefield like a thunder-cloud.

"The business we have to discuss concerns the young people, General."

"Yes," brightened by this, he assented: "Yes, dear Lady Camper; it is a part of the business; it is a secondary part; it has to be discussed; I say I subscribe beforehand. I may say that honouring, esteeming you as I do, and hoping ardently for your consent . . ."

"They must have a home and an income, General."

"I presume, dearest lady, that Elizabeth will be welcome in your home. I certainly shall never chase Reginald out of mine."

Lady Camper threw back her head. "Then you are not yet awake, or you practise the art of sleeping with open eyes! Now listen to me. I rouge, I have told you. I like colour, and I do not like to see wrinkles or have them seen. Therefore I rouge. I do not expect to deceive the world so flagrantly as to my age, and you I would not deceive for a moment. I am seventy."

The effect of this noble frankness on the General, was to raise him from his chair in a sitting posture as if he had been blown up.

Her countenance was inexorably imperturbable under his alternate blinking and gazing that drew her close and shot her distant, like a mysterious toy.

"But," said she, "I am an artist; I dislike the look of extreme age, so I conceal it as well as I can. You are very kind to fall in with the deception: an innocent and, I think, a proper one, before the world, though not to the gentleman who does me the honour to propose to me for my hand. You desire to settle our business first. You esteem me; I suppose you mean as much as young people mean when they say they love. Do you? Let us come to an understanding."

"I can," the melancholy General gasped, "I say I can—I cannot—I cannot credit your ladyship's . . ."

"You are at liberty to call me Angela."

"Ange . . ." he tried it, and in shame relapsed. "Madam, yes. Thanks."

"Ah," cried Lady Camper, "do not use these vulgar contractions of decent speech in my presence. I abhor the word 'thanks.' It is fit for fribbles."

"Dear me, I have used it all my life," groaned the General.

"Then, for the remainder, be it understood that you renounce it. To continue, my age is . . ."

"Oh, impossible, impossible," the General almost wailed; there was really a crack in his voice.

"Advancing to seventy. But, like you, I am happy to say I have not a malady. I bring no invalid frame to an union that necessitates the leaving of the front door open day and night to the doctor. My belief is, I could follow my husband still on a campaign, if he were a warrior instead of a pensioner."

General Ople winced.

He was about to say humbly, " As General of Brigade . . ."

" Yes, yes, you want a commanding officer, and that I have seen, and that has caused me to meditate on your proposal," she interrupted him ; while he, studying her countenance hard, with the painful aspect of a youth who lashes a donkey memory in an examination by word of mouth, attempted to marshal her signs of younger years against her awful confession of the extremely ancient, the witheringly ancient. But for the manifest rouge, manifest in spite of her declaration that she had not yet that morning proceeded to her paint-brush, he would have thrown down his glove to challenge her on the subject of her age. She had actually charms. Her mouth had a charm ; her eyes were lively ; her figure, mature if you like, was at least full and good ; she stood upright, she had a queenly seat. His mental ejaculation was, " What a wonderful constitution ! "

By a lapse of politeness, he repeated it to himself half aloud ; he was shockingly nervous.

" Yes, I have finer health than many a younger woman," she said. " An ordinary calculation would give me twenty good years to come. I am a widow, as you know. And, by the way, you have a leaning for widows. Have you not? I thought I had heard of a widow Barcop in this parish. Do not protest. I assure you I am a stranger to jealousy. My income . . ."

The General raised his hands.

" Well, then," said the cool and self-contained lady, " before I go farther, I may ask you, knowing what you have forced me to confess, are you still of the same mind as to marriage? And one moment, General. I promise you most sincerely that your withdrawing a step shall not, as far as it touches me, affect my neighbourly and friendly sentiments, not in any degree. Shall we be as we were ? "

Lady Camper extended her delicate hand to him. He took it respectfully, inspected the aristocratic and unshrunken fingers, and kissing them, said, " I never withdraw from a position, unless I am beaten back. Lady Camper, I . . ."

" My name is Angela."

The General tried again : he could not utter the name.

To call a lady of seventy Angela is difficult in itself. It is, it seems, thrice difficult in the way of courtship.

" Angela ! " said she.

" Yes. I say, there is not a more beautiful female name, dear Lady Camper."

"Spare me that word 'female' as long as you live. Address me by that name, if you please."

The General smiled. The smile was meant for propitiation and sweetness. It became a brazen smile.

"Unless you wish to step back," said she.

"Indeed, no. I am happy, Lady Camper. My life is yours. I say, my life is devoted to you, dear madam."

"Angela !"

General Ople was blushingly delivered of the name.

"That will do," said she. "And as I think it possible one may be admired too much as an artist, I must request you to keep my number of years a secret."

"To the death, madam," said the General.

"And now we will take a turn in the garden, Wilson Ople. And beware of one thing, for a commencement, for you are full of weeds, and I mean to pluck out a few: never call any place a gentlemanly residence in my hearing, nor let it come to my ears that you have been using the phrase elsewhere. Don't express astonishment. At present it is enough that I dislike it. But this only," Lady Camper added, "this only if it is not your intention to withdraw from your position."

"Madam, my lady, I was saying—hem !—Angela, I *could* not wish to withdraw."

Lady Camper leaned with some pressure on his

arm, observing, "You have a curious attachment to antiquities."

"My dear lady, it is your mind ; I say, it is your mind : I was saying, I am in love with your mind," the General endeavoured to assure her, and himself too.

"Or is it my powers as an artist?"

"Your mind, your extraordinary powers of mind."

"Well," said Lady Camper, "a veteran General of Brigade is as good a crutch as a childless old grannam can have."

And such, as a crutch, General Ople, parading her grounds with the aged woman, found himself used and treated.

The accuracy of his perceptions might be questioned. He was like a man stunned by some great tropical fruit, which responds to the longing of his eyes by falling on his head ; but it appeared to him, that she increased in bitterness at every step they took, as if determined to make him realize her wrinkles.

He was even so inconsequent, or so little recognized his position, as to object in his heart to hear himself called Wilson.

It is true that she uttered Wilsonople as if the names formed one word. And on a second occasion (when he inclined to feel hurt) she remarked, " I fear me, Wilsonople, if we are to speak plainly, thou art but a fool." He, perhaps, naturally objected to that. He was, however, giddy, and barely knew.

Yet once more the magical woman changed. All semblance of harshness, and harridan-like spike-tonguedness vanished when she said adieu.

The astronomer, looking at the crusty jag and scoria of the magnified moon through his telescope, and again with naked eyes at the soft-beaming moon, when the crater-ridges are faint as eyebrow-pencillings, has a similar sharp alternation of prospect to that which mystified General Ople.

But between watching an orb that is only variable at our caprice, and contemplating a woman who shifts and quivers ever at her own, how vast the difference!

And consider that this woman is about to be one's wife!

He could have believed (if he had not known full surely that such things are not) he was in the hands of a witch.

Lady Camper's " adieu " was perfectly beautiful —a kind, cordial, intimate, above all, to satisfy his present craving, it was a lady-like adieu—the adieu of a delicate and elegant woman, who had hardly left her anchorage by forty to sail into the fifties.

Alas! he had her word for it, that she was not less than seventy. And, worse, she had betrayed most melancholy signs of sourness and agedness as soon as he had sworn himself to her fast and fixed.

" The road is open to you to retreat," were her last words.

" My road," he answered gallantly, "is forward."

He was drawing backward as he said it, and something provoked her to smile.

CHAPTER V

IT is a noble thing to say that your road is forward, and it befits a man of battles. General
Ople was too loyal a gentleman to think of any
other road. Still, albeit not gifted with imagination, he could not avoid the feeling that he had set
his face to Winter. He found himself suddenly
walking straight into the heart of Winter, and a
nipping Winter. For her ladyship had proved
acutely nipping. His little customary phrases, to
which Lady Camper objected, he could see no
harm in whatever. Conversing with her in the
privacy of domestic life would never be the flowing
business that it is for other men. It would demand
perpetual vigilance, hop, skip, jump, flounderings,
and apologies.

This was not a pleasing prospect.

On the other hand, she was the niece of an earl.
She was wealthy. She might be an excellent
friend to Elizabeth ; and she could be, when she
liked, both commandingly and bewitchingly lady-
like.

Good! But he was a General Officer of not
more than fifty-five, in his full vigour, and she a
woman of seventy !

The prospect was bleak. It resembled an outlook on the steppes. In point of the discipline he was to expect, he might be compared to a raw recruit, and in his own home!

However, she was a woman of mind. One would be proud of her.

But did he know the worst of her? A dreadful presentiment, that he did not know the worst of her, rolled an ocean of gloom upon General Ople, striking out one solitary thought in the obscurity, namely, that he was about to receive punishment for retiring from active service to a life of ease at a comparatively early age, when still in marching trim. And the shadow of the thought was, that he deserved the punishment!

He was in his garden with the dawn. Hard exercise is the best of opiates for dismal reflections. The General discomposed his daughter by offering to accompany her on her morning ride before breakfast. She considered that it would fatigue him. "I am not a man of eighty!" he cried. He could have wished he had been.

He led the way to the park, where they soon had sight of young Rolles, who checked his horse and spied them like a vedette, but, perceiving that he had been seen, came cantering, and hailing the General with hearty wonderment.

"And what's this the world says, General?" said he. "But we all applaud your taste. My aunt Angela was the handsomest woman of her time."

The General murmured in confusion, "Dear me!" and looked at the young man, thinking that he could not have known the time.

"Is all arranged, my dear General?"

"Nothing is arranged, and I beg—I say I beg . . . I came out for fresh air and pace."

The General rode frantically.

In spite of the fresh air, he was unable to eat at breakfast. He was bound, of course, to present himself to Lady Camper, in common civility, immediately after it.

And first, what were the phrases he had to avoid uttering in her presence? He could remember only the "gentlemanly residence." And it was a gentlemanly residence, he thought as he took leave of it. It was one, neatly named to fit the place. Lady Camper is indeed a most eccentric person! he decided from his experience of her.

He was rather astonished that young Rolles should have spoken so coolly of his aunt's leaning to matrimony; but perhaps her exact age was unknown to the younger members of her family.

This idea refreshed him by suggesting the extremely honourable nature of Lady Camper's uncomfortable confession.

He himself had an uncomfortable confession to make. He would have to speak of his income. He was living up to the edges of it.

She is an upright woman, and I must be the same! he said, fortunately not in her hearing.

The subject was disagreeable to a man sensitive on the topic of money, and feeling that his prudence had recently been misled to keep up appearances.

Lady Camper was in her garden, reclining under her parasol. A chair was beside her, to which, acknowledging the salutation of her suitor, she waved him.

"You have met my nephew Reginald this morning, General?"

"Curiously, in the park, this morning, before breakfast, I did, yes. Hem! I, I say I did meet him. Has your ladyship seen him?"

"No. The park is very pretty in the early morning."

"Sweetly pretty."

Lady Camper raised her head, and with the mildness of assured dictatorship, pronounced: "Never say that before me."

"I submit, my lady," said the poor scourged man.

"Why, naturally you do. Vulgar phrases have to be endured, except when our intimates are guilty, and then we are not merely offended, we are compromised by them. You are still of the mind in which you left me yesterday? You are one day older. But I warn you, so am I."

"Yes, my lady, we cannot, I say we cannot check time. Decidedly of the same mind. Quite so."

'Oblige me by never saying 'Quite so.' My

lawyer says it. It reeks of the City of London. And do not look so miserable."

" I, madam ? my dear lady ! " the General flashed out in a radiance that dulled instantly.

" Well," said she, cheerfully, " and you're for the old woman ? "

" For Lady Camper."

" You are seductive in your flatteries, General. Well, then, we have to speak of business."

" My affairs——" General Ople was beginning, with perturbed forehead ; but Lady Camper held up her finger.

" We will touch on your affairs incidentally. Now listen to me, and do not exclaim until I have finished. You know that these two young ones have been whispering over the wall for some months. They have been meeting on the river and in the park habitually, apparently with your consent."

'" My lady ! "

" I did not say with your connivance."

" You mean my daughter Elizabeth ? "

" And my nephew Reginald. We have named them, if that advances us. Now, the end of such meetings is marriage, and the sooner the better, if they are to continue. I would rather they should not ; I do not hold it good for young soldiers to marry. But if they do, it is very certain that their pay will not support a family ; and in a marriage of two healthy young people, we have to assume the existence of the family. You have allowed matters to go so far that the boy is hot in love ; I suppose the girl is, too. She is a nice girl. I do not object to her personally. But I insist that a settlement be made on her before I give my nephew one penny. Hear me out, for I am not fond of business, and shall be glad to have done with these explanations. Reginald has nothing of his own. He is my sister's son, and I loved her, and rather like the boy. He has at present four hundred a-year from me. I will double it, on the condition that you at once make over ten thousand —not less ; and let it be yes or no !—to be settled on your daughter and go to her children, independent of the husband—*cela va sans dire*. Now you may speak, General."

The General spoke, with breath fetched from the deeps :

"Ten thousand pounds ! Hem ! Ten ! Hem, frankly—ten, my lady ! One's income—I am quite taken by surprise. I say Elizabeth's conduct— though, poor child ! it is natural to her to seek a mate, I mean, to accept a mate and an establishment, and Reginald is a very hopeful fellow—I was saying, they jump on me out of an ambush, and I wish them every happiness. And she is an ardent soldier, and a soldier she must marry. But ten thousand ! "

" It is to secure the happiness of your daughter, General."

" Pounds! my lady. It would rather cripple me."

" You would have my house, General ; you would have the moiety, as the lawyers say, of my purse ; you would have horses, carriages, servants ; I do not divine what more you would wish to have."

" But, madam—a pensioner on the Government! I can look back on past services, I say old services, and I accept my position. But, madam, a pensioner on my wife, bringing next to nothing to the common estate! I fear my self-respect would, I say would . . ."

" Well, and what would it do, General Ople ? "

" I was saying, my self-respect as my wife's pensioner, my lady. I could not come to her empty-handed."

" Do you expect that I should be the person to settle money on your daughter, to save her from mischances? A rakish husband, for example, for Reginald is young, and no one can guess what will be made of him."

" Undoubtedly your ladyship is correct. We might try absence for the poor girl. I have no female relation, but I could send her to the sea-side to a lady-friend."

" General Ople, I forbid you, as you value my esteem, ever—and I repeat, I forbid you ever—to afflict my ears with that phrase, ' lady-friend ! ' "

The General blinked in a state of insurgent humility.

These incessant whippings could not but sting

the humblest of men ; and "lady-friend," he was
sure, was a very common term, used, he was sure,
in the very best society.   He had never heard Her
Majesty speak at levées of a lady-friend, but he
was quite sure that she had one ; and if so, what
could be the objection to her subjects mentioning
it as a term to suit their own circumstances ?

He was harassed and perplexed by old Lady
Camper's treatment of him, and he resolved not to
call her Angela even upon supplication—not that
day, at least.

She said, " You will not need to bring property
of any kind to the common estate ; I neither look
for it nor desire it.   The generous thing for you to
do would be to give your daughter all you have,
and come to me."

" But, Lady Camper, if I denude myself or cur-
tail my income—a man at his wife's discretion, I
was saying a man at his wife's mercy !   .   .   ."

General Ople was really forced, by his manly
dignity, to make this protest on its behalf.   He did
not see how he could have escaped doing so ; he
was more an agent than a principal.   " My wife's
mercy," he said again, but simply as a herald proclaiming superior orders.

Lady Camper's brows were wrathful.   A deep
blood-crimson overcame the rouge, and gave her a
terrible stormy look.

" The congress now ceases to sit, and the treaty
is not concluded," was all she said.

She rose, bowed to him, "Good morning, General," and turned her back.

He sighed. He was a free man. But this could not be denied—whatever the lady's age, she was a grand woman in her carriage, and when looking angry, she had a queen-like aspect that raised her out of the reckoning of time.

So now he knew there was a worse behind what he had previously known. He was precipitate in calling it the worst. "Now," said he to himself, " I know the worst ! "

No man should ever say it. Least of all, one who has entered into relations with an eccentric lady.

CHAPTER VI

POLITENESS required that General Ople should not appear to rejoice in his dismissal as a suitor, and should at least make some show of holding himself at the beck of a reconsidering mind. He was guilty of running up to London early next day, and remaining absent until night-fall; and he did the same on the two following days. When he presented himself at Lady Camper's lodge-gates, the astonishing intelligence, that her ladyship had departed for the Continent and Egypt gave him qualms of remorse, which assumed a more definite shape in something like awe of her triumphant constitution. He forbore to mention her age, for he was the most honourable of men, but a habit of tea-table talkativeness impelled him to say and repeat an idea that had visited him, to the effect, that Lady Camper was one of those wonderful women who are comparable to brilliant generals, and defend themselves from the siege of Time by various aggressive movements. Fearful of not being understood, owing to the rarity of the occasions when the squat plain squad of honest Saxon regulars at his command were called upon to explain an idea, he re-cast the sentence.   But, as it happened that the regulars of his vocabulary were not numerous, and not accustomed to work upon thoughts and images, his repetitions rather succeeded in exposing the piece of knowledge he had recently acquired than in making his meaning plainer.   So we need not marvel that his acquaintance should suppose him to be secretly aware of an extreme degree in which Lady Camper was a veteran.

General Ople entered into the gaieties of the neighbourhood once more, and passed through the Winter cheerfully.   In justice to him, however, it should be said that to the intent dwelling of his mind upon Lady Camper, and not to the festive life he led, was due his entire ignorance of his daughter's unhappiness.   She lived with him, and yet it was in other houses he learnt that she was unhappy.   After his last interview with Lady Camper, he had informed Elizabeth of the ruinous and preposterous amount of money demanded of him for a settlement upon her : and Elizabeth, like the girl of good sense that she was, had replied immediately, " It could not be thought of, papa." He had spoken to Reginald likewise.   The young man fell into a dramatic tearing-of-hair and long-stride fury, not ill becoming an enamoured dragoon. But he maintained that his aunt, though an eccentric, was a cordially kind woman.   He seemed to feel, if he did not partly hint, that the General might have accepted Lady Camper's terms.   The young officer could no longer be welcome at Douro Lodge, so the General paid him a morning call at his quarters, and was distressed to find him breakfasting very late, tapping eggs that he forgot to open—one of the surest signs of a young man downright and deep in love, as the General knew from experience—and surrounded by uncut sporting journals of past weeks, which dated from the day when his blow had struck him, as accurately as the watch of the drowned man marks his minute. Lady Camper had gone to Italy, and was in communication with her nephew : Reginald was not further explicit.   His legs were very prominent in his despair, and his fingers frequently performed the part of blunt combs, consequently the General was impressed by his passion for Elizabeth.   The girl who, if she was often meditative, always met his eyes with a smile, and quietly said " Yes, papa," and " No, papa," gave him little concern as to the state of her feelings.   Yet everybody said now that she was unhappy.   Mrs. Barcop, the widow, raised her voice above the rest.   So attentive was she to Elizabeth that the General had it kindly suggested to him, that someone was courting him through his daughter.   He gazed at the widow.   Now she was not much past thirty ; and it was really singular— he could have laughed—thinking of Mrs. Barcop set him persistently thinking of Lady Camper. That is to say, his mad fancy reverted from the lady of perhaps thirty-five to the lady of seventy! Such, thought he, is genius in a woman! Of his neighbours generally, Mrs. Baerens, the wife of a German merchant, an exquisite player on the pianoforte, was the most inclined to lead him to speak of Lady Camper. She was a kind prattling woman, and was known to have been a governess before her charms withdrew the gastronomic Gott-fried Baerens from his devotion to the well-served City club, where, as he exclaimed (ever turning fondly to his wife as he vocalized the compliment), he had found every necessity, every luxury, in life, " as you cannot have dem out of London—all save de female!" Mrs. Baerens, a lady of Teutonic extraction, was distinguishable as of that sex ; at least she was not masculine. She spoke with great respect of Lady Camper and her family, and seemed to agree in the General's eulogies of Lady Camper's constitution. Still he thought she eyed him strangely.

One April morning the General received a letter with the Italian postmark. Opening it with his usual calm and happy curiosity, he perceived that it was composed of pen-and-ink drawings. And suddenly his heart sank like a scuttled ship. He saw himself the victim of a caricature.

The first sketch had merely seemed picturesque, and he supposed it a clever play of fancy by some travelling friend, or perhaps an actual scene slightly exaggerated. Even on reading, " A distant view of the city of Wilsonople," he was only slightly enlightened.   His heart beat still with befitting regularity.   But the second and the third sketches betrayed the terrible hand.   The distant view of the city of Wilsonople was fair with glittering domes, which, in the succeeding near view, proved to have been soap-bubbles, for a place of extreme flatness, begirt with crazy old-fashioned fortifications, was shown ; and in the third view, representing the interior, stood for sole place of habitation, a sentry-box.

Most minutely drawn, and, alas ! with fearful accuracy, a military gentleman in undress occupied the box.   Not a doubt could exist as to the person it was meant to be.

The General tried hard to remain incredulous. He remembered too well who had called him Wilsonople.

But here was the extraordinary thing that sent him over the neighbourhood canvassing for exclamations : on the fourth page was the outline of a lovely feminine hand, holding a pen, as in the act of shading, and under it was written these words : " *What I say is, I say I think it exceedingly unladylike.*"

Now consider the General's feelings when, turning to this fourth page, having these very words in his mouth, as the accurate expression of his thoughts, he discovered them written !

An enemy who anticipates the actions of our

mind, has a quality of the malignant divine that may well inspire terror. The senses of General Ople were struck by the aspect of a lurid Goddess, who penetrated him, read him through, and had both power and will to expose and make him ridiculous for ever.

The loveliness of the hand, too, in a perplexing manner contested his denunciation of her conduct. It was ladylike eminently, and it involved him in a confused mixture of the moral and material, as great as young people are known to feel when they make the attempt to separate them, in one of their frenzies.

With a petty bitter laugh he folded the letter, put it in his breast-pocket, and sallied forth for a walk, chiefly to talk to himself about it. But as it absorbed him entirely, he showed it to the rector, whom he met, and what the rector said is of no consequence, for General Ople listened to no remarks, calling in succession on the Pollingtons, the Goslings, the Baerens', and others, early though it was, and the lords of those houses absent amassing hoards ; and to the ladies everywhere he displayed the sketches he had received, observing that Wilsonople meant himself ; and there he was, he said, pointing at the capped fellow in the sentry-box, done unmistakably. The likeness indeed was remarkable. "She is a woman of genius," he ejaculated, with utter melancholy. Mrs. Baerens by the aid of a magnifying glass, assisted him to read a line under the sentry-box, that he had taken for a mere trembling dash ; it ran, *A gentlemanly residence.*

"What eyes she has !" the General exclaimed ; " I say it is miraculous what eyes she has at her time of . . . I was saying I should never have known it was writing."

He sighed heavily. His shuddering sensitiveness to caricature was increased by a certain evident dread of the hand which struck ; the knowing that he was absolutely bare to this woman, defenceless, open to exposure in his little whims, foibles, tricks, incompetencies, in what lay in his heart, and the words that would come to his tongue. He felt like a man haunted.

So deeply did he feel the blow, that people asked how it was that he could be so foolish as to dance about assisting Lady Camper in her efforts to make him ridiculous ; he acted the parts of publisher and agent for the fearful caricaturist. In truth, there was a strangely double reason for his conduct ; he danced about for sympathy, he had the intensest craving for sympathy, but more than this, or quite as much, he desired to have the powers of his enemy widely appreciated ; in the first place, that he might be excused to himself for wincing under them, and secondly, because an awful admiration of her, that should be deepened by a corresponding sentiment around him, helped him to enjoy luxurious recollections of an hour when he was near making her his own—his own, in the holy abstract contemplation of marriage, without realizing their probable relative conditions after the ceremony.

" I say, that is the very image of her ladyship's hand," he was especially fond of remarking, " I say it is a beautiful hand."

He carried the letter in his pocket-book ; and beginning to fancy that she had done her worst, for he could not imagine an inventive malignity capable of pursuing the theme, he spoke of her treatment of him with compassionate regret, not badly assumed from being partly sincere.

Two letters dated in France, the one Dijon, the other Fontainebleau, arrived together ; and as the General knew Lady Camper to be returning to England, he expected that she was anxious to excuse herself to him. His fingers were not so confident, for he tore one of the letters to open it.

The City of Wilsonople was recognisable immediately. So likewise was the sole inhabitant.

General Ople's petty bitter laugh recurred, like a weak-chested patient's cough in the shifting of our winds eastward.

A faceless woman's shadow kneels on the ground near the sentry-box, weeping. A faceless shadow of a young man on horseback is beheld galloping toward a gulf. The sole inhabitant contemplates his largely substantial full fleshed face and figure in a glass.

Next, we see the standard of Great Britain furled ; next, unfurled and borne by a troop of shadows to the sentry-box. The officer within says, " I say I should be very happy to carry it, but I cannot quit this gentlemanly residence."

Next, the standard is shown assailed by popguns. Several of the shadows are prostrate. " I was saying, I assure you that nothing but this gentlemanly residence prevents me from heading you," says the gallant officer.

General Ople trembled with protestant indignation when he saw himself reclining in a magnified sentry-box, while detachments of shadows hurry to him to show him the standard of his country trailing in the dust ; and he is maliciously made to say, " I dislike responsibility. I say I am a fervent patriot, and very fond of my comforts, but I shun responsibility."

The second letter contained scenes between Wilsonople and the Moon.

He addresses her as his neighbour, and tells her of his triumphs over the sex.

He requests her to inform him whether she is a " female," that she may be triumphed over.

He hastens past her window on foot, with his head bent, just as the General had been in the habit of walking.

He drives a mouse-pony furiously by.

He cuts down a tree, that she may peep through.

Then, from the Moon's point of view, Wilsonople,

a Silenus, is discerned in an arm-chair winking at a couple too plainly pouting their lips for a doubt of their intentions to be entertained.

A fourth letter arrived, bearing date of Paris. This one illustrated Wilsonople's courtship of the Moon, and ended with his " saying," in his peculiar manner, " *In spite of her paint I could not have conceived her age to be so enormous.*"

How break off his engagement with the Lady Moon? Consent to none of her terms !

Little used as he was to read behind a veil, acuteness of suffering sharpened the General's intelligence to a degree that sustained him in animated dialogue with each succeeding sketch, or poisoned arrow whirring at him from the moment his eyes rested on it ; and here are a few samples :—

"Wilsonople informs the Moon that she is 'sweetly pretty.'

He thanks her with 'thanks' for a handsome piece of lunar green cheese.

He points to her, apparently telling some one, 'my lady-friend.'

He sneezes ' Bijou ! bijou ! bijou !'"

They were trifles, but they attacked his habits of speech ; and he began to grow more and more alarmingly absurd in each fresh caricature of his person.

He looked at himself as the malicious woman's hand had shaped him. It was unjust ; it was no resemblance—and yet it was! There was a corner of likeness left that leavened the lump ; henceforth he must walk abroad with this distressing image of himself before his eyes, instead of the satisfactory reflex of the man who had, and was happy in thinking that he had, done mischief in his time. Such an end for a conquering man was too pathetic.

The General surprised himself talking to himself in something louder than a hum at neighbours' dinner-tables. He looked about and noticed that people were silently watching him.

CHAPTER VII

LADY CAMPER'S return was the subject
of speculation in the neighbourhood, for
most people thought she would cease to per-
secute the General with her preposterous and
unwarrantable pen-and-ink sketches when living
so closely proximate; and how he would behave
was the question. Those who made a hero of
him were sure he would treat her with disdain.
Others were uncertain. He had been so severely
hit that it seemed possible he would not show
much spirit.

He, for his part, had come to entertain such
dread of the post, that Lady Camper's return relieved him of his morning apprehensions; and he
would have forgiven her, though he feared to see
her, if only she had promised to leave him in peace
for the future. He feared to see her, because of
the too probable furnishing of fresh matter for her
ladyship's hand. Of course he could not avoid
being seen by her, and that was a particular
misery. A gentlemanly humility, or demureness
of aspect, when seen, would, he hoped, disarm his
enemy. It should, he thought. He had borne

unheard-of things.   No one of his friends and acquaintances knew, they could not know, what he had endured.   It had caused him fits of stammering.   It had destroyed the composure of his gait. Elizabeth had informed him that he talked to himself incessantly, and aloud. She, poor child, looked pale too.   She was evidently anxious about him.

Young Rolles, whom he had met now and then, persisted in praising his aunt's good heart. So, perhaps, having satiated her revenge, she might now be inclined for peace, on the terms of distant civility.

"Yes! poor Elizabeth!" sighed the General, in pity of the poor girl's disappointment; "poor Elizabeth! she little guesses what her father has gone through. Poor child! I say, she hasn't an idea of my sufferings."

General Ople delivered his card at Lady Camper's lodge gates, and escaped to his residence in a state of prickly heat that required the brushing of his hair with hard brushes for ten minutes to comfort and re-establish him.

He fell to working in his garden, when Lady Camper's card was brought to him an hour after the delivery of his own, a pleasing promptitude, showing signs of repentance, and suggesting to the General instantly some sharp sarcasms upon women, which he had come upon in quotations in the papers and the pulpit, his two main sources of information.

Instead of handing back the card to the maid, he stuck it in his hat and went on digging.

The first of a series of letters containing shameless realistic caricatures was handed to him the afternoon following. They came fast and thick. Not a day's interval of grace was allowed. Niobe under the shafts of Diana was hardly less violently and mortally assailed. The deadliness of the attack lay in the ridicule of the daily habits of one of the most sensitive of men, as to his personal appearance, and the opinion of the world. He might have concealed the sketches, but he could not have concealed the bruises, and people were perpetually asking the unhappy General what he was saying, for he spoke to himself as if he were repeating something to them for the tenth time.

" I say," said he, " I say that for a lady, really an educated lady, to sit, as she must—I was saying, she must have sat in an attic to have the right view of me. And there you see—this is what she has done. This is the last, this is the afternoon's delivery. Her ladyship has me correctly as to costume, but I could not exhibit such a sketch to ladies."

A back view of the General was displayed in his act of digging.

"I say I could not allow ladies to see it," he informed the gentlemen, who were suffered to inspect it freely.

Y

"But you see, I have no means of escape ; I am at her mercy from morning to night," the General said, with a quivering tongue, "unless I stay at home inside the house ; and that is death to me, or unless I abandon the place, and my lease ; and I shall—I say, I shall find nowhere in England for anything like the money or conveniences such a gent—a residence you would call fit for a gentleman. I call it a bi . . . it is, in short, a gem. But I shall have to go."

Young Rolles offered to expostulate with his aunt Angela.

The General said, "Tha . . . I thank you very much. I would not have her ladyship suppose I am so susceptible. I hardly know," he confessed pitiably, "what it is right to say, and what not— what not. I—I—I never know when I am not looking a fool. I hurry from tree to tree to shun the light. I am seriously affected in my appetite. I say, I shall have to go."

Reginald gave him to understand that if he flew, the shafts would follow him, for Lady Camper would never forgive his running away, and was quite equal to publishing a book of the adventures of Wilsonople.

Sunday afternoon, walking in the park with his daughter on his arm, General Ople met Mr. Rolles. He saw that the young man and Elizabeth were mortally pale, and as the very idea of wretchedness directed his attention to himself, he addressed them conjointly on the subject of his persecution, giving neither of them a chance of speaking until they were constrained to part.

A sketch was the consequence, in which a withered Cupid and a fading Psyche were seen divided by Wilsonople, who keeps them forcibly asunder with policeman's fists, while courteously and elegantly entreating them to hear him. "Meet," he tells them, "as often as you like, in my company, so long as you listen to me ;" and the pathos of his aspect makes hungry demand for a sympathetic audience.

Now, this, and not the series representing the martyrdom of the old couple at Douro Lodge Gates, whose rigid frames bore witness to the close packing of a gentlemanly residence, this was the sketch General Ople, in his madness from the pursuing bite of the gadfly, handed about at Mrs. Pollington's lawn-party. Some have said, that he would not have betrayed his daughter ; but it is reasonable to suppose he had no idea of his daughter's being the Psyche. Or if he had, it was indistinct, owing to the violence of his personal emotion. Assuming this to have been the very sketch ; he handed it to two or three ladies in turn, and was heard to deliver himself at intervals in the following snatches : "As you like, my lady, as you like ; strike, I say strike ; I bear it ; I say I bear it. . . . If her ladyship is unforgiving, I say I am enduring. . . . I may go, I was saying I may go mad, but while I have my reason I walk upright, I walk upright."

Mr. Pollington and certain City gentlemen hearing the poor General's renewed soliloquies, were seized with disgust of Lady Camper's conduct, and stoutly advised an application to the Law Courts.

He gave ear to them abstractedly, but after pulling out the whole chapter of the caricatures (which it seemed that he kept in a case of morocco leather in his breast-pocket), showing them, with comments on them, and observing, "There will be more, there must be more, I say I am sure there are things I do that her ladyship will discover and expose," he declined to seek redress or simple protection ; and the miserable spectacle was exhibited soon after of this courtly man listening to Mrs. Barcop on the weather, and replying in acquiescence : "It is hot.—If your ladyship will only abstain from colours. Very hot as you say, madam,—I do not complain of pen and ink, but I would rather escape colours. And I dare say you find it hot too ?"

Mrs. Barcop shut her eyes and sighed over the wreck of a handsome military officer.

She asked him : "What is your objection to colours ?"

His hand was at his breast-pocket immediately, as he said : "Have you not seen ?"—though but a few minutes back he had shown her the contents of the packet, including a hurried glance of the famous digging scene.

By this time the entire district was in fervid sympathy with General Ople. The ladies did not, as their lords did, proclaim astonishment that a man should suffer a woman to goad him to a state of semi-lunacy ; but one or two confessed to their husbands, that it required a great admiration of General Ople not to despise him, both for his susceptibility and his patience. As for the men, they knew him to have faced the balls in bellowing battle-strife ; they knew him to have endured privation, not only cold but downright want of food and drink—an almost unimaginable horror to these brave daily feasters ; so they could not quite look on him in contempt ; but his want of sense was offensive, and still more so his submission to a scourging by a woman. Not one of them would have deigned to feel it. Would they have allowed her to see that she could sting them ? They would have laughed at her. Or they would have dragged her before a magistrate.

It was a Sunday in early Summer when General Ople walked to morning service, unaccompanied by Elizabeth, who was unwell. The church was of the considerate old-fashioned order, with deaf square pews, permitting the mind to abstract itself from the sermon, or wrestle at leisure with the difficulties presented by the preacher, as General Ople often did, feeling not a little in love with his sincere attentiveness for grappling with the knotty point and partially allowing the struggle to be seen.

The Church was, besides, a sanctuary for him. Hither his enemy did not come. He had this one place of refuge, and he almost looked a happy man again.

He had passed into his hat and out of it, which he habitually did standing, when who should walk up to within a couple of yards of him but Lady Camper. Her pew was full of poor people, who made signs of retiring. She signified to them that they were to sit, then quietly took her seat among them, fronting the General across the aisle.

During the sermon a low voice, sharp in contra-distinction to the monotone of the preacher's, was heard to repeat these words: " I say I am not sure I shall survive it." Considerable muttering in the same quarter was heard besides.

After the customary ceremonious game, when all were free to move, of nobody liking to move first, Lady Camper and a charity boy were the persons who took the lead. But Lady Camper could not quit her pew, owing to the sticking of the door. She smiled as with her pretty hand she twice or thrice essayed to shake it open. General Ople strode to her aid. He pulled the door, gave the shadow of a respectful bow, and no doubt he would have withdrawn, had not Lady Camper, while acknowledging the civility, placed her Prayer-book in his hands to carry at her heels. There was no choice for him. He made a sort of slipping dance back for his hat, and followed her ladyship. All present being eager to witness the spectacle, the passage of Lady Camper dragging the victim General behind her was observed without a stir of the well-dressed members of the congregation, until a desire overcame them to see how Lady Camper would behave to her fish when she had him outside the sacred edifice.

None could have imagined such a scene. Lady Camper was in her carriage; General Ople was hat in hand at the carriage step, and he looked as if he were toasting before the bars of a furnace; for while he stood there, Lady Camper was rapidly pencilling outlines in a small pocket sketch-book. There are dogs whose shyness is put to it to endure human observation and a direct address to them, even on the part of their masters; and these dear simple dogs wag tail and turn their heads aside waveringly, as though to entreat you not to eye them and talk to them so. General Ople, in the presence of the sketch-book, was much like the nervous animal. He would fain have run away. He glanced at it, and round about, and again at it, and at the heavens. Her ladyship's cruelty, and his inexplicable submission to it, were witnessed of the multitude.

The General's friends walked very slowly. Lady Camper's carriage whirled by, and the General came up with them, accosting them and himself alternately. They asked him where Elizabeth was, and he replied, " Poor child, yes ! I am told she is pale, but I cannot believe I am so perfectly, I say so perfectly ridiculous when I join the responses." He drew forth half a dozen sheets, and showed them sketches that Lady Camper had taken in church, caricaturing him in the sitting down and the standing up. She had torn them out of the book, and presented them to him when driving off. " I was saying, worship in the ordinary sense will be interdicted to me if her ladyship . . ," said the General, woefully shuffling the sketch-paper sheets in which he figured.

He made the following odd confession to Mr and Mrs. Gosling on the road :—that he had gone to his chest, and taken out his sword-belt to measure his girth, and found himself thinner than when he left the service, which had not been the case before his attendance at the last levée of the foregoing season. So the deduction was obvious, that Lady Camper had reduced him. She had reduced him as effectually as a harassing siege.

" But why do you pay attention to her? Why ! . . ," exclaimed Mr. Gosling, a gentleman of the City, whose roundness would have turned a rifle-shot.

" To allow her to wound you so seriously ! " exclaimed Mrs. Gosling.

" Madam, if she were my wife," the General explained, " I should feel it. I say it is the fact of it ; I feel it, if I appear so extremely ridiculous to a human eye, to any one eye."

"To Lady Camper's eye !"

He admitted it might be that. He had not thought of ascribing the acuteness of his pain to the miserable image he presented in this particular lady's eye. No ; it really was true, curiously true : another lady's eye might have transformed him to a pumpkin shape, exaggerated all his foibles fifty-fold, and he, though not liking it, of course not, would yet have preserved a certain manly equanimity. How was it Lady Camper had such power over him ?—a lady concealing seventy years with a rouge-box or paint-pot ! It was witchcraft in its worst character. He had for six months at her bidding been actually living the life of a beast, degraded in his own esteem ; scorched by every laugh he heard ; running, pursued, over-taken, and as it were scored or branded, and then let go for the process to be repeated.

OUR young barbarians have it all their own way with us when they fall into love-liking ; they lead us whither they please, and interest us in their wishings, their weepings, and that fine performance, their kissings. But when we see our veterans tottering to their fall, we scarcely consent to their having a wish ; as for a kiss, we halloo at them if we discover them on a byway to the sacred grove where such things are supposed to be done by the venerable. And this piece of rank injustice, not to say impoliteness, is entirely because of an unsound opinion that Nature is not in it, as though it were our esteem for Nature which caused us to disrespect them. They, in truth, show her to us discreet, civilized, in a decent moral aspect : vistas of real life, views of the mind's eye, are opened by their touching little emotions ; whereas those bully youngsters who come bellowing at us and catch us by the senses plainly prove either that we are no better than they, or that we give our attention to Nature only when she makes us afraid of her. If we cared for her, we should be up and after her reverentially in her sedater steps, deeply studying her in her slower paces.   Whirling she teaches nothing.   Our closest instructors, the true philosophers—the story-tellers, in short—will learn in time that Nature is not of necessity always roaring, and as soon as they do, the world may be said to be enlightened.   Meantime, in the contemplation of a pair of white whiskers fluttering round a pair of manifestly painted cheeks, be assured that Nature is in it : not that hectoring wanton—but let the young have their fun.   Let the superior interest of the passions of the aged be conceded, and not a word shall be said against the young.

If, then, Nature is in it, how has she been made active ?   The reason of her launch upon this last adventure is, that she has perceived the person who can supply the virtue known to her by experience to be wanting.   Thus, in the broader instance, many who have journeyed far down the road, turn back to the worship of youth, which they have lost. Some are for the graceful worldliness of wit, which they have just share enough of to admire it.   Some are captivated by hands that can wield the rod, which in earlier days they escaped to their cost. In the case of General Ople, it was partly her whippings of him, partly her penetration : her ability, that sat so finely on a wealthy woman, her indifference to conventional manners, that so well beseemed a nobly-born one, and more than all, her correction of his little weaknesses and incompetencies, in spite of his dislike of it, won him.   He began to feel a sort of nibbling pleasure in her grotesque sketches of his person; a tendency to recur to the old ones while dreading the arrival of new. You hear old gentlemen speak fondly of the swish; and they are not attached to pain, but the instrument revives their feeling of youth; and General Ople half enjoyed, while shrinking, Lady Camper's foregone outlines of him. For in the distance, the whip's-end may look like a clinging caress instead of a stinging flick. But this craven melting in his heart was rebuked by a very worthy pride, that flew for support to the injury she had done to his devotions, and the offence to the sacred edifice. After thinking over it, he decided that he must quit his residence; and as it appeared to him in the light of duty, he, with an unspoken anguish, commissioned the house-agent of his town to sell his lease or let the house furnished, without further parley.

From the house-agent's shop he turned into the chemist's, for a tonic—a foolish proceeding, for he had received bracing enough in the blow he had just dealt himself, but he had been cogitating on tonics recently, imagining certain valiant effects of them, with visions of a former careless happiness that they were likely to restore. So he requested to have the tonic strong, and he took one glass of it over the counter.

Fifteen minutes after the draught, he came in sight of his house, and beholding it, he could have

called it a gentlemanly residence aloud under Lady
Camper's windows, his insurgency was of such violence.   He talked of it incessantly, but forbore to
tell Elizabeth, as she was looking pale, the reason
why its modest merits touched him so.   He longed
for the hour of his next dose, and for a caricature to
follow, that he might drink and defy it.   A caricature was really due to him, he thought ; otherwise
why had he abandoned his bijou dwelling.   Lady
Camper, however, sent none.   He had to wait a
fortnight before one came, and that was rather a
likeness, and a handsome likeness, except as
regarded a certain disorderliness in his dress, which
he knew to be very unlike him.   Still it despatched him to the looking-glass, to bring that
verifier of facts in evidence against the sketch.
While sitting there he heard the housemaid's knock
at the door, and the strange intelligence that his
daughter was with Lady Camper, and had left
word that she hoped he would not forget his engagement to go to Mrs. Baerens' lawn-party.

The General jumped away from the glass, shout-
ing at the absent Elizabeth in a fit of wrath so
foreign to him, that he returned hurriedly to have
another look at himself, and exclaimed at the pitch
of his voice, " I say I attribute it to an indigestion
of that tonic. Do you hear ? " The housemaid
faintly answered outside the door that she did,
alarming him, for there seemed to be confusion
somewhere.   His hope was that no one would

mention Lady Camper's name, for the mere thought of her caused a rush to his head. "I believe I am in for a touch of apoplexy," he said to the rector, who greeted him, in advance of the ladies, on Mr. Baerens' lawn. He said it smilingly, but wanting some show of sympathy, instead of the whisper and meaningless hand at his clerical band, with which the rector responded, he cried, "Apoplexy," and his friend seemed then to understand, and disappeared among the ladies.

Several of them surrounded the General, and one inquired whether the series was being continued. He drew forth his pocket-book, handed her the latest, and remarked on the gross injustice of it; for, as he requested them to take note, her lady-ship now sketched him as a person inattentive to his dress, and he begged them to observe that she had drawn him with his necktie hanging loose. "And that, I say that has never been known of me since I first entered society."

The ladies exchanged looks of profound concern; for the fact was, the General had come without any necktie and any collar, and he appeared to be unaware of the circumstance. The rector had told them that, in answer to a hint he had dropped on the subject of neckties, General Ople expressed a slight apprehension of apoplexy; but his careless or merely partial observance of the laws of buttonment could have nothing to do with such fears. They signified rather a disorder of the intelligence. Elizabeth was condemned for leaving him to go about alone. The situation was really most painful, for a word to so sensitive a man would drive him away in shame and for good ; and still, to let him parade the ground in the state, compared with his natural self, of scarecrow, and with the dreadful habit of talking to himself quite raging, was a horrible alternative. Mrs. Baerens at last directed her husband upon the General, trembling as though she watched for the operations of a fish torpedo ; and other ladies shared her excessive anxiousness, for Mr. Baerens had the manner and the look of artillery, and on this occasion carried a surcharge of powder.

The General bent his ear to Mr. Baerens, whose German-English and repeated remark, " I am to do it wid delicassy," did not assist his comprehension, and when he might have been enlightened, he was petrified by seeing Lady Camper walk on the lawn with Elizabeth. The great lady stood a moment beside Mrs. Baerens ; she came straight over to him, contemplating him in silence.

Then she said, " Your arm, General Ople," and she made one circuit of the lawn with him, barely speaking.

At her request he conducted her to her carriage. He took a seat beside her, obediently. He felt that he was being sketched, and comported himself like a child's flat man, that jumps at the pulling of a string.

"Where have you left your girl, General?"

Before he could rally his wits to answer the
question, he was asked:

"And what have you done with your necktie
and collar?"

He touched his throat.

"I am rather nervous to-day, I forgot Elizabeth,"
he said, sending his fingers in a dotting run of
wonderment round his neck.

Lady Camper smiled with a triumphing humour
on her close-drawn lips.

The verified absence of necktie and collar
seemed to be choking him.

"Never mind, you have been abroad without
them," said Lady Camper, "and that is a victory
for me.   And you thought of Elizabeth first when
I drew your attention to it, and that is a victory
for you.   It is a very great victory.   Pray do not
be dismayed, General.   You have a handsome
campaigning air.   And no apologies, if you please;
I like you well enough as you are.   There is my
hand."

General Ople understood her last remark.   He
pressed the lady's hand in silence, very nervously.

"But do not shrug your head into your shoulders
as if there were any possibility of concealing the
thunderingly evident," said Lady Camper, electri-
fying him, what with her cordial squeeze, her
kind eyes, and her singular language.   "You have
omitted the collar.   Well?   The collar is the fatal

finishing touch in men's dress; it would make Apollo look bourgeois."

Her hand was in his: and watching the play of her features, a spark entered General Ople's brain, causing him, in forgetfulness of collar and caricatures, to ejaculate, " Seventy?   Did your ladyship say seventy?   Utterly impossible! You trifled with me."

" We will talk when we are free of this accompaniment of carriage-wheels, General," said Lady Camper.

" I will beg permission to go and fetch Elizabeth, madam."

" Rightly thought of.   Fetch her in my carriage. And, by the way, Mrs. Baerens was my old music-mistress, and is, I think, one year older than I.   She can tell you on which side of seventy I am."

" I shall not require to ask, my lady," he said, sighing.

" Then we will send the carriage for Elizabeth, and have it out together at once.   I am impatient; yes, General, impatient: for what?— forgiveness."

" Of me, my lady? "   The General breathed profoundly.

" Of whom else?   Do you know what it is?— I don't think you do. You English have the smallest experience of humanity.   I mean this: to strike so hard that, in the end, you soften your

heart to the victim. Well, that is my weakness.
And we of our blood put no restraint on the blows
we strike, so we are always overdoing it."

General Ople assisted Lady Camper to alight
from the carriage, which was forthwith despatched
for Elizabeth.

He prepared to listen to her with a disconnected
smile of acute attentiveness.

She had changed. She spoke of money. Ten
thousand pounds must be settled on his daughter.
" And now," said she, " you will remember that you
are wanting a collar."

He acquiesced. He craved permission to retire
for ten minutes.

"Simplest of men! what will cover you ? " she
exclaimed, and peremptorily bidding him sit down
in the drawing-room, she took one of the famous
pair of pistols in her hand, and said, " If I put myself in a similar position, and make myself *décolletée*
too, will that satisfy you ? You see these mur-
derous weapons. Well, I am a coward. I dread
fire-arms. They are laid there to impose on the
world, and I believe they do. They have imposed
on you. Now you would never think of pretending
to a moral quality you do not possess. But, silly,
simple man that you are ! You can give yourself
the airs of wealth, buy horses to conceal your
nakedness, and when you are taken upon the standard of your apparent income, you would rather
seem to be beating a miserly retreat than behave

frankly and honestly. I have a little overstated it, but I am near the mark."

"Your ladyship wanting courage!" cried the General.

"Refresh yourself by meditating on it," said she. "And to prove it to you, I was glad to take this house when I knew I was to have a gallant gentleman for a neighbour. No visitors will be admitted, General Ople, so you are bare-throated only to me: sit quietly. One day you speculated on the paint in my cheeks for the space of a minute and a half:—I had said that I freckled easily. Your look signified that you really could not detect a single freckle for the paint. I forgave you, or I did not. But when I found you, on closer acquaintance, as indifferent to your daughter's happiness as you had been to her reputation . . . "

"My daughter! her reputation! her happiness!" General Ople raised his eyes under a wave, half uttering the outcries.

"So indifferent to her reputation, that you allowed a young man to talk with her over the wall, and meet her by appointment: so reckless of the girl's happiness, that when I tried to bring you to a treaty, on her behalf, you could not be dragged from thinking of yourself and your own affair. When I found that, perhaps I was predisposed to give you some of what my sisters used to call my spice. You would not honestly state the proportions of your income, and you affected to be faithful to the woman of seventy. Most preposterous! Could any caricature of mine exceed in grotesqueness your sketch of yourself? You are a brave and a generous man all the same: and I suspect it is more hoodwinking than egotism—or extreme egotism — that blinds you. A certain amount you must have to be a man. You did not like my paint, still less did you like my sincerity; you were annoyed by my corrections of your habits of speech; you were horrified by the age of seventy, and you were credulous—General Ople, listen to me, and remember that you have no collar on!—you were credulous of my statement of my great age, or you chose to be so, or chose to seem so, because I had brushed your cat's coat against the fur. And then, full of yourself, not thinking of Elizabeth, but to withdraw in the chivalrous attitude of the man true to his word to the old woman, only stickling to bring a certain independence to the common stock, because—I quote you! and you have no collar on, mind—'*you could not be at your wife's mercy,*' you broke from your proposal on the money question. Where was your consideration for Elizabeth then?

"Well, General, you were fond of thinking of yourself, and I thought I would assist you. I gave you plenty of subject matter. I will not say I meant to work a homœopathic cure. But if I drive you to forget your collar, is it or is it not a triumph?

"No," added Lady Camper, "it is no triumph for me, but it is one for you, if you like to make the most of it. Your fault has been to quit active service, General, and love your ease too well. It is the fault of your countrymen. You must get a militia regiment, or inspectorship of militia. You are ten times the man in exercise. Why, do you mean to tell me that you would have cared for those drawings of mine when marching?"

"I think so, I say I think so," remarked the General seriously.

"I doubt it," said she. "But to the point; here comes Elizabeth. If you have not much money to spare for her, according to your prudent calculation, reflect how this money has enfeebled you and reduced you to the level of the people round about us here—who are what? Inhabitants of gentlemanly residences, yes! But what kind of creature? They have no mental standard, no moral aim, no native chivalry. You were rapidly becoming one of them, only, fortunately for you, you were sensitive to ridicule."

"Elizabeth shall have half my money settled on her," said the General; "though I fear it is not much. And if I can find occupation, my lady . . ."

"Something worthier than *that*," said Lady Camper, pencilling outlines rapidly on the margin of a book, and he saw himself lashing a pony; "or *that*," and he was plucking at a cabbage; "or *that*," and he was bowing to three petticoated posts.

"The likeness is exact," General Ople groaned.

"So you may suppose I have studied you," said she. "But there is no real likeness. Slight exaggerations do more harm to truth than reckless violations of it. You would not have cared one bit for a caricature, if you had not nursed the absurd idea of being one of our conquerors. It is the very tragedy of modesty for a man like you to have such notions, my poor dear good friend. The modest are the most easily intoxicated when they sip at vanity. And reflect whether you have not been intoxicated, for these young people have been wretched, and you have not observed it, though one of them was living with you, and is the child you love. There, I have done. Pray show a good face to Elizabeth."

The General obeyed as well as he could. He felt very like a sheep that has come from a shearing, and when released he wished to run away. But hardly had he escaped before he had a desire for the renewal of the operation. "She sees me through, she sees me through," he was heard saying to himself, and in the end he taught himself to say it with a secret exultation, for as it was on her part an extraordinary piece of insight to see him through, it struck him that in acknowledging the truth of it, he made a discovery of new powers in human nature.

General Ople studied Lady Camper diligently

for fresh proofs of her penetration of the mysteries in his bosom ; by which means, as it happened that she was diligently observing the two betrothed young ones, he began to watch them likewise, and took a pleasure in the sight. Their meetings, their partings, their rides out and home furnished him themes of converse. He soon had enough to talk of, and previously, as he remembered, he had never sustained a conversation of any length with composure and the beneficent sense of fulness. Five thousand pounds, to which sum Lady Camper reduced her stipulation for Elizabeth's dowry, he signed over to his dear girl gladly, and came out with the confession to her ladyship that a well-invested twelve thousand comprised his fortune. She shrugged : she had left off pulling him this way and that, so his chains were enjoyable, and he said to himself: "If ever she should in the dead of night want a man to defend her !" He mentioned it to Reginald, who had been the repository of Elizabeth's lamentations about her father being left alone, forsaken, and the young man conceived a scheme for causing his aunt's great bell to be rung at midnight, which would certainly have led to a dramatic issue and the happy re-establishment of our masculine ascendency at the close of this history. But he forgot it in his bridegroom's delight, until he was making his miserable official speech at the wedding-breakfast, and set Elizabeth winking over a tear. As she stood in the hall

ready to depart, a great van was observed in the
road at the gates of Douro Lodge ; and this, the
men in custody declared to contain the goods and
knick-knacks of the people who had taken the
house furnished for a year, and were coming in
that very afternoon.

"I remember, I say now I remember, I had a
notice," the General said cheerily to his troubled
daughter.

"But where are you to go, papa?" the poor girl
cried, close on sobbing.

"I shall get employment of some sort," said he.
"I was saying I want it, I need it, I require it."

"You are saying three times what once would
have sufficed for," said Lady Camper, and she asked
him a few questions, frowned with a smile, and
offered him a lodgement in his neighbour's house.

"Really, dearest Aunt Angela?" said Elizabeth.

"What else can I do, child?   I have, it seems,
driven him out of a gentlemanly residence, and I
must give him a ladylike one.   True, I would
rather have had him at call, but as I have always
wished for a policeman in the house, I may as
well be satisfied with a soldier."

"But if you lose your character, my lady?"
said Reginald.

"Then I must look to the General to restore it."

General Ople immediately bowed his head over
Lady Camper's fingers.

"An odd thing to happen to a woman of forty-one !" she said to her great people, and they submitted with the best grace in the world, while the General's ears tingled till he felt younger than Reginald. This, his reflections ran, or it would be more correct to say waltzed, this is the result of painting!—that you can believe a woman to be any age when her cheeks are tinted !

As for Lady Camper, she had been floated accidentally over the ridicule of the bruit of a marriage at a time of life as terrible to her as her fiction of seventy had been to General Ople ; she resigned herself to let things go with the tide. She had not been blissful in her first marriage, she had abandoned the chase of an ideal man, and she had found one who was tuneable so as not to offend her ears, likely ever to be a fund of amusement for her humour, good, impressible, and above all, very picturesque. There is the secret of her, and of how it came to pass that a simple man and a complex woman fell to union after the strangest division.

www.ingramcontent.com/pod-product-compliance
Lightning Source LLC
Chambersburg PA
CBHW031127120726
47905CB00006B/1589